How to Shield an ASSASSIN

UNHOLY TRIFECTA HEIST 1

AJ SHERWOOD

HOW TO SHIELD AN ASSASSIN
Unholy Trifecta Heist 1

PRINTING HISTORY
Oct 2019

www.ajsherwood.com

PART ONE

1

He was being tailed.

Ari walked steadily, easily, not letting on he knew he was being followed. Badly being followed, at that. The street was narrow—more alley than anything—with most of the lights flickering or out altogether. Abandoned trash littered the sides, and he kicked it absently out of the way as he moved. It wouldn't take much to disappear here. The shadows were thick, he was wearing dark clothes. He had a parked SUV waiting not far away. It was the perfect combination for a disappearing act and easy enough to pull off.

Two things stopped him: curiosity and a nagging sense something was off.

The footsteps were light, barely heard on the pavement. Like there was no weight in them, rather than being merely silent. No matter how well trained, an adult man couldn't walk like that. Ari walked half a block, his ears trained on his tail, becoming slowly convinced it wasn't an adult following him.

A child?

What kind of fucked up adult sent a child to tail an assassin?

Ari had been in the business for nearly twelve years. He didn't have a lot of morals, maybe a handful, but kids featured at the top of his very short list. He didn't do kids. He didn't hurt them, he sure as hell didn't kill them, and he'd been known a time or two to step in and teach a lesson to any adult who thought kids made a good toy. Having this kid out on his tail at nearly eleven o'clock at night, in one of the worst sections of Memphis, made rage crawl up his throat and choke him.

He finally couldn't take it anymore. He either had to find the adult who'd set the kid on him and beat the ever-living shit out of him, or take the kid to a safer place—no, scratch that. He'd do both. But it was time to end this madness. At the next working streetlight, he stopped dead, not turning around, and waited.

The footsteps stopped too.

"Hey," he said calmly. "This whole cat and mouse thing ain't cool, okay? How about you come over here, in the light, and you tell me what you need. I might be able to help you out."

Ten seconds passed, a weighty pause while the kid figured out what to do. Ari half-expected flight, but instead the footsteps firmed, no longer trying to sneak. A smile twitched his lips up. This one had guts. He loved gutsy kids. World needed more of them.

Ari was well aware of how he looked. At thirty, he was young, but his profession had left its mark. He wasn't ugly—his Italian blood made him look like a '50s era bad boy—but his vibe scared people off. Most people looked at his rangy frame, the scars along his arms, the flat look in his dark brown eyes, and found other places to be. As he didn't want to scare the kid, he turned slowly, kept his hands well away from the weapons tucked up under his leather jacket, and tried a smile on for size.

Then she stepped into the light, and the smile abruptly dropped.

The little girl couldn't have hit double digits yet. Eight, maybe, but it was hard to tell. She might've been a beautiful child but it was hard to see that, too. Bruises littered her face, neck, and hands—some of them yellow with age, others fresh enough to be mottled purple. Her tangled, butterscotch-colored hair fell all around her face and down to her waist. Her clothes were obviously someone's cast-offs. They hung poorly on her. The thin denim jacket actually looked like an adult's, as it swarmed her and did little to keep her warm in the cold November weather. One look at her and he wanted to kill the SOB who had made her his punching bag.

She was scared, he could see it in her shaking hands, but she faced him squarely, which was more than most adults could manage. Looking up at him, she swallowed hard before speaking, words raspy. "I'm Sarah. I saw you beat up Hardy back there."

Ari slowly sank to one knee, putting them on the same eye level. It helped. She stopped shaking, looking relieved he no longer loomed over her. So she'd seen him beat up the local drug dealer, had she? Ari was actually only here on a job, a quick in and out to kill a serial rapist. He'd stumbled across the drug dealer trying to force himself on a girl because her father was an addict needing his fix. Ari had made sure the dealer would be in the hospital for the next six months, and the girl had enough money to make a run for it, maybe make herself a new life in a different city. He was proud of both deeds tonight, but why would a little girl watch that kind of violence and decide to approach him?

"Yeah, honey, I did. He was a bad man. His face needed rearranging."

"Do you beat up bad men as your job?"

Just what the hell was that she thinking? She thought that of him and still approached? Alarm bells started blaring in the back of Ari's head. "Yeah, honey, I do. Why?"

From the pocket of her sagging pants, she drew out something that made a lot of clinking noises, and held out both hands to him. It was a jumbled collection of change, perhaps two dollars altogether. With her chocolate brown eyes, she looked up at him, pleading. "Can I hire you? Will you stop him?"

Despite the fact Ari routinely killed people in his line of work, he didn't actually feel murderous most of the time. Right now, the rage that rushed over him threatened to overtake his common sense. He had to choke it back, bitter as it was. "Who's hurting you, honey?"

"My stepfather. Momma left last year, and when she did, he got mad. He..." she trailed off, eyes falling to the pavement. Then her chin firmed and she squared her shoulders, meeting his eyes once more. "I need you to stop him."

Oh, Ari would stop him, alright. He held out both hands, taking the change from her. "You just hired yourself an assassin, sweetheart."

She lit up in relief, dumping the change in his hands. "He lives at 314A Osborne Way."

"Tell you what, kiddo. You come with me and stand just outside the house, okay?" No way in hell he was going to leave her standing on a dark street in Memphis. She'd be kidnapped and have even worse done to her. Ari wasn't taking that chance. He pocketed the change, standing.

Sarah nodded, fell into step with him, taking two steps for his one. He noticed, and slowed down so she wasn't jogging to keep up with him. Ari might like kids but he didn't have a lot of experience with them—mostly because no sane adult would trust him with their kid. As they walked, his thoughts raced ahead. After he dealt with her stepfather, then what? What happened to her when her mom was already out of the picture? "Honey, you got any relatives? Grandma, grandpa, uncles, anything like that?"

Shaking her head no, she kept walking.

Shit. With no relatives, that meant she'd go straight into foster care. And fosters were a crap shoot. Ari knew from personal experience.

An insane thought nudged into his brain. He nearly paused mid-stride when it hit. Maybe he could adopt her. Ari could admit that sounded crazy on the surface. No one sane would look at him and think dad material—much less him—and he was half-convinced he'd screw up any child handed to him. But when he looked down at the child walking so trustingly at his side, the thought occurred to him that even if he screwed up royally, he was still better than what she'd had. Ari wouldn't beat her, he'd make sure she was fed and protected. That alone made him a hundred times better than the bastard claiming to be her father.

And it wouldn't be entirely for her. Ari had great friends, and a brother, but he was alone a lot. Sometimes that loneliness got to him. It wouldn't hurt for him to raise her, would it?

They reached the house before he could really make a decision one way or another. It honestly looked like an abandoned house. There was a broken-down stove on the front porch, dead flowers in pots scattered about, and someone's dirty laundry on the ground. The only sign of life came from the light in the window, flickering, clearly from a TV. Kneeling, he put a light hand on Sarah's back, drawing her eyes up to him. She was back to being scared, staring at the house like it contained the boogeyman. To her, it likely did. "You change your mind, sweetie?"

Shaking her head, she pointed to the door. "It's not locked."

Right. "You stay on the porch, okay? If someone comes to get you, you scream for me. I'm going to take you to a safe place after this."

"You are?" Her expression was hard to see in the dim lighting, but he could hear her surprise clearly enough.

"Yeah, honey. Can't leave a kid on the streets. That's quello non va bene, you get me?" With a pat on her head, he moved toward the house, stride becoming quiet as he moved. Not that he worried about the bastard hearing him approach, but occupational habits kicked in. Ari briefly debated putting the silencer back on his Glock and then shrugged. Ah well, it didn't matter.

The door was indeed unlocked, although it stuck a little, warped with time. He shoved it aside, one hand already on the gun strapped to his back. Ari really wanted to kill this SOB, but at the same time, he was of two minds about killing in front of a child. Was that the right thing to do? His alternate plan was to put a bullet in each of the asshole's shoulders, keep him out of action for a while, then take off.

A heavy man with a three-day beard and beer belly slouched in the single easy-boy in the living room. At Ari's entrance, he lifted his head blearily to stare at Ari. "Who the fuck're you?"

"I'm here because of Sarah," Ari answered calmly, loosening the gun holstered at his back.

"That runt? You into kids?"

Ari froze mid-motion, the gun still under his jacket. What the hell had he just said?

Jumping to the wrong conclusion, the drunkard lifted a lip, his leer truly repugnant. "Five hundred dollars, you can have'er."

Red washed over his vision like a riptide. Ari didn't even remember moving, his gun coming up automatically and putting two bullets in the man's head in a quick double-tap. The stepfather never saw it coming, his eyes wide with surprise as life faded out of them. Ari stood there a second, shaking, bile rising in his throat. This filthy sack of shit was willing to sell his eight-year-old daughter to a pimp?

Never had two dollars been put to such excellent use.

Holstering the gun, he stepped back out, straight to the little girl obediently waiting for him on the porch. With the dry-rotted curtains hanging in front of the window, she'd not been able to see the murder, but she didn't need to see to know. Ari stared at her, waiting for some sort of emotional response on her part. Anger, fear, tears, something.

She smiled up at him in relief. "Thank you."

Oh hell. Ari remembered being there, a child at the mercy of adults more likely to use fists than words. He looked at her and saw himself at that age, and his whole being rebelled. He really couldn't leave her alone now. "Tell you what, kiddo. How about I adopt you? I can't trust you to the foster system. I gotta tell you, I'm probably not good dad material, but you'll be safe with me. And no douchebag will get his hands on you again, I can promise you that."

She cocked her head up at him, her face becoming gradually more expressive with hope. "You're an assassin, right? Can you teach me to be like Black Widow?"

Was that her hero? Her lack of fear of him now made more sense. "Yeah, kid, I can teach you the moves."

Her smile was lopsided, impeded on one side because of the bruises, but it spoke of pure joy. "Then please adopt me."

"Sure thing." Ari reached out with both hands, picking her up, feeling nothing more than skin and bones. The urge to go kick the corpse inside a few times rose. Damn him and the mother who had abandoned her to him. "Anything you want from inside?"

Shaking her head no, she latched onto his collar with both hands, fingers tangled in the fabric. "You really, really want to keep me?"

"Kid, I like your guts," he admitted honestly. "Not many adults have your kind of savvy, to walk up and make a deal with me. But let's discuss details after we get out of here, okay?"

"Okay," she agreed blithely.

He stretched out his legs, eating up the ground while keeping a firm grip on her. Ari's SUV was actually parked in front of the supermarket down the street. He'd headed a little away from it earlier, when Sarah started tailing him, but it was to their benefit to blow this popsicle stand quickly. Not that the neighborhood wasn't used to gunshots, but he liked to avoid the pesky police when he could.

"What's your name?" she asked him, keeping her voice to a loud whisper.

Ari appreciated her attempt at being quiet. His name wasn't something he used all that often and he liked it that way. "Ari. Aristide, really, but everyone calls me Ari. We'll need to change your name, and mine, so that we're family on paper. That okay?"

"Yeah. I don't like the name Sarah anyway. Momma once said the nurse at the hospital named me cause no one else did."

Maybe he needed to track down her mother, Ari mused. Just so he could put a bullet in the woman. It would make him feel better. "Okay. We'll think up a different name for you. Tonight, though, let's head to a Walmart and get you some different clothes and toys and shit."

Someone would think he'd offered her the holy grail. "You're going to buy me stuff?"

"Yeah, duh," he answered with a wink, startling a smile out of her. "Look, I know you got the raw end of the deal when it came to parents, and I'm not saying I'll be any good at this father thing, but taking care of you? That's my pleasure, princess. So you get clothes, and toys, and stuff. Just make it portable, capiche? We gotta boogey sometimes. You've got a two-bag limit."

"Okay," she promised faithfully.

He reached the SUV. The people in the neighborhood had been smart enough to leave it alone, fortunately. Unlocking it with the fob on his keychain, he popped her into the front seat, buckled her in, then darted around to the driver's side. As he started up the engine, another thought occurred, and he ordered her, "And call me Dad, okay? Especially in public. People will assume I've kidnapped you if they think I'm not your dad."

She gave him a cheeky grin. "But you did kidnap me."

"Po-tay-to, po-tah-to," he dismissed with an airy wave.

Giggling, she touched the leather interior of the car with wonder. "You're a good assassin."

"One of the best in the business." He wasn't surprised she'd leapt to that conclusion. The car wasn't a cheap one, after all. "Okay, squirt, let's go shopping."

Ari focused on getting them out of the area quickly, not wanting to linger in this bad section of town. Putting distance between himself and that corpse was the priority for a good half hour. But he heard no sirens, saw no sign of police heading in. It could well be no one had bothered to report it. Only after he'd gone some distance did he realize the little girl at his side was deadly still and quiet.

He was no expert on kids. But an eight-year-old just sitting in a seat without even fidgeting was weird, right? In her shoes, he'd at least be asking questions, but she wasn't doing that either. Had she been trained by that abusive asshole to stay still and quiet? Or had she learned to behave this way to avoid his fists?

Whichever the reason, it pissed Ari off royally. There was no way he could fix what had been done to her, but at least he could help her now. "Hey, gattina. You got a name you want to be called by?"

She looked at him curiously. "You're not going to choose for me?"

"Seems like someone already did that once and picked a name you didn't like. I think it's your turn." Ari slowed for a red light and gave her his best smile. "Benelli's your last name. Whatever you pick, try to think of something that works with it."

"Benelli?"

"Yeah. My mother...that was her maiden name." Ari had only recently figured this out. He didn't know a lot about his mother's people, as he'd lost her so young and had no records from her. He and Luca had chosen to do some investigation, as what they remembered from childhood was sketchy at best. It had taken digging to find her name, and he wanted to use it now. To have some connection to the warm mother he'd lost. It seemed appropriate. "I thought I'd take it."

"Benelli," she repeated thoughtfully.

Ari let her mull on the question as he consulted his phone's GPS for a Walmart. There was one ten minutes away, and he punched it in, taking the next turn to wind his way that direction. When she didn't say anything else for several minutes, he prompted her, "Nothing springing to mind?"

"I want a strong name. An assassin name." She trailed off, becoming quieter with each word. "I don't know...what's good."

Ari was a little stuck on that himself. "Maybe take a name from one of the gun companies? Smith and Wesson, Glock, Remington—"

"Remington?"

Stopping at another light, Ari darted her a look. "You heard of Remington?"

"Yeah, there was a news report. Kelly Clarkson's baby is named Remington, right?"

News to Ari, but then, he didn't follow celeb news. "Really? Well, I mean, all of the gun companies are basically named after the men who designed the guns. So I guess it makes sense it's a real name."

"Remington Benelli," she whispered to herself.

That didn't quite jive to Ari's ear. He played around with it mentally for a minute before offering, "Maybe Remi Benelli?"

Remi gave him one of those rare, genuine smiles again. "Remi Benelli. I like that."

"You like it enough to keep it? Or do you want to keep thinking about it?"

"No, I like it. Remi." She repeated to herself again, like she was getting used to it. "Remi. Remi."

They arrived at the partially filled parking lot for the supercenter. Ari pulled in near the front, under a street light, because doing otherwise was stupid. You didn't have enough light to see what might be hiding in the backseat otherwise. Coming around, he caught Sa-Remi as she slid out of the seat. "Climb in under my jacket, gattina. You're not dressed for this cold."

She snuggled underneath, her arms wrapped around his neck, legs around his waist. He kept an arm under her as a support, the other clutching his jacket closed. She still shivered even then, and he swore to get warm clothes on her as quickly as possible. Maybe pay out, then take her into the bathroom, let her change.

As he speed-walked into the store, he tried to get her to open up a little more, as this quiet routine of hers really alarmed him. "What's your favorite color, gattina?"

"Blue," she said shyly against his neck.

"Yeah? Any colors you don't like to wear?"

"Pink."

"Really? I thought girls like pink."

"Pink's too girly."

Ari nodded hello to the Walmart greeter, pausing a moment to get his bearings. Let's see, little girl's section was—there. "Too girly, huh? Okay, we can do without the pink. Damn, I should probably get a buggy. You'll need lots of stuff."

Her tiny hands dug into his shirt as she whispered doubtfully, "But you said I can't buy a lot."

"I said you got a two-bag limit. They can be big bags, you know. Bags I can carry." His heart felt like someone jabbed it repeatedly with a hot iron poker. God, he remembered being there. Being told he couldn't have things. Being told he was only allowed so much. Bad memories from his own childhood rushed to the forefront and Ari shoved them ruthlessly down. He wasn't going to let her stew in the same nightmare he'd lived through. Like hell would Ari let that happen.

He fetched the buggy and maneuvered it with one hand a little awkwardly. Remi refused to let go of him, even after they reached the right section and he'd put her down. She kept a hand on his pant leg at all times, pointing to things she liked. Ari didn't chide her for it. She was likely still reeling after the events of the past hour. He certainly was.

Ari picked up the first sweater she pointed out and then paused. "Wait. Remi, what size are you?"

She shook her head in ignorance and gave him an uncertain look.

Of course she wouldn't know. "Huh. Gattina, you might need to try things on until we figure that out. Let's see...this one looks like it might fit? Let's grab that one, and maybe the next size up. We'll try both, yeah?"

"Excuse me," an icy voice demanded from behind him.

Ari didn't do well with people coming in from behind and he whirled quickly, barely checking the impulse to pull a gun.

The woman behind him skittered a foot back in alarm, no doubt from the expression on his face, but she stood her ground, bag clutched in front of her like a broadsword. She wore nurses' scrubs, her black hair in a multitude of braids swept up in some sort of bun thing, and there was a hard expression on her face.

"Why is this child covered in bruises?"

Oh shit. A good Samaritan. Ari was really bad at dealing with this type. The woman had every right to question Remi's state, but how did he respond and get her to go away?

Remi latched onto his hand. "My stepfather was beating me. Daddy found out and came and got me."

The woman's ire doubled. But she bent down to Remi's level and asked her, "And he's good to you?"

Remi nodded fervently. "Daddy won't ever hit me. He said I won't go back there."

The woman gave Ari a sidelong look. "You got custody of her?"

"Yes." Which was true. Sorta.

She seemed to believe it, at least enough to stop glaring at him. "Why don't you know her sizes?"

"I lived with Mom before this," Remi answered again, truthfully.

"I see. Well, it's true a lot of men aren't good with shopping for girl's clothes anyway. What's your name, sweetie?"

"Remi."

"Remi, how about I stay and help you figure stuff out a little?"

Ari really wished the woman would just go away. But he also sort of needed her help because he was seriously out of his depth. He had no doubt she was lingering to make sure Remi really had told her the truth, but he'd deal with that as he went. "That'd be great, ma'am. Maybe you can figure out what size she is?"

Someone should have warned him how *expensive* little girls were. His credit card actually flinched after the total rang out.

It took three hours in Walmart to figure out what all to get his new daughter and stick it in the cart. Figuring out her sizes alone was a pain in the ass, and it would have been downright impossible without the nurse's help.

Bless Remi for her quick thinking and brains in answering the many, many questions posed to them. The woman had finally turned sympathetic towards Ari instead of calling the cops, and she'd even stayed to help Remi figure out which shampoos and conditioners and other hair things a little girl needed.

Now they were at a nice hotel, Remi all scrubbed up and passed out in the middle of the queen-sized bed. Her hair was still wet and tangled, and only time could heal the bruises, but at least she was clean. She had a giant unicorn with a purple horn firmly clutched in her arms, the only large toy she'd asked for. Everything else could be crammed into a duffle bag.

He sat on the edge of the other queen, watching her sleep, and wondered for the *nth* time what the hell he thought he was doing. Four hours he'd had her, and Ari was clearly out of his depth, but...the way she looked at him. As if he were a hero. As if he were *her* hero. And there was a part of him, the part still a child, that would have given anything to be in her shoes. To have a dedicated protector looking out for him.

All he could do was his level best to give her what she needed. Ari didn't have any role models to go off of, but maybe he didn't need one in this case. Remi, fortunately, was street savvy enough to fill in for him when he fumbled. Like at Walmart, she'd known exactly what to say to get the nurse off Ari's back. Bless her.

But that didn't mean he could just let things ride. There were things only he could handle, and that meant making a few phone calls. Sighing, he snagged his phone before heading into the bathroom and shutting the door. Sitting on the edge of the tub, he dialed his brother's phone.

Unlike him, Luca had managed to get through the foster care system firmly still believing in justice and fairness and all of that. He was determined to make changes to the system so that it worked better. Ari had gotten to eighteen not giving a rat's ass about the law, but his brother had become a lawyer, as straight as a bleeding arrow. Most of the time they agreed to not talk about Ari's profession and got along alright. The fact they barely saw each other more than three times a year also helped their relationship stay steady.

This? Well, this would make his twin contemplate murder himself.

The call finally picked up with a groggy, "*Hello? Oh dammit, Ari. Really, you can't remember what time zone I'm in?*"

"I did remember," Ari defended himself. "I'm just in a spot and need your magic touch."

"*I'm so not making bail for you.*"

"Not bail. And I resent the implication anyone can catch me long enough to get me in jail." Ari paused, trying to decide how to word this so Luca didn't hang up on him and call for the National Guard. "I, ah, adopted a little girl today."

The other end went dead silent.

"Luca? You still breathing, man?"

"*Aristide. Who in their ever-loving mind would give you a little girl to raise? Wait, you didn't buy her off some slave market, did you?*"

"You do know me well. I'd totally do that. But no, I didn't. She was abandoned by her mom, her dad was shot tonight—"

"*Wait. Wait, her dad 'was shot' or you shot her dad?*"

"To be fair, he was a bad man."

"*Oh god. Why do I pick up your phone calls? Why do I do that to myself?*"

Ari grinned at the bland hotel wall. "You know, that's a very excellent question. I do wonder that some days."

"*Aristide. I want you to listen to me. You can't adopt a child out of guilt. Alright? That's not the right response here.*"

"Naw, it's not guilt. She actually hired me to stop him from beating her. I knew what I was walking into."

An audible silence rang over the line. "*You're telling me she hired an assassin. To kill her father.*"

"Stepfather. Stepfather who was beating her, starving her, and tried to sell her to me."

"*Oh hell. This now makes perfect sense. Still, Ari, have you considered turning her into Child Services? That's the correct, responsible thing to do in this case.*"

"Are you done with your last-ditch effort now?"

"*Yeah,*" Luca sighed in defeat. "*I'm done. Thank you for*

calling me on my cell and not at the office. I would hate to have this recorded in company logs."

"See? I do look out for you."

"*You lying liar. Alright, I assume you want me to make a new identity for you two so no one comes looking for her?*"

Ari grinned. He did love his brother. "Yup."

"*What would you do without me?*"

"Go to illegal sources."

"*I will hang up on you. Right the fuck now, I will hang up on you.*"

"Luca," he softened his voice, not quite pleading. "She literally has no family. You really want to throw her to the wolves?"

"*You really think you can do better than foster care?*"

"Well, I'll feed her, won't beat her, and make sure she can do the things little girls like. What do you think? That sound better than foster care?"

There was a pregnant pause on the other end of the line. "*You know, I assumed that because you're gay, I'd never have any nieces or nephews. Way to make an uncle out of me without giving me a head's up first, bro.*"

Ari grinned. "Love you too."

Something flopped, like a pillow hitting the floor, followed by the rustling of sheets. "*I don't know what crime I committed in a previous life to deserve you, but it must have been a doozy. Alright, give me particulars. Name, birthdate, and what city hospital should she be born in? Mother's name?*"

"She wants to be called Remi. She's eight, birthday is today. The rest, we don't care. Ah, give me a new last name too: Benelli."

"*Aristide and Remi Benelli. It does roll off the tongue, I give you that.*" Luca paused and the next words were spoken more carefully. "*Are you intending to connect with the family, now that we've found them?*"

"Naw. I mean, they're so uptight, no way they'd accept me. You can try, though."

"*I'll pass. I'm not eager to meet people who threw a pregnant teenager out of the house. I'm just surprised you want to take on the name.*"

"I'm doing it more to honor Mom."

"*Ah. Should have figured. I'll work it up, but it might take a few weeks. Nothing about the government is fast. What are you going to do in the meantime?*"

"Find a nice place to settle in for a bit, give normal life a try."

Luca busted out laughing.

Ari pulled the phone away from his ear long enough to stick his tongue out at his phone. "Stop laughing. I'm a professional assassin, how hard can it be?"

2

A scream woke him out of a sound sleep. Ari dove for the gun under the other pillow first, trying to open his eyes in the process. What was it? What was happening? Why was he even hearing screaming when he lived alone in this house—shit, what house was he in again?

Sobbing followed the screaming, then abrupt silence.

Remi. The name barreled through his barely conscious mind, and he was alert in a split second like he had never been before. Ari scrambled out of bed, shaking off a clinging top sheet as he did and almost nose diving into the carpet. In a less than graceful move, he got out of his bedroom and into the one across the hall, hitting the light as he did so. The single bed in the middle of the room was empty, the Black Widow blanket missing and the pillow half-way to the floor.

Alarm shot through him all over again to see that empty bed. Terrible visions of someone managing to get through his security and grabbing Remi scrambled his brain. It took far longer than it should have to spot the huddled form crammed between wall and dresser in the far corner.

"Rems?" He cautiously approached, fear dissipating, but worry rising. He saw no signs someone had broken in, but his little girl was terrified of something.

There was another muffled sound, like a sob choked back, and he belatedly realized what this must be. A bad nightmare. Ari ached in brutal sympathy because he still had those—even as an adult. Putting the gun down on her nightstand, he slowly came around and sank onto his knees in front of her. "Remi, gattina, come out of there. Was it a bad dream?"

The blanket completely covered her from head to toe but he saw the dip as she nodded.

"Okay. Bad dreams happen sometimes."

A threadbare whisper came from the blanket. "You too?"

"Yeah, gattina, me too. I have them sometimes." What was the right tactic here? Did he force the issue of her coming out of the corner? Let her take it at her own pace? Just sit and talk to her for a while?

Ari really wished he had someone to talk to about this. His brother was flat out. Luca was still uneasy about leaving a kid in his care and was about one trigger away from coming and getting Remi himself. Ari hadn't told his two closest friends about her yet. Ivan and Kyou were two people he trusted the most in the world, but he didn't know how the thief or hacker would take the news of him picking up a child. Well, Ivan might take it well. The man was supportive when it came to family. Kyou was so anti-social some days it was hard to predict which way he'd jump. Even if he told them, Ari didn't expect a lot of help. They wouldn't know any better than he what to do with an abused child.

Sometimes, he really wanted a listening ear as he figured this out.

Remi still wasn't budging. Ari didn't know what to say to her, really. Maybe if he shared a little of his past, she'd realize they were more alike than she thought? "Some of my dreams are about jobs I've been on, jobs that went really wrong. But most of 'em, they're about when I was younger. More your age. See, I lost my mom when I was just shy of eight years old."

The blanket slowly came down, revealing a disheveled head of hair and two red rimmed eyes peeking over it at him. "Really? What happened?"

Ari wet his lips and answered, although part of him would really rather not. Since this conversation would apparently take more than a few seconds, he settled more comfortably, crossing his legs. "My mom was from Italy. She got pregnant with me and Luca, and her boyfriend wouldn't marry her. Her family kicked her out because of it, and she came to America. She didn't make it big over here or anything. She was a waitress, but we did okay. She was always able to feed us. But one night while she was working, the restaurant had a mob family inside having dinner. The place got shot up. She was hit in the crossfire."

The blanket came down a little further. "No one helped her?"

What an innocent question. "Nothing to help. She was struck in the heart. Dead before she hit the floor. At least, that's what the cop told me when I asked. After that, Luca and I were sent into foster. They tried to find relatives for us, but...well. Mom had burned that bridge pretty thoroughly. They wouldn't take us. Foster was...not good. Sometimes I stayed somewhere decent. But most of the time, it wasn't good. It's why I couldn't let you go into it, gattina."

Remi scooted out from her hole and came closer, although she didn't touch him. Her eyes were wide, penetrating in a way he'd never seen from a child's face before. "That's why?"

"Why did you think I took you in?" he asked softly.

"I don't know. I was just happy you did."

Ari blew out a low breath and kicked himself for not explaining things better to her before. "Remi, this world is a shitty, shitty place. I looked at you and saw me, all those years ago. I was afraid, if I didn't take you in, that you wouldn't survive it. That you'd not be given the chance. And I was maybe—just a little, mind you—but maybe a bit lonely."

There was that smile. When Remi was happy, her smile could light up the room. "I can stay with you forever and ever, if you want."

Tears burned in his eyes. "Forever and ever? Wow, that's an amazing offer. You know, I might take you up on that. Tonight, though, how about we bunk together? Maybe that will keep the nightmare from coming back."

She nodded, and he lifted the burrito wrapped child into his arms. Remi's grip on his shirt nearly strangled him. It was odd, actually, now that he thought of it. She never initiated contact, but if he reached for her first, she'd cling to him like an octopus. Surely that would ease as she found her rhythm with him.

Ari shut her light off on the way back to his room and they snuggled into his bed, Remi still clinging to him. Ari didn't think he'd be able to sleep with her doing so, but he didn't breathe a word of that to her. He could go without a few hours of sleep, that wasn't a big deal. The nightmare worried him. The clinginess worried him. Hell, all of this worried him. But Ari didn't know what to do aside from what he was already doing—giving her time, patience, and steady attention. Hoping she'd work through it.

Right then, he decided to not take any jobs for a month or so. Give them both a chance to get to know each other better. And even then, he'd take day jobs, quick in and outs until she got settled.

This parenting thing was harder than it looked.

The nightmares didn't return that night. Or the next. Ari took that as a good sign, or would have, if Remi hadn't invaded his bed. Right now, that was fine, but she'd need to learn to sleep in her own at some point.

Ari didn't think he'd have to kick her out anytime soon. For one thing, he was very, very single. Ari wasn't the type to have one-night stands—he literally couldn't. It took a great deal of trust to let someone else into his personal space. It had taken a few years with Ivan to get really comfortable with the man. Kyou he'd known as a kid, so that hadn't been as hard. Remi, of course, was a no brainer. But picking someone up at a bar or a club? Flat out. No way in hell could he relax enough with a stranger to have sex. Most of his dates involved getting close to a target.

He was the type of person who needed to date and really get to know someone before he could let his guard down. Hard enough to do as an assassin. As a single father as well? If Ari hadn't already been resigned to going it alone, he'd have made the choice the day he got Remi. It wasn't worth the possible danger to her to bring some stranger in. Ari would just have to make do with late night showers.

After four days of having her, Ari felt tired of winging it. He needed a game plan. He had to figure out how to tell Ivan and Kyou he now had a daughter. He had to figure out school for her—and that alone threatened to give him a migraine. Regular school meant she needed a regular address. Ari had homes in Seattle, Halifax, Italy, and London. The one they were currently in was a rental; he'd move out of it as soon as he figured out where to go. Maybe the east coast? Ivan had a house somewhere in North Carolina. Kyou was in New York, not too far off. If shit really hit the fan, it might be better to have his friends nearby.

Although how to tell them...that was the kicker.

On autopilot, he put bacon, scrambled eggs, and toast on two plates and carried them to the bar. Remi hopped up onto the bar stool and gave him a shy smile.

"Morning, gattina. Eat quick, we've got some serious decisions to make today."

She dug into the eggs obediently. "Like what?"

"Well, like school. No way in hell can I homeschool you, I barely passed high school as it was. In order for school to happen, we need to figure out an address. Your Uncle Luca says the paperwork for our new identities are almost done. I want to be in our new place when it arrives so we can get the ball rolling."

Remi nodded, following, chewing on bacon. "So where are we going?"

"Well, now, here's the thing. I've got two really good friends I do jobs with. And I haven't told them about you yet, but I figure I will pretty soon. One of them lives in New York, the other one in North Carolina at the moment. The one in North Carolina got hurt a few days ago, so he's resting. I think when he's well, I want the two of you to meet. New York's a bit too congested for me, I don't like staying there for long." And the crime rate was pretty insane. "I'm leaning toward North Carolina."

Remi looked up at him through her lashes, biting her bottom lip. "You're still going to train me, right?"

"What? Yeah, of course. I just can't homeschool you. Everything else I can do." Ari focused on his own breakfast for a few minutes before it got cold. He was anxious to move now that he had a good idea of what to do. House hunting and picking out a good school would eat up several days at least. Once they had their identities, he'd need to find a doctor too, because apparently shots were a serious business with schools. The research he'd done yesterday about what all was required to get a child enrolled in school was just ridiculous.

Glancing over, he saw that half of her plate was still full. Remi had slowed down considerably, mostly pushing her eggs around the plate with a fork. "You done?"

For some reason she flinched, eyes turning bright with unshed tears. The expression was made worse because her eye wasn't healed yet, and the tears made it look fresh. "I can finish it."

Why was she...shit. She was cowering like she expected a solid slap in the face. "Whoa, gattina, calm down. If you're full, you're full. It's fine, you don't have to finish."

Remi took in a deep breath sounding like a half-sob, still staring at him as if judging his sincerity on this. Ari wished he'd done more to her stepfather than put two bullets into that son of a bitch. No kid should be this scared about finishing a plate. Broadcasting every movement, he leaned in and hugged her around the shoulders, not relaxing until she wrapped both arms around him too. Okay, that was better. She always calmed down a little once he hugged her.

"Next time, you fill your own plate, yeah? That way you can judge how much you want."

She nodded against his shirt but didn't utter a peep.

Ari let his head drop back, staring blindly at the ceiling. He had this. He really did. Just one issue at a time. "How about we do dishes, then sit in front of the computer for a while and house hunt?"

Remi lifted her face a whole millimeter to answer him. "It's really fine if I don't finish?"

"Forcing yourself to finish means you're overeating and not listening to your body. If you're not listening to your body, you can make yourself sick. Black Widow doesn't make herself sick, right?"

"Right."

"Then no forcing yourself. Bene?"

"What's that mean?"

"Good, or okay."

"Bene," she answered, sounding firmer now.

"That's my girl." Ari let go of her and picked up both of their plates, heading for the sink. "Get the laptop and plug it in.

House hunting takes a while. And we have to figure out which town we'll be in. I want a good school for you."

Remi paused in the kitchen doorway, watching him carefully. "Can I do ballet?"

Hands covered in soap and water, he blinked at her. Where had this even come from? "Ballet?"

She wrapped both arms around her chest, uncertain, but gamely explained. "Black Widow does ballet."

"Ah." Ari thought about it. Ballet developed core strength, flexibility, and muscle mass which was all good for MMA fighting. "Sure. We'll look up ballet studios too."

Beaming at him, she darted in for a thigh hug. "Thanks, Ari."

"You're welcome, gattina." It really meant that much to her? Ari still hadn't figured out how much of her obsession with Black Widow was hero worship and how much of it was her fixation on wanting to be strong enough to protect herself. At this point, it might not even matter. "You remember the password for the laptop?"

"Malvagio."

"Right." Ari washed the last dish and put it on the rack to dry. Should he even bother packing up the utensils and kitchen stuff? Or just their personal gear? Let the next occupants deal with whatever he'd left behind.

Carrying the laptop back in, Remi asked, "Was Malvagio your old name?"

"What, before I took on Benelli? No, Malvagio is my street name. Kinda like a code name."

"Like Black Widow?"

"Exactly like that." Ari sat on the stool, putting Remi up on his knee so she could see the laptop too. Since she was still curiously looking up at him, he further explained, "You don't want to give people your real name. Makes it easy for them to find you. And it's a pain in the ass to create a new identity on the fly. So most people go by a street name, or some sort of nickname, to avoid that. There's some exceptions—mercenaries tend to just use their real name. But they're hired for retrievals and quick jobs, they're not normally breaking laws. So people aren't really after them much. One of my friends uses his real name half the time, but he's an adrenaline junkie. He finds it funny when people come after him. Me, I go by nickname 'cause I'm paranoid."

"What's it mean, though?"

"It's Italian for 'wicked.'" Ari had been all of nineteen when he'd come up with it. There were days he second-guessed the decision but it was too late now. Everyone knew him by that handle. "We should probably think up a code name for you, too. Or do you want to be called Widow?"

Remi bounced once in place, for a moment forgetting her normal caution as excitement took over. "Widow would be lit!"

"Then Widow it is." Ari laid a personal bet with himself whether she'd regret that in her twenties. He'd be there to rub it in, regardless. "Alright, Widow. Aside from a ballet studio, and a good school, what else does our new home need to have?"

3

The move had been...interesting. Interesting about covered it. Ari bought a house in a small town in North Carolina, one town over from where Ivan lived. He'd still not found the right timing to tell either Kyou or Ivan about Remi. Luca had given him such grief, he'd not found the emotional strength to battle it out with the other men. And honestly, the move and Christmas had sort of wiped him out. Too many feels.

Christmas hadn't been a thing for him since his mother died, so Ari hadn't really been sure what to do about it, at first. But he'd eventually decided that for Remi's sake, the holiday should happen. She'd been alright with the tree decorating, and the store-bought dinner. But come Christmas morning, she'd at first been confused, then alarmed, by getting multiple presents. Luca had mailed her something—a pink tutu of all things—and she'd liked it. She'd liked the ballet slippers, too, that Ari'd gotten her. But by present four, she'd stopped, the brightly wrapped present in her hand and a bewildered look on her face. She'd asked him: "But I can't keep a lot of stuff, right?"

Her expression had just about KO'd him on the spot. Ari'd wanted to punch himself in the face. He should never have told her she had to stay within a two-bag limit—she was right to be confused.

He'd quickly scrambled and explained that no, what he'd meant was she could only have two bags while they were on a job. But now they had a house, they could have more than just two bags worth of stuff. Didn't she have a bed, and a dresser, and all that? And he had lots of weapons and stuff too, right?

Not all of that would fit in two bags, not even close.

She'd eventually nodded, accepting this new logic, but the excitement of Christmas never quite materialized. She was too wary to think all of this was really hers.

They'd skyped Luca, and she'd been happier then, seeing her uncle for the first time. Family connection meant more to her than pretty, wrapped presents. Luca had been full of questions for her, too: How was the new school? Dance lessons? Did she like the new house?

Since she'd not started school or dance yet—that was next week—she could only really talk about the house and how much she looked forward to ballet. Still, they'd chattered happily and Ari only had to throw in a word here and there. Luca no doubt wondered why he'd waited so long to get her enrolled in school. If he'd seen her before Christmas Day, he wouldn't have wondered. It had taken that long for the bruises to fade and to get enough weight on her so she didn't look like an abused skeleton.

They weren't in a pattern, not yet, but the house was mostly unpacked and she was enrolled in both school and dance. And he still had to figure out how to tell Kyou and Ivan, which... yeah. He had no idea how to even approach that.

Longing for his own brand of normalcy, Ari dared to take a job on New Year's Day.

Ari went through a mental checklist in his head, his gear in hand as he prepared to leave. The job would be a quick in and out, basically a day job, as long as the stars aligned and his intel stayed good. Sometimes old intel was worse than bad intel. This had come from Kyou, though, and the hacker was good about updating him when the situation changed. He'd probably be back by dinner—

"Daddy? Are you going somewhere?" A sleepy voice asked him from the stairs.

His head snapped around to see his daughter in her Batman pajamas standing on the bottom stair, rubbing at one eye sleepily, a worried expression on her face. Mentally, he started swearing up a storm. How had he forgotten an eight-year-old who couldn't just be left home alone? Had he just fallen into pre-job habits? Ari kicked himself a few times. "In a bit, yeah. I have a quick job. Don't worry, gattina." He formed a plan on the fly even as he reassured her. "I'm going to call my friend to stay with you while I'm gone."

She came up to him and wrapped both arms around his thigh, pressing her face into his leg. "Friend?"

Shit, he'd scared her. After a month of having her, Ari had seen her gradually come out of her shell a bit. The move had helped. At least, she'd been more stable since the move. She wasn't always quiet and contained; she'd actually ask him questions without prompting sometimes. If she were back to clinging like a koala bear, then she was feeling insecure again. "Yeah, the good friend I told you about? The one who lives nearby? He's a professional thief. We do a lot of jobs together. His name's Ivan. We call him Eidolon in the criminal underworld because the man basically walks through walls like they're not even there."

She tilted her head up, looking intrigued. "Kind of like Black Widow can?"

"Yup. I bet, if you ask him, he'll teach you some of his tricks. Ivan's a really nice guy." In fact, one of the reasons why they got along so well was that he and Ivan shared the same moral code: you don't prey on the weak. "Let me call him, see where he is, okay?"

"Okay."

"Maybe you should get dressed while we're waiting."

Nodding, she reluctantly let go of him and headed back upstairs. Ari waited until she was out of earshot before heading into the kitchen. He took a moment to bang his head against the fridge. Smooth, man, real smooth. Apparently, that old adage about habits being a dangerous thing was dead on. It had blindsided him this time neatly enough. As he pulled his phone free, he tried to remember how long Ivan had spent recuperating. His last job had gotten him injured, but he was mostly on the mend at this point. Hadn't Kyou said he would only be out of commission for two months? Were they at the end of two months yet?

The phone rang twice before it was picked up. Ivan sounded fuzzy and cotton-mouthed as he groaned, "*Svoloch. Why are you calling me at six in the morning, you have death wish?*"

"Uh, Ivan. I, um, maybe need a favor."

The Russian accent only deepened. *"This favor better pay well. I do not like being called in at last minute."*

That Ari knew. "Yeah, that's my bad. I'm...not used to this yet."

There was a digestive pause. He could practically hear Ivan becoming more alert. *"We're not talking about a job, are we."*

"Um, no. No, we're not. This was not how I wanted to let you know, I swear I was going to tell you, and we moved here to be closer to you for a reason—"

"We?"

"Yeah, we. I have a daughter."

"You. Have a daughter? How?"

"It's a really long story. Short version, I adopted her. She's a really great kid, Ivan, I couldn't let her go into foster, and that's where she was heading. She wants to be an assassin when she grows up. Thinks it's totally cool I took her in. Look, I'll tell you the full story later, but I've got a job today, and I kinda forgot to arrange a sitter for her. Aside from you, the only person who knows about her is my brother."

"Chert dura. How can you leave that for last minute? Why did you not tell me about her sooner?"

"I'm well aware I'm an idiot, okay? Can you watch her until I get the job done?"

There was a great deal of cloth rustling and thumps on the other end of the line. *"Da. This girl, I must meet her. I will be there in...wait, where are you?"*

Ari rattled off the address.

"Da, good, I can be there in forty-five minutes. Have coffee for me. She knows about you and me, right?"

"Yeah, she knows the basics. She'll probably ask you how to do stealth stuff. It's fine if you want to teach her. I'll leave cash on the table for pizza and stuff."

"We will talk about that when I get in."

"Thanks man, really."

"You owe me."

"Absolutely."

With a grunt, Ivan hung up. Ari turned to find his daughter hovering in the kitchen doorway, staring at him with big, chocolate eyes and shifting anxiously from foot to foot. He gave her a reassuring smile. "Ivan's really eager to meet you. He'll be here in about an hour, maybe less."

She nodded and didn't look the slightest bit relieved.

Ari couldn't exactly blame her. "Why don't you eat breakfast while we're waiting?"

Ivan showed up precisely forty-five minutes later. Ari expected he'd need to brace Remi and maybe hang out for a few minutes with them because Ivan looked intimidating at first glance. The Russian had grown up in a rough environment, and it had left its mark. The hint of a gold tooth in his smile and the tattoo on his collarbone peeking out were eye-catching in the wrong ways, but the man's tall, rangy build and penetrating grey eyes unnerved people. For some reason, his acorn brown hair was in a buzz cut at the moment, which didn't help his initial intimidating impression.

He came in, gave Ari an exasperated look, then knelt down to put himself on eye level with Remi. "Hello."

Remi had a firm grip on Ari's pant leg but still regarded Ivan with a sort of fascination. "Hello."

"Remi, Ivan. Eidolon, this is Black Widow in training." Ari ruffled her hair, hoping the affectionate gesture would relax her a little.

"I'd not heard my comrade has a daughter."

Remi whispered, "Is that bad?"

"What, that he has you? No, no, cute girls are always a blessing, da?" Ivan grinned at her. "I'm just surprised."

"I met and adopted her recently," Ari explained, as he had promised to fill Ivan in. "About a month ago, actually. That job I took in Memphis, that's where I met her."

"My stepfather was hitting me," Remi surprised Ari by saying. "I asked Daddy to help."

"What!" Ivan soothed her with a hand petting her hair, outrage all over his face. "How can any man hit such pretty solnishko? Ari, this zasranets, he's dealt with?"

Over her head, Ari mouthed the assurance: *He's dead.*

Looking satisfied, Ivan listened to Remi's response.

"Daddy made sure he won't hurt me. Then he took me away with him."

"I'm very glad to hear it." Ivan gave her a serious look. "Solnishko, you're an assassin in training? Your father, he's teaching you how to fight?"

She nodded wordlessly.

"He teaching you how to get through locks?"

Now intrigued, she shook her head no.

"What? How can you reach a target if you can't get through locked doors?" Ivan gave Ari an exasperated look, but it was clear the man was teasing and trying not to laugh. "You're not teaching her the important things. You, go. I need time with my solnishko. We will start with something easy, da? Locks on this house."

Ari looked down to see how Remi was taking this, but she was unclenching, drawn to Ivan's offer and curious. Ivan's lure was successful, then. Good. "Okay. Well, you've got till dinner. I should be back by then. But Ivan, the locks on this house aren't exactly simple. I doubt she can crack these even with one of your lessons."

Behind a hand, Ivan whispered to her, "He's not an expert. Ignore him."

Rolling his eyes, Ari gave Remi a last pat on the head and went for his duffle. "I'll be back. Remi, don't break him, okay?"

"Okay. Have fun, Daddy!"

There, that sounded more her normal self. Ari gave her a last smile and wink as he sauntered through the door.

Hopefully they didn't do anything drastic. Like decide to rob a bank. Ivan, when bored, could not be trusted.

Maybe he should have called Kyou instead.

The job went well enough that Ari was indeed back by dinner, the restlessness under his skin eased. He came in to find his lovely daughter attacking the back door with lockpicks and opening it in ten seconds flat. It both alarmed and impressed him, because if an eight-year-old with only a day of training under her belt could get through his locks, then they were obviously *not* as secure as Ari had assumed them to be.

Ivan hung out for dinner, promised to come back tomorrow to play some more, and even got a hug in with Remi before he left. Remi was all smiles as Ari tucked her into bed that night, and he lingered, sitting next to her on the bed. "You like Ivan?"

"Uncle Ivan's super fun," Remi informed him, animated in a way he'd never seen before. "He taught me all about how locks work, and how to swear in Russian, and promised to get me lock picks and show me how to hide them in my hair."

He breathed out in silent relief. Ari had felt bad about leaving her with Ivan all day, but apparently they got along swimmingly. "I'm glad you like him. He clearly likes you, if he's coming back to play tomorrow."

"He said, whenever you have a job, he'll hang out with me. He said I've got another uncle too, a hacker uncle, that I should meet."

"Yeah, Uncle Kyou, the one in New York. He may or may not meet you in person. He's kinda like Batman, although he likes to stay in the batcave most of the time."

"Oh." She looked a little disappointed by that. "So he won't want to play with me?"

"He might, gattina. We'll have to see. Even I have a hard time getting him to leave his cave, and I've known him for years and years." Frankly, now that he thought about it, Remi might work as a lure to get Kyou out of his house for once. "Anyway, I'll call and ask him. When you do meet him, remember his code name is K. Use that in front of other people, okay?"

"Okay." She plucked at her blanket and chewed on her bottom lip. "Daddy, you don't have a girlfriend?"

Sometimes (and by sometimes he meant most of the time), Ari had no clue how ideas connected in Remi's head. This was one of them. "No, and how did we jump to this subject?"

"Uncle Ivan said you had to call him because you didn't have anyone else to call except Uncle Luca."

"Ah." Praise be, there was an actual connection. "Well, you're half-right."

"So you don't have a girlfriend?"

"No, gattina. But I don't like girls that way. I like boys

better." Wait, should he be explaining what gay is to an eight-year-old?

Remi took this in a single blink. "Okay. But you don't have a boyfriend?"

Well, clearly children had an easier time accepting than adults. Ari was a bit nonplussed at how effortlessly she'd accepted that. "Naw, not right now. I haven't met anyone I like."

"But will you get one?"

"Eh, maybe." Definitely not.

That wasn't the answer she'd expected. Or maybe she wanted something different. Either way, Remi frowned in a dissatisfied manner.

Ari really didn't want to get stuck on this topic, so he changed it. "Go to sleep, kiddo. I'll see if you can't meet Uncle Kyou at some point." After he figured out how to tell him.

"Okay. Night, Daddy."

"Night." He slipped out of her room, hitting the light switch as he went. Ari absently thought about maybe picking up one of those parenting books. Today had been a clear example that he didn't have a handle on this father thing yet. Maybe he should sit and make a game plan with Ivan. If he could get both Ivan and Kyou on board to help him watch Remi while on jobs, things would go a whole lot smoother.

Couldn't someone out there write how an assassin should raise a child? If they did, Ari would be ever so grateful and read all ten volumes of it assiduously.

4

Kyou stared down at Remi with the most discombobulated expression to ever grace a human face. The hacker looked a little wild, his blue-black hair sticking up in every possible direction, and he wore a faded sweater that said: *Some days I wish I were a missing person.* He had that look of three-day old bread. He wasn't moldy yet, but give it a bit more time in a dark corner, and he'd get there.

"What is this short, human-shaped creature?" Kyou asked in honest bewilderment.

Ari rolled his eyes. "You'd think you'd never seen a child before."

Remi leaned into him and whispered loudly, "This is my Uncle Kyou?"

"The under-caffeinated version. It's why he's not tracking right now. Let me pour a gallon of coffee down him, maybe a few energy drinks, then he'll make more sense."

Kyou spluttered, still staring at Remi as if she were the boogeyman. "Wait. Wait, you're real?"

"What, you thought I was messing with you?"

"Ivan kept spouting off all these stories about her, of course I thought you were messing with me!" Kyou protested in a wail. "He's not trustworthy!"

"Okay, I give you that." Ari started to see the humor in this. "You gonna let us in? Uncle Kyou?"

The hacker spluttered again, still staring down at Remi as if doubting his sanity. But he did move back three steps to give them the room necessary to come inside.

Kyou's place this time was a converted warehouse with I-beams stretching across the ceiling and polished cement floors. He favored the aesthetic, as most of his safehouses were like this. Ari personally thought it had more to do with the apartment leaning towards naturally cold, and better for a computer setup. Kyou had at least chosen to buy a couch this time. Last two places, there'd only been a giant bed and TV screen. The rest of the apartment furniture was all Kyou's baby—aka the computer.

The hacker retreated to his computer like a baby turtle heading for the sea. Only once he was in his seat did he settle and look less on the verge of a panic attack. His basilisk stare at Remi didn't unnerve the little girl, but it started to do so with Ari. Just when had Kyou last slept?

"K? You okay, man?"

Kyou blinked three times before he seemed to register the question. "What? Oh. Yeah, I slept."

Yeah, that was an obvious lie. When he volunteered sleeping information without being asked, he'd not slept in days. "Was that this week or last week?"

Remi came around to stare at the many, many monitor screens and the giant CPU on top of the desk, her eyes wide with wonder. "You really are like Batman. Daddy said you were." Seriously, she informed Kyou, "I'm going to be like Black Widow when I grow up."

Kyou cocked his head at her, finally speaking to her directly. "Are you? Why, cause your dad is an assassin?"

"Naw. I just really like her. She's so tough people can't hurt her. I want to be like that too."

An odd expression came over his face. "Was someone hurting you?"

"It's okay. Daddy took care of it." She gave him a small smile, and then abruptly changed topics, pointing to the computer. "Who's that man?"

Kyou gave the monitor in question a glance. "Ah, that's the bad man Ari—ah, your daddy needs to take care of. I've been watching him so Ari knows where to find him."

"You can do that from a computer?"

"Yeah, sure. It's just a matter of finding the right camera

and connecting to it."

"Can you show me?"

With an odd look on his face, Kyou slowly dipped his head. "Yeah. Yeah, sure, I guess. Ari, is this age appropriate?"

Ari shrugged, because fuck if he knew. "Ivan's taught her how to pick locks, pickpocket, and swear in Russian. Hasn't done any damage that I can see."

"I feel like using Ivan as a baseline for sanity is a really poor life decision, but okay. Come here, Remi. What you do is—"

Ari more or less left them to it and headed for the opposite side of the room. He normally wouldn't do this, but considering the state Kyou was in, it was better to have a backup plan. He called Ivan and watched the two in front of the computer as the phone rang.

"*How's my solnishko?*"

"I love that's how you now answer the phone."

"*She's more fun than you are.*"

"Uh-huh. Well, your solnishko has finally met her Uncle Kyou."

"*Ahhh. How did that go?*"

"Kyou thought we were playing an elaborate prank on him this whole time. Didn't think she was real."

Ivan roared with laughter.

"You're really something, you know that? Here I thought Kyou would know everything about her before I even got them face to face, but because you told him about her, he assumed we were pulling his leg."

"*I am the master of pranks.*"

"You must be, to fool him. Anyway, I'm calling because he's seriously sleep deprived."

Ivan abruptly stopped laughing. "*How bad?*"

"He told me without my asking that he slept."

"*Ouch. Da, not good. Last time he was that bad off, he was hallucinating sounds.*"

"And I have to leave your solnishko with him to do a job." Ari waited. Three, two, one....

"*Chert. You tell me this now. Where are you?*"

"Up in Cincinnati for a job. You're up here somewhere too, right? Kyou said he was providing support for you."

"*Da, I'm not far from his rental.*"

"I'm reasonably sure Remi can keep him from doing something insane until you can get here. But I need to leave in five, so hurry it up."

Ivan swore some more and abruptly hung up.

Ari really liked having Remi. This whole daughter thing was working out well for him. He'd never been able to get Ivan to cooperate like this before, not without more bribes involved.

He returned to the duo at the computer, taking a moment to appreciate the sight of his very introverted friend with a child in his lap, typing around her and seriously showing her how to hack traffic cameras and hijack them. He took a picture, too, as Ivan would be sorry later he'd missed this.

Hearing the click, Kyou looked up and made a face at him. "Why are you still here, you pest? Go away."

"I kinda need to know where my target is?"

"I've pinged that into your phone already."

Ari lifted his phone to check and sure enough, his GPS was already up and running with the address loaded. How Kyou managed to do that while teaching his child how to hack cameras, he had no idea. But then, Kyou often did stuff like this. He didn't really question it anymore. "'Kay. I'm off, then. Rems, Ivan's on his way in. Don't let Uncle Kyou have anymore coffee, order computer parts, or call that guy he's stalking. He says weird stuff when he's this sleep deprived."

Kyou snapped upright, outrage scrawled all over his face. "Excuse you, I told you I slept!"

"Uh-huh. You sure did. Unprompted." Ari gave him a pointed look, and Kyou at least had the decency to look abashed. "And Rems, remember what I said before."

"When you're close to the target, I'm not allowed to look," she parroted back faithfully, her attention only partially on him, eyes still on the screen.

"That's my girl." He ducked down and kissed her forehead. Kyou had a peculiar expression on his face and Ari paused, still leaning over, not sure how to interpret it. "I'm sorry, did you need a kiss bye too?"

Kyou swatted him on the ass without hesitation. "Get out of here."

Laughing, Ari sauntered out, sliding an earbud into his ear as he went. Then it was a simple matter of hopping into his SUV and heading off. Fortunately, Cincinnati traffic wasn't too bad this time of the day. The potholes were something else, though. Not to mention the black ice and the slush on the road. January always made for interesting road conditions up here.

This wasn't going to be a drive-by, he'd need to set up somewhere with a good vantage point. Ari had been stalking his target for the past week with Kyou's help, getting the target's patterns down well enough to anticipate where he'd be. A certain rooftop promised the right angle for a snipe, which was what he preferred. Especially in cases like this, when the target had enough bodyguards to be the president of a small country.

"Ari, we might have some trouble."

Ari slowed to a stop at a light and frowned. "Define trouble."

"Your contract just went open."

"The hell? My client gave me two weeks to get this guy. I'm well within schedule."

"Yeah, I don't know what to tell you. He either got impatient or something changed. But it went open...shit, six hours ago. Why am I only getting the notification now?"

Six hours? A lot could change in six hours in their business. "So am I facing competition on this or not?"

"Maybe. I don't see any movement at the moment, no one's asking questions on the contract...wait. Wait a sec. Shiiiit. They've disabled comments."

"So people could be messaging the broker directly but we wouldn't know," Ari translated wearily.

"Basically. I mean, I can hack the site and tell you, but I'd need like two days. The security on this site is no joke."

"And I'd have the job well done by then. It's okay, just try to watch my six. It looks like I'll only get one shot at this."

"Naw, he's got this, Remi. He's taken tougher jobs before. He's just suddenly got a much closer deadline."

Ari wished Remi had an earbud in, but at the same time she shouldn't actually listen in on this job. Oh well. Next job, maybe, assuming it wasn't another assassination. He'd see if the guys wanted support on one of their jobs so she could see him in action. Ari kept his eyes peeled as he found an open slot on the street and parked.

"*Wave to the camera, Ari.*"

Snorting, he did as bid, then pulled his case out of the back seat. Kyou was either more punch drunk than expected or he was hamming it up for Remi's benefit. He put them temporarily out of mind as he started for the four-story building that would be his temporary sniper's nest. As he slipped into the narrow alley between buildings, he caught movement up ahead as someone else entered the alley at the same time. Ari took his measure in a split second, but it wasn't hard to recognize someone else in the same line of business.

Shit.

The man was already reaching for the inside of his jacket. Ari didn't have anything on him except his trusty knife, a Glock, and the sniper rifle in the case. Swearing, he immediately ducked back around the side of the building. He had more of an arsenal in the SUV, but he was suddenly aware how much open ground was between here and there. Not that he'd had much choice on that, but still. This suddenly looked like a very bad predicament.

"*Ari, I've got two on the other side of the street closing in, someone else on your side approaching from the north side.*"

"In other words, I'm about to be pinched." Ari made a snap decision and hoofed it for the SUV. He had no cover here, and a shootout near the target was a bad idea anyway. That meant the target's bodyguards would get involved as well, and it would all go to hell rather spectacularly.

He threw open the door, tossing the case into the passenger side, and as he did so he heard the bark of a gun. His window shattered in a spray of glass and a burning pain creased the side of his neck. Swearing, he dove into the driver's side, heedless of the glass. He had maybe three seconds to get out of here before he really got caught in some stupid shootout and the half mil pay was so not worth it.

Another report of a gun, and this time it hit his back window, again breaking out the glass. Ari kept his head down as he floored it. The adrenaline ran hot in his veins, his heartbeat a war drum in his ears, so it took a few seconds before he could hear Kyou's voice again.

"*—he's okay, Remi. Look, princess, watch. He's driving, right? He's driving right through a red light, granted, but driving regardless. Malvagio? Say something, you're scaring the fuck out of your daughter.*"

"I'm okay," he rasped, hand clamped to the freely bleeding wound on the side of his neck. Shit, shit, shit, it was a mistake for him to let Remi watch this time. "Remi, breathe, I'm alright. It's just a graze."

"*Sorry, man. Those guys obviously knew the blind spots, as they slid in between the cameras way too smoothly. I did not see them coming until they were right on you. You coming back or swinging around for a re-approach?*"

Ari was tempted to try again but...naw. This had become a crapshoot and he really had no respect for his client setting him up like this. "Coming back. The client fucked himself by opening up the contract; I'm not lying in that shit."

"*Don't blame you. Okay, I've got the first aid kit out for you.*"

"Thanks." Ari focused on driving and losing anyone who might be following him. It was colder than a brass toilet seat in the Yukon out here, and he was shivering pretty hard even with the heat blasting, but he couldn't take chances. Paranoia was not only a healthy habit in his profession but a way of life. When he was satisfied it was alright, he chose the back way into Kyou's place, down the alley he knew his friend had complete control over, and into the parking garage underneath. The glass and the damage to his SUV he'd have to deal with later. For now, he took his gear out and lugged it up the flight of stairs and into the apartment.

Remi waited in the open doorway, dancing in place, tears silently streaming down her cheeks. Ari's heart about broke seeing that terrified expression on her face. He'd never wanted to see that. "Ahhh, Rems. I'm okay. Honest, it's just a scratch."

She more or less launched herself at him, hugging him tightly around his waist, tears wetting his shirt. Ari switched the case to his other hand so he could stroke her hair back without getting blood all over her.

Kyou appeared as well, looking him over with a critical eye. "Yeah, you're mostly okay. Give me the gear. Ivan called and demanded an update while you were out. I told him, so now he's pissed. I think he's gone hunting."

"You sicced Ivan on them?" Ari grinned in delight. "You got popcorn?"

"It's definitely going to be a show."

Remi pulled back and frowned at both of them. But the banter was working, she wasn't as upset as she had been a moment before. "But what if Uncle Ivan gets hurt too?"

"Won't happen," Kyou assured her blithely. "Trust me, they'll never see him coming. Your dad's good, he's stealthy. But Ivan's a fucking ghost. Let's get Ari patched up so we can sit in front of the monitors and watch Ivan take them all down."

This offer more or less dried up the tears. Remi's face stuck with the frown as she played assistant for Kyou, handing him alcohol wipes and gauze and tape as requested. Patching Ari up seemed to alleviate most of her concerns as she saw it really wasn't that serious. Ari was still kicking himself about this whole ordeal. Why the hell hadn't he really considered what this would do to Remi? Ari was careful, of course he was—being careless meant a quick death in this business. But still, as careful as he was, he got hurt. Not regularly, but it wasn't uncommon. If she saw him harmed, of course it would terrify her. Remi had no other person to depend on but him.

He really, truly needed to find a way to loop his brother more firmly into this. Just so Remi had a proper safety net if something happened to him.

Kyou popped a bag of popcorn into the microwave, found a few beers and one coke, and brought it all out for his guests. As he did, Ari spoke up. "Hey, Eidolon."

"*Malvagio, you alright?*"

"Just a scratch, man. Thanks for being my avenging angel and all. Remi saw me take the hit and it rattled her some. I didn't want to stick around."

Ivan was quick on the uptake. "*It was good call. She still watching, I take it?*"

"Yeah, we all are."

"*Then I not shoot to kill. Just rough them up, da?*"

"I'd appreciate it."

"*Anything for my solnishko.*"

Ari rolled his eyes. Of course. Did he expect Ivan to say anything else?

Kyou found another computer chair and pulled it up, and they sat side by side, munching on popcorn with Remi in Ari's lap. She watched without any comment as Ivan did indeed wound the two men who had shot at Ari previously. Ari felt vindicated but also a little miffed he hadn't been able to close the job or get his own revenge. Oh well. It wasn't like he and Ivan didn't regularly swap favors anyway. He'd repay the man in some future time.

As Ivan waved at the camera in a smug manner, Remi finally spoke. "Daddy? Next time, will you take Uncle Ivan too?"

"Ah..." Ari drew the sound out, buying himself a second to think. He exchanged a look with Kyou, but the hacker just shrugged, leaving him on his own. The rat. "Well, gattina, we do a lot of jobs together. But we can't always take all the same jobs."

"Why not?"

"Well, the jobs don't always need a hacker, thief, and assassin. Sometimes it just needs one. And sometimes the others have things they have to do too."

She didn't look up at him, staring hard at the blood staining his shirt. "But...if it's dangerous, like this time, will you ask?"

Ari hadn't thought it dangerous at all. This job should have been easy. But he knew better than to say that. "Sure. Sure, I'll ask."

Maybe he shouldn't try to work and figure out this parenting thing at the same time. Ari had enough socked away that he could afford to lay low for a few months, let Remi go to school. Maybe he'd read a few parenting books, and they'd figure more stuff out before trying to leap back into the underworld.

Yeah. Yeah, that sounded like a good idea.

Seeing that white expression on her face put it into perspective for Ari that what he did wasn't safe. He'd known that—of course he had—but he now had a deeper understanding of the fallout. Of what could happen to Remi if he wasn't careful. He really needed to sit down and carefully think this all through, put in better safety nets, plan for the future better. He absolutely did not want a repeat of today ever again. His heart hurt to see Remi stare at him with fear and alarm filled eyes.

Hugging her hard to him, he kissed Remi's temple and murmured, "Ti voglio bene cucciola di papà."

"Love you too," she whispered back, snuggling in.

For her sake, Ari promised himself then and there to really get his shit together.

PART TWO

5

CARTER

Carter was fairly sure that this qualified as a terrible, awful, no good, very bad day.

He'd had bad team-ups before. Every mercenary had at some point or another. But this one, this one might well take the cake. It wasn't a string of bad luck that did them in, either. Carter could forgive that. Bad luck was bad luck, no way around it but through it. But these guys hadn't been professional at all, constantly falling short and blowing off the job as no big deal. Getting drunk without caring if they were hungover in the morning. And the behind the scenes support? Nil.

Carter looked down at the little girl hanging so tightly to his fingers, her stuffed bunny clutched in her other hand in a death grip. The sad thing was, the job hadn't really been difficult. The little girl had been lost during the rush of evacuees and landed in the wrong place. It had been a simple retrieval mission when all legalities had failed to come through. What *should* have taken four days of prep and twenty-six hours to complete had instead taken a full week. In the end, Carter had just taken her and ditched the rest of the guys. They could fight out who would get paid later. He didn't give a shit at this point. He wanted this little girl properly in her mother's arms.

And then he was going to have a long, painful chat with the man who had arranged for this team-up to begin with.

"Mr. Harrison, are we almost there?" Libby asked him hopefully. Olivia was all of five, but she was very firm about being called Libby. Olivia, apparently, was a name for old ladies.

"Almost, pumpkin." Carter kept an automatic watch on their surroundings as they passed through the airport. It should be an easy enough walk out the doors, as no one checked passengers who disembarked, not unless they were coming from a foreign country. He'd already cleared customs with her at the previous airport. New York was their last stop, and hopefully her mother was already waiting near baggage claim. "I texted your mom before we got on board, and she said she'd meet us here. We're in the home stretch."

Libby bounced happily, much like the bunny she held in her arm, giggling.

Carter felt like giggling himself, for that matter. Seriously, he never wanted to work with men like that again.

Because he'd been in this business a while, he knew better than to relax his guard. He stayed vigilant as they weaved their way through the wide hallways and to the baggage claim area. Carter looked for his client, trying to match a face with the picture he had of her, but he didn't get a chance to spot her before he heard a happy voice calling over the crowd.

"LIBBY!"

"Mommy, Mommy, Mommy," Libby chanted back, already trying to tug free.

A woman with the same blond hair and freckles skidded to a stop on her knees, catching her daughter up in a fierce embrace, lifting Libby clean off her toes. She was sobbing and kissing her daughter everywhere she could reach even as Libby giggled and squirmed and hugged her back.

Carter enjoyed the scene, as it was heartwarming, but still kept an eye around them. He didn't think they'd have trouble at this point, but he was a little worried about his 'team' figuring out he'd taken off with their target and chasing after them. He'd really have to deal with them. But first, he wanted these two safely in a taxi and on their way home.

The mother finally pulled herself together enough to look up at him. Her eyes were red rimmed but she was smiling, joyfully. "Thank you so much, Mr. Harrison. I was worried you'd not be able to bring her to me."

"It did get a bit dicey at one point," he admitted frankly. Although it shouldn't have, dammit. "But I'm glad I could get her here safely. Ma'am, let's move this along. I want you safely in a taxi and on your way home."

She nodded in agreement, getting to her feet, bringing her daughter up with her. Libby settled into her mother's arms with a happy sigh, pillowing her head on the woman's shoulder.

Carter stayed a half-step behind as they went through the automatic glass doors. A line of taxis waited, and the pair slid into the backseat of one without issue. Carter waved them off and finally relaxed a hair. He was, frankly, exhausted. Libby had gotten to sleep on the plane, but aside from cat naps, he hadn't slept at all in three days.

His phone rang with a non-disclosed number. Growling, since he knew exactly who it was, he answered with a curt, "Harrison."

"*Mr. Harrison. You violated the terms of our agreement.*"

"My agreement with you didn't include working with a bunch of frat boys who got drunk every night and were trigger happy. My agreement didn't cover making bail for them because of a drunk and disorderly. IN A FOREIGN COUNTRY. My agreement with you didn't cover leaving a little girl stranded because they couldn't pull their acts together long enough to do a simple retrieval."

There was a pregnant moment of silence. "*They failed to mention the drunk and disorderly.*"

"I fucking bet they did. Let's be clear on this. I'm taking full payment for this job, because frankly they didn't do anything to earn it, and I'm the one who got the job done. And this is the last time you get to contact me for a job. I don't trust your judgement, Baker. I don't trust the men you hire. The next time I take a team assignment, I'm damn well going to form my own team. You've got one hour to pay me." Carter hung up the phone with a punch of the thumb. He seriously missed the good old days where you could slam a receiver down. It was so much more viscerally satisfying.

He'd been forced to abandon most of his gear in order to move lightly and get Libby out, so he definitely needed that full paycheck to replace stuff. His brand new laptop had been part of the sacrifice, which just pissed him off. He'd really splurged when buying that, and he'd barely been able to get it set up before the job started. Growling, he went to the next taxi in line and slung himself into the back seat. "Take me to the nearest Marriott, please."

"Sure thing," the driver called back. She cast him a glance as the car pulled away from the curb. "I saw the little girl and her mom. Not yours?"

Carter had a pat answer for questions like this. "I'm a retrieval specialist. The little girl was stuck in foreign customs, and I was the one to get her back to her mom."

"Oh. Cool beans, that's great. I love guys like you who cut the red tape. You look beat, man, was it rough?"

"Yeah, it wasn't a great trip. But successful, which is what counts, right?"

"Right. No luggage?"

"Like I said, rough trip."

"Ouch, man, that bites."

"Tell me about it." Carter's phone rang and he groaned. Please not another job, he'd barely gotten off the last one. Swearing a few choice words, he pulled it out of his pocket and let his head rest against the cool glass of the window as he put it up to his ear. "Harrison."

"Mr. Harrison. This is the first time we've spoken. I'm Emura, a broker."

"Yeah, hi. I have to tell you, this isn't a good time. I just came off a job."

"Fortunately, this isn't an immediate time limit. You have three months to do this in."

That should have sounded good, but it was conversely worrying. Jobs that came with long deadlines meant they were stupidly difficult enough that even the client didn't expect you to get it done anytime soon. "What's the job?"

"A certain painting has been illegally acquired, shall we say, and is currently in Knowles."

Carter let out a low whistle. The three months deadline now made perfect sense. Knowles was a very famous private art gallery owned by the wealthy Knox family. The Knoxes liked to throw parties to display all of their shinies, and Knowles was the place they hosted them in. It was, in a word, a fortress of security. Carter had never even attempted to access the place, and he'd only heard of one person who had successfully gotten in and out.

Malvagio.

"Emura, do you mind if I ask a frank question? Why are you contacting me? This isn't exactly my skillset."

A low chuckle answered him. *"I don't mind, Mr. Harrison. In truth, Eidolon would be my first choice, but he is not accepting contracts at this time. But the reason why I've called you is very simple. You know how to get the job done. You're good at collecting the right people for the job, at wrangling them, and completing a task. I have faith that even if this isn't exactly in your skillset, you can still find the right people to team up with you and accomplish it."*

Okay, in that context, it made more sense. That was exactly Carter's reputation. He'd worked damn hard to have it, too. The problem was, he didn't really know who to call. He'd worked with many people over the years, but they were basically split into three categories for him: 1) Hell no, 2) Maybe, but not for this, and 3) Would love to, but have no idea how to reach him/her. Carter himself was a friendly guy and always wanted to make friends, but most of the people he worked with were private and sort of lone wolves by nature. They didn't want to stay in contact after the job was done. There were a few exceptions, but not many.

"Emura, I may or may not know the right people to help me pull this off. Tell you what, give me a few weeks to research this and see if I can pull a team together. If I can, I'll take a crack at it. If I can't, I'll tell you and let someone else have a crack at it."

"Fair enough, Mr. Harrison. For your information, I'm taking a one percent fee for this particular task."

Only one percent? That was either very generous of him or this was a doozy of a target. "And what's the job exactly?"

"Monet's Bridge Over a Pond of Water Lilies."

Carter let out a low whistle. The painting was worth forty-three million. But it was also supposed to be in the Metropolitan Museum of Art, if memory wasn't mistaken. "Who's my client?"

"The Metropolitan Museum of Art. The fee for the job is ten million."

Ouch. Now that was just embarrassing, having to steal back your own property. Carter assumed someone had screwed up royally if they were quietly trying to steal it back instead of just reporting it. "Wow. Okay, the terms are good. For now, consider the contract taken."

"I'll do so. I'll be in touch, Mr. Harrison."

"Yup, you bet." Carter hung up the call and saved the contact under Emura so he could find it again.

The driver, a curious soul, asked, "Another job already?"

"Looks like it. Reward for a job well done is another job, right?"

She snorted a laugh. "Yup, that's how it goes."

Carter stared out at the passing buildings and streetlights, mentally putting together a plan. The assassin known as Malvagio wouldn't be easy to find. But Carter really had no idea how to breach Knowles without his help. Emura was right on that point—this wasn't a one-man job anyway. It would take at least two people, and likely a team, to get in through Knowles' security.

The question was, how did he find an assassin?

6

ARI

Ari was willing to admit he might, possibly, have failed to think this through.

Normal might perhaps be outside of his skillset. The making pancakes in the morning, and teaching Remi computer hacking, and MMA—all of that was easy. After six months he still hadn't figured out the magic for a little girl's hair, but combing it seemed to work for now. And Remi was golden about being patient while he figured crap out.

School. School was definitely the issue.

His perfectly adorable little girl was sitting in the principal's office with a belligerent look on her face, eyes squinting evilly at the mother of her assailant. The mother glared right back at her, looking very upper middle class. The principal—who had her grey hair in a bun and wore a cardigan—was either exasperated or alarmed in turns. Neither woman seemed at all pleased to see him, which was unfair, in Ari's opinion. *He* hadn't hit anyone. (Yet.)

The mother, one Mrs. Pritchard, turned her steely-eyed glare at him, a visible tic at the corner of her mouth. "And where is Mrs. Benelli?"

"There is no Mrs. Benelli," Ari responded levelly. He was less focused on the women and more on his little girl as he took the hard plastic chair next to her. "Just me and Remi. Rems, what went down?"

Tilting in her chair, she looked up at him, still mad enough to spit nails. "That idjut Davy tried to put a hand up my shirt—"

Mrs. Pritchard tried to overrule her. "I'm sure you misunderstood—"

Giving her a look that could kill, Remi kept right on rolling, "—and he'd already done it to three other girls and got a warning for it, and a timeout, but he did it to me 'cause he thought I was an easy mark. I showed him different."

Ari beamed at her proudly. "That's my girl."

"*Mister* Benelli," the principal started in a hard tone. "I do not condone violence in my school."

"Yeah? What's your take on sexual harassment?" he countered easily, kicking back in his chair. He'd noted Mrs. Pritchard was now flushed with embarrassment. Didn't know her son was a letch, eh?

"Of course we don't condone that behavior either," Principal Walsh responded, irritated. "But the correct course of action in this case was for Remi to report Davy's behavior, not attack him."

"Seems like it already had been reported, by other girls, and Davy didn't care if he got a timeout or not. My daughter's well within her rights to punch anyone who puts a hand on her."

Principal Walsh ground her teeth audibly. "I quite disagree, and she did more than punch him."

"Yeah?" That was news to Ari. Then again, he'd only been in the office for two minutes and still hadn't gotten the full story yet. Looking at his Remi, he asked, "Whatcha do, kiddo?"

"Widow combo," she informed him proudly.

Ouch. The 'widow combo,' as Remi called it, was an MMA combination of strikes—a three-pointer designed to take an opponent down quickly and ruthlessly. It started with a knee to the groin, slamming the opponent's head down onto that same knee to break the nose, and then striking an elbow into the nape of the neck to take them down completely. Yeah, okay, widow's combo might have been a touch overkill. "Is he out?"

"Like a light," Remi confirmed, still proud of herself.

He didn't want to dissuade his daughter from defending herself, but he'd apparently failed to give her limits when teaching her martial arts. That was his bad. Ari tried to mitigate this a little without sounding like Remi was in trouble. "Yeah, okay, I agree he had it coming, but kiddo? It's kinda hard to get someone reported if they're not awake enough to answer questions."

Remi blinked up at him with her chocolate brown eyes, mouth forming a perfect *o*. "Rats, I didn't think of that."

"Yeah, maybe consider that next time," he counselled, relieved she saw his point. "You know, leave it at a blow to the groin if he's weak enough to go down with that."

"*Mister* Benelli," Principal Walsh snapped, looking horrified. "I don't want her hitting anyone at all!"

"And I don't want her in a position where she has to defend herself," he responded mildly. "Look, Principal, I know you got rules here. And I agree with most of 'em. But my little girl had another guy's hand up her shirt, which is non va bene. And if he's a repeat offender, I can see why she laid the guy out flat. She can't trust the teachers to stop him. So, if you don't want her hitting people? Maybe you should make sure the boys aren't doing bad-touches."

Both Walsh and Pritchard looked horrified by his logic. Ari briefly toyed with pointing out he routinely killed people who pissed him off, but figured that was too hardcore for elementary school. Also not helpful in this case. "Make you two a deal. I'll teach her to hold back, you teach Davy not to sexually harass the girls."

Walsh, at this point, had her head in both hands. "Mr. Benelli. By any chance, are you a soldier?"

"Was, yeah." Briefly. Before he got kicked out for insubordination.

"That explains a great deal," Walsh grumbled to the top of her desk. "I'm afraid I have to suspend Remi for a week for violence."

"Yeah, that's okay," Ari assured her. It likely would take him a week to teach Remi the appropriate amount of force to use in different circumstances.

"And Mrs. Pritchard," Principal Walsh continued, tone hardening, "While I am sorry Davy was hurt, I'm afraid Remi did have a point. We have tried multiple ways of disciplining your son without any effect. He is also suspended for a week, and if he touches another person inappropriately, I'm afraid I'll have to expel him."

Mrs. Pritchard was not happy—she was nearly purple with anger—but she managed a tight nod. "I understand."

"Good. Thank you both for coming in."

Glad to escape, Ari ducked out with Remi close on his heels. He now remembered why he'd ditched school more often than not. Taking Remi's hand, he held onto it as they walked to the parking lot. "You're lethal, kiddo."

She grinned up at him, pleased at this praise. "Am I like Black Widow?"

"You sure are getting there. You just gotta remember, Black Widow only uses full on force against guys trained to take the punishment."

Remi nodded agreeably. "I'll remember that next time."

"Okay." Ari took his first easy breath in the past half hour. Getting called into the principal's office was never a good thing, no matter what age a man was at. Although, he was proud of himself for getting them both out of there as he had.

See? He totally had a handle on this whole parenting thing. "Let's get ice cream, then you've got dance."

Still holding onto his hand, Remi did one of those ballet lunge things. "I like ballet."

"Yeah, honey, I know." It was a little expensive, what with the tutus and shoes and tights and all, but it helped her balance and developed her core strength. Worth it, in his opinion. Besides, Remi had so much fun with it, he loved watching her.

They got ice cream at the local mom and pop shop on the corner, basically killing time. Remi was all over the place, as usual, talking about anything that occurred to her. And a lot occurred to her, most of it random and disconnected. Some kind of switch had flipped in her head about two and a half months into their relationship. An *it's alright now,* and she turned almost overnight into this child who chattered and cuddled and was at ease with him. He much, much preferred this chatterbox over that silent child who flinched at everything.

There were still days he felt lost—like he had no idea what the fuck he was doing—and he knew he needed to get back in the game soon and take some jobs. But at least for the rest of the month he'd just focus on Remi. If today was any example, she wasn't quite ready to face the wide green world yet.

Or, he should say, the world wasn't ready for her.

They went to dance class. Mrs. Nelson was a genuinely nice woman who had been teaching dance for twenty years. She cut him some slack for being a single dad, always taking five minutes to put Remi's hair up in a bun before class started. He mostly felt awkward, sitting in the chairs off to the side of the long room. Pink tutus weren't exactly in his wheelhouse. But Remi loved having him there, and he was still new enough at this parenting thing, he didn't want her to think he'd gotten tired of her or some shit. It was easy enough to sit there and look at jobs on his phone, keep his ear to the ground.

They were learning pirouettes today, which Remi got down before any of the other girls. Ari felt a little smug about that. His Remi was a natural athlete. It made teaching her MMA really fun. She'd be terrifying in another ten years.

Class ended, the girls dispersed. Remi routinely spent ten minutes after class practicing what she'd learned, just to make sure she had it all down, so Ari didn't move. Mrs. Nelson, used to her, waved at Ari as she ducked into her office in the back of the building.

Ten minutes came and went, so he left the chair, intent on moving things along. "Come on, princess. Time's up."

"I don't have this down yet. There should be more of a *wooosh* feeling."

"Yeah, I'm feeling the *wooosh*, but you can practice at home if you want to keep going," he informed her. "The kitchen—" From the corner of his eye, he saw the door open, and he automatically tracked who had just entered. He knew the face well, even though he'd never actually crossed paths with the man in person. Whirling, he drew and leveled his Glock at the mercenary who had just walked in, keeping Remi behind him. "Harrison."

Splaying both hands to his sides, Harrison said evenly, "Hey, Malvagio."

Ari felt Remi put both hands on his waist and lean around him to get a look at the man. Harrison looked good, five-foot-ten of muscle and lethal grace. Salt and pepper highlights streaked his hair in the high faded sides, gelled-back top strands, and the stubble ringing his mouth. His skin glowed with a healthy tan, indicating he'd been somewhere warm recently. Rumor had it he'd started out as an Army Ranger before leaving. Now he was the mercenary people hired when they absolutely had to have the job done right the first time. Ari appreciated not only the professionalism of the man, but the rugged beauty he sported. For the first time in a long time, Ari's libido piped up and waved a flag of approval and interest, which was interesting.

It was just a shame he might have to kill him.

Mentally, Ari swore up a blue streak. How in hell had anyone—even Carter Harrison, who was admittedly very good at his job—found him? Ari had taken special pains to move into this small southern town without leaving a trace of his whereabouts, and he'd let it be known he was taking a few months break. He did *not* appreciate anyone showing up like this and blowing his cover, not to mention seeing Remi's face. He never wanted the underworld to be able to ID her. Although if he had to pick someone to stumble across them, Harrison was at the top of a short list. The man had a thing about kids, too.

Still, fear coursed through his veins like molten lava and left a bitter aftertaste in the back of his throat. Ari was abso-fucking-lutely not ready for someone aside from Ivan and Kyou to be around his daughter. His finger on the trigger spasmed with the need to pull it and not take any chances. Only Ari's common sense kept him from doing so. Carter hadn't done anything (yet) to deserve a head shot, and he didn't want Remi to see someone killed in front of her. Still, it was hard to curb the instinct.

"Daddy," Remi whispered in a carrying tone, "is he a good bad guy or a bad bad guy?"

"Totally depends if he's carrying right now, sweetie," Ari answered levelly. If the man had the stupidity to be packing in front of his little girl, Ari'd put a bullet in his leg. Just for the principle of it.

Harrison grinned down at her, as if he found her charming. Which was the correct response. Remi was charming. Harrison lifted his shirt hem, showing he was clean, then turned and lifted the back up enough to show he hadn't tucked something into his waist either. The jeans were a slim fit, not disguising any muscle, and making it clear he didn't have something strapped to his ankle, either. "Not packing," he reassured them both in a mellow baritone.

Only slightly relieved, Ari lowered the gun, aiming at the floor, but he didn't holster it. Not yet. Harrison didn't actually need a weapon. He *was* a weapon. He kept an ear out for Mrs. Nelson, who was still in the office, aware they had maybe five minutes to hash this out before they had to move. Or draw the wrong attention from the class of kids coming in next. "Why are you here, Harrison?"

"Need help on a job," Harrison admitted, finally bringing his eyes up to Ari's. Those slate blue eyes held a shade of disbelief, as if he couldn't quite reconcile the myth with the man standing in front of him. "Far as I know, you're the only one with the experience I need."

Ari knew he couldn't stay out of the game completely, and he hadn't been intending to really try, but this was sucky timing. He also had to appreciate Harrison's nerve in still standing there, calmly, because he had to sense that Ari really wanted to put a bullet in him. It made him want to hear the man out. "This something I can just walk you through?"

"Yeah, probably not. It's a two-man job, at least."

"What are we talking about, man?"

"Knowles."

Letting out a whistle, Ari rocked back on his heels. Knowles Museum and the Knox family did not play by the rules when it came to their collection, routinely pulling things out of people's estates and forging provenance papers stating they'd always had it. They had enough judges, policemen, and money that they got by with it. Ari had taken a job about nine months ago to crack Knowles and slip inside. It was one of the few times he'd been hired not to kill someone, but to retrieve a diamond ring the target wore. It had taken him a solid month of planning to even get into the mansion, and if he were being honest about it, he'd never have made it in without the help of both Kyou and Ivan. Thankfully, they'd been able to avoid breaking into the vault.

"Knowles is not easy to crack," Ari acknowledged slowly.

"Two-man job, you said. You coming out with something heavy?"

"More like awkward, but yeah."

"What's the pay?"

"Ten mil."

Ari knew better than to ask any further questions, not without some sort of understanding between them. He'd already pushed Harrison a touch too far as it was. Harrison likely gave him a pass on that because Remi stood right there, giving him good reason to ask questions.

The man still stood there calmly. Ari, in his shoes, would not have. Now that some of his initial panic had eased, Ari tried to consider this more rationally. Was he comfortable that someone aside from his inner circle knew about his daughter? No way in hell. But Harrison wasn't 'someone.' The man's reputation spoke for itself: he was a retrieval specialist who didn't betray anyone. Could Ari trust that reputation blindly? Probably not. But he was alright playing this out a little longer, getting a better read on the situation. Ari could always shoot the man later if he was a problem.

Besides, that payout...that was damn tempting. Ten million. Split two ways, five million. Damn, he could really go for five million. A little rainy-day money for both him and Remi if they needed it would be good. Sliding the gun back into its holster, he suggested, "Let's get an early dinner somewhere and talk this over. Remi, grab your stuff."

"Okay." Delighted, she skipped off to the cubby holes to grab her backpack and pull on street clothes.

Harrison watched her go, the tip of his tongue worrying his top lip. "You, ah, got someone who can watch her?"

"My current relationship status is that last night I slept with the clothes I was too lazy to fold; does that answer your question?" Ari responded dryly. Pulling out his phone, he shot off a quick text to Kyou to look up Carter Harrison. "It's fine, she's not a snitch. Are you, princess?"

"Rule two!" she agreed promptly, tugging on shorts over her tights.

"Rule one's don't be an asshole," Ari explained to the now bemused Harrison. "Rule two's don't be a snitch."

"You got many of these rules?"

"Just those two so far. Although I think rule three needs to be don't use deadly combos on the pleebs." Ari waved away the man's curiosity. "School. Long story. My name's Ari. Use that."

"Sure."

7

CARTER

Carter had heard the rumors, of course, that Malvagio wasn't in the game at the moment. No one quite knew why, just that he'd moved to the southern side of the United States and was being extremely closed mouthed about his exact location. It had taken Carter a month to track the man—a very frustrating, harrowing, headache inducing month, as Malvagio had taken extreme care to make sure no one knew where he was. Finding him in the dance studio was more fluke than anything. Carter had been walking the street and just so happened to spot Malvagio through the big open paned windows.

Of course, Carter finally understood exactly why Malvagio— Ari—had taken all of those precautions.

Who'd have thought the assassin known as 'Wicked' would be a father?

Remi was quite possibly the most beautiful little girl Carter had ever seen. He stared at her in bemusement as she pulled on her last tennis shoe. She was graceful for her age, not a wasted movement, slender like an athlete, with a doll shaped face, butterscotch colored hair, and warm chocolate brown eyes. She looked nothing like her father, who resembled more a dark, swarthy Italian pirate. Remi had to take after her mother.

He was under no illusions about the situation. Carter might have stumbled across them by accident, but if he dared to breathe a word about Remi to anyone, he'd have an enraged assassin after his head. In their world of violence, she was a very soft target. Carter was frankly lucky Ari hadn't shot him on sight. If their positions had been reversed, he probably wouldn't have hesitated.

Catching Ari's eye, he said quietly, "She's beautiful." The words conveyed what he didn't say: *I won't breathe a word about her. Sorry for seeing her, man, my bad.*

Ari relaxed a fraction of a hair and gave him a tight smile. "She is. And charming. And knows it."

Bouncing up to Ari, Remi caught his hand and batted her big brown eyes at him beseechingly. "Fries?"

"Why do you always want fries after dance? It's like an addiction." Rolling his eyes, Ari asked casually, "Want burgers and fries? There's a good joint about a block down; we can walk to it."

Carter was less concerned about food and more focused on getting this man's help. He nodded. "That's fine."

They left the studio, Remi on Ari's other side, Ari acting as a buffer between her and Carter. Carter was aware that just being near his daughter set the man on edge, so he tried to offset that a little. "I had no idea you had a daughter, and I've been looking for you for the past month."

Ari cast him a sharp glance from the corner of his eye. "Yeah? No one's heard about her yet, then?"

"Not a peep. All I had to go off at first was that you were in the Carolinas somewhere taking a break and wouldn't accept any contracts until June."

"I'm surprised you heard even that."

"It was a whisper, really, more of a rumor. Someone who knew someone spotted you coming through this area kind of thing. Seeing you in the dance studio was pure luck. I stopped here for gas."

Ari grunted satisfaction. "I worked hard to manage that."

"I could tell. It was a pain in the as—" Carter belatedly remembered a young child listened and wasn't sure if cussing was an okay thing, amending to, "—butt to find you. Where's Waldo has nothing on you."

Ari snickered.

Leaning around her sire, Remi informed him, "You can

cuss. Daddy does it all the time."

It was really giving him a headache, trying to fit the concept of 'daddy' and 'Malvagio, deadly assassin' in the same brain space. Carter went with the easier section of that sentence. "Okay. Thanks."

"And you can tell me stuff," she continued cheerfully. "I'm going to be like Black Widow when I grow up, so it's okay to talk about assassin stuff in front of me."

Ari caught his eye and gave him a minute shake of the head, indicating Carter better not just tell his little girl everything. Carter gave him a minute nod back to show he understood, but answered Remi, "Sure. Wait, really? You want to be like Black Widow?"

"Yeah, she's *awesome*," Remi enthused, bouncing for two steps, pulling at Ari in the process.

"Well, yeah, she's badass," Carter agreed. She wanted to be like Black Widow, but not her dad, who was an actual assassin? Kid logic hurt his brain.

The diner was a '50s mockup, with pink walls and blue barstools, serving an (un)healthy mix of greasy and fried foods. They settled into a back-corner booth, a waitress in roller skates took their orders, then they waited long enough for her to wheel out of earshot. Something about Ari and Remi looked entirely perfect sitting in the booth. It could have been their familiarity with the place, or that Ari had the right style to look like he was part of the scenery with his blue wash jeans and white t-shirt, but it was interesting either way. Carter did not feel as comfortable, but he put that down to knowing he had to state his offer carefully or risk getting shot. What didn't help his comfort level was finding Ari attractive. He'd always favored dark brunets. Ari's golden, sun-kissed skin and rangy build drew Carter's eye and attention. His ink black hair waving messily around his ears and intelligent espresso colored eyes ensured his attraction. The man looked downright edible, really. Carter gave the possibility of them getting it on a zero percent possibility with a chance of Hell Nopus, which was a shame. Because he'd so love to tap that.

He internally sighed, tapped down his libido before it could start whining, and firmly put himself into a more professional headspace. After their drinks arrived, he leaned in a little and said in a carefully low tone, "Job's a month out. I've got two months to complete it, but the best window I've found is in a month. I can show you the schedule I dug up, see if you disagree, but that's my time frame at the moment."

"Okay." Ari watched him like a hawk, idly playing with the strawberry milkshake in his hand. "What's the target?"

"A painting. *Bridge Over a Pond of Water Lilies.*"

"Monet's *Water Lilies*?" Ari hissed, surprise flaring those espresso eyes wide. "Isn't that supposed to be in the Met?"

"Yeah. Well, actually, it's still supposedly in the Met." Carter quirked an eyebrow and waited.

It didn't take Ari long. Whistling, he bit his lip to stifle a chuckle. "Now that's embarrassing."

Remi's eyes bounced between them and, growing impatient with the cryptic talk, finally tugged at Ari's sleeve. "What's going on?"

"A bad man stole a very famous painting," Ari explained rapidly in a whisper, "from a very famous museum of art. But the museum doesn't want to admit it's stolen, so they put a forgery up in its place."

"Ohhhh," Remi said in understanding. "Did the museum hire you, Mr. Harrison?"

He blinked at being so politely addressed. The idea of Malvagio having a daughter still messed with Carter's head something fierce, but they did make for a very cute picture. With their heads put together like that, the sunlight coming in from the window gleaming in their hair, they looked picturesque. Carter found himself smiling without intentionally meaning to. "Yes, that's right. They want this handled quietly. A quick swap, before their insurance is due to be updated and the painting tested."

"Ah." A small smile played around Ari's lips. "Therefore the deadline. Who took it?"

"Tricksy."

"Damn, that woman is good." Shaking his head in wonder, Ari confided to Remi, "Tricksy is one of the best thieves in the known world. I've only worked with her twice before, and it was a thing of beauty, watching her work. So we're undoing her hard work, huh?"

"You know that's only going to amuse her." Fortunately, Tricksy didn't care about what was stolen or if her colleagues put stolen property back. As long as she got her paycheck, she was good. Did that mean Carter wouldn't send her a head's up? Of course not. There were professional courtesies if nothing else to observe. Tricksy was not a woman you wanted to piss off.

Ari canted his head at Carter, clearly thinking hard, and coming to some internal decision. "I'll be honest with you, Harrison. I didn't get into Knowles alone last time. Frankly, I wouldn't have been able to."

Carter wasn't actually surprised to hear that. Knowles was worse than Fort Knox. It made sense Ari'd had help. "Who helped you?"

"Two friends. A professional thief and a hacker." Ari rubbed a hand along his jaw, the barely there stubble rasping audibly against his palm. "If you only have a month to pull this off? Then I highly suggest pulling them in. It's going to be a pain in the ass otherwise."

"It'll mean splitting the payment," Carter pointed out. He was intrigued, because if Ari was volunteering the information, it meant he was less inclined to shoot Carter. Something he'd said had pinged the man's curiosity enough that he wanted to actually take the job. It made him wonder who, exactly, Ari trusted enough to work with. The possibility of working with competent people was icing on the figurative cake after the last shit show Carter'd been on.

Ari shrugged. "Yeah. But I don't see how just the two of us can get in there without them. You a hacker?"

"I know a few tricks but I'm not *that* good."

"Yeah, me neither. I know you're just taking my word for it, but I trust these guys with my life. Better, I trust them with hers," he inclined his head down at Remi, who listened to them intently, "and they have the experience to get us in, as they've already done it once before."

That spoke well of them, alright. Still, Carter wasn't going to just blithely agree. "Will you tell me who they are?"

"K and Eidolon."

Carter let out a low whistle. "Damn, you know all the right

people, don't you?"

Ari grinned and shrugged as if this wasn't any big deal.

K was notorious—one of the best hackers in the business—and very, very private. Few knew his real name. No one knew where he lived or even what he looked like. In fact, this was the first time Carter had met someone who actually knew the hacker personally. The thief Eidolon was more visible. Harrison hadn't met him personally, but he knew of him. Knew that people called him Eidolon for a reason. The man could get in anywhere, as if walls didn't even pose a challenge. It was remarkable how many things he had stolen in his career, and Carter knew the man couldn't be over thirty. "I'm curious. Did it really take all three of you to get in?"

"Yeah. That's how difficult Knowles is." Ari gave him a pointed look and didn't say another word.

Carter had suspected Ari hadn't done the job alone, but the story he'd heard had only mentioned the assassin. Carter was just as glad rumor had chosen to pick out Malvagio and not the other two. Carter would still be looking next century if he tried to lay hands on either Eidolon or K.

"I'll be honest. I like working with teams. I especially like working with competent teams who already know the lay of the land. I'd rather split it four ways than not get a payout at all."

"That's about your only choices in the matter. Okay, in that case, let's pause this conversation until we can get the other two on the phone."

"Both uncles are coming in to work with you?" Remi asked in growing excitement. "Can I help Uncle K again?"

"You'll probably end up with him," Ari responded thoughtfully. "Best place for you during this job."

Since the hacker would be working remote, not inside with them. Yes, that was obvious. What startled Carter was that Remi called both of these men 'uncles.' She knew them. When Ari said he trusted both of these men with his daughter, he hadn't been just throwing words around. If Ari trusted him enough to offer all of this, did that mean he could finally relax and move his hands off the table? Carter visually imagined doing that and then re-considered, keeping them carefully in sight.

"Where you staying?" Ari asked casually.

"I don't have anywhere at the moment," Carter admitted slowly, trying to figure out what this question led to. That was supposed to be a casual question, correct? Carter's instincts didn't throw up a red flag, but he still found it impossible to really relax on the bench. "I just drove into town this morning. All of my gear is still in the car."

"Hmm. Alright, let's go to the park after this and get those two on the phone. They'll likely have a safe house you can crash at. It'll be smarter to stay there, all things considered. And we'll move there too after we get school done." Ari sighed and gave his daughter a long look. "Two more weeks."

She grinned back up at him. "Then summer vacation!"

"You have no idea how relieved I am by that, kiddo. You're brutal on the pleebs." Ari commiserated to Carter, "Some moron tried to stick his hand up her shirt. She flattened him."

Huffing on her nails, Remi buffed them against her shirt, chest sticking out proudly. "I sure did."

Carter considered the facts. Daughter raised by notorious assassin. Unarmed/unskilled eight-year-old boy. "Is he still breathing?"

"Yeah, although I understand she broke his nose." Ari tried to look put upon but he still had a proud gleam in his eye.

Carter found the expression humanizing. Ari truly looked like a father, and only a father, in that moment. The tension keeping Carter stiff in his seat finally unwound enough he dared to drop a hand to rest casually on his lap. Ari didn't even seem to notice. (Which was a lie, of course he did, but it didn't make the man nervous.) Carter relaxed a notch further and studied Remi thoughtfully. If she was already doing this at eight, what would she be like at eighteen...? Carter looked at the little girl sharing a booth with him and the word 'formidable' floated in his mind. "Good for you."

Remi beamed at him. "Mr. Harrison, do you have kids?"

"Ah, no. I'm single. No kids."

She sighed, thin shoulders slumping. "No one has kids."

Carter looked to Ari for a translation on that one. Ari gave his daughter a consoling pat on the shoulder. "She really wants a playmate. Someone who's in a similar situation that she doesn't have to pretend with. But most people in our profession don't really have families. Or if they do, they're certainly not going to advertise it. Too dangerous."

He saw the problem but really, there wasn't a good solution. "Sorry, Remi."

"It's okay," she sighed again.

Their food arrived, and everyone dug in. The topic shifted to different things, mostly about what was happening in the world and news stories. They finished up and walked out casually, like any couple out with their daughter, and down the street another block. A small park surrounding the old train station— now gift shop—lay devoid of people. They settled on a green, metal bench with Remi sitting on her father's knee. Ari pulled his phone up and called K, putting the phone to his ear. Carter watched curiously and kept his mental fingers crossed that both pros would agree to the contract.

Ari's demeanor softened as he answered, "Hey, K. Yeah, professional call this time. Yeah, that text. He found me today."

Carter's mouth went dry. Shit. Ari had shot off a quick text to someone at the dance studio. Carter hadn't thought much of it, too busy reeling from seeing Remi. But of course Ari would have alerted someone that Carter was there. K would be the obvious choice—the one who could remotely keep track of the situation. Just how close had he already come to being targeted by *two* criminals?

Maybe he should buy a lottery ticket. His luck was proving phenomenal today.

Ari shot him a dry glance. "Yeah, tell me about it. Anyway, he came looking for a reason. He's got a job involving Knowles that he wants help with. Two-month deadline, but best opening to get the job done is in a month, according to him. Contract's 10 mil. You up for it? Okay, hang on." Putting the phone on his knee, he hit speaker. "Alright, you're on speaker."

"Hello, Harrison."

"Hello, K." He sounded...young? If he was older than his twenties, Carter would eat his boots. He also didn't sound ready to take Carter out. Maybe even friendly, which was a good sign. Carter went with being extra polite, just in case. "Thanks for speaking with me."

"I admit I'm intrigued. Ari's clearly agreed to work with

you, otherwise we wouldn't be having this conversation. I'm not inclined to let him go back into Knowles alone, especially with his current situation."

"He knows about me," Remi pitched in.

There was an audible hiccup. *"Well, hell. That puts a spin on things. Princess, how'd you get discovered?"*

"He found us at my dance class."

"Ah. Harrison, you're lucky you're still breathing right now."

"Trust me, I feel my luck," Carter assured him, meaning every word. "And I know better than to breathe a word about her. K, in the interest of full disclosure, do you want me to tell you the target before you agree?"

"I do want to know, but it's not necessary. I've read your file, Harrison. You're not the type to betray people. You've got my help and I expect one-fourth of your payment."

Carter took the first full breath he'd managed in the past half hour. "I have no problem with that. We have an agreement. Target's Monet's *Bridge Over a Pond of Water Lilies.*"

K put the pieces together rather quickly and started laughing. *"Oh, now that's embarrassing. The Met's focus this month is on Monet. And what's up right now in their gallery is a forgery? Priceless. I can guess who our client is, but who stole it to begin with?"*

"Tricksy."

"Ah? Well, that'll make our thief friend happy, as he loves ribbing her. Have you spoken with Eidolon yet?"

"No," Ari said, "I called you first. Want to pull him in for a conference call? You know he'll agree."

"Of course he'll agree. He loves working with the princess and he's always ready for a challenge. I think he's been bored the past two weeks, too. And you know what he's like when he's bored."

Ari shuddered. "And the eastern seaboard is still intact?"

"Yeah. Barely. Call him, see if he picks up."

Ari punched a few buttons on the phone, adding 'Eidolon' into the call. Harrison appreciated that even on his personal phone, Ari was cautious enough to not use anyone's real name. That kind of paranoia kept people alive.

The phone rang three times before a deep, rough voice answered brightly, "*Ari!* *How is my solnishko?*"

"Your solnishko is fine and dandy but I've got you on speaker with Carter Harrison," Ari informed him quickly. "K's with us on the call too. We've got a job we want to run past you."

"*Da*," Eidolon said instantly.

"Is that a 'yes, go ahead and speak' or 'yes, I'll do it?'" Ari asked dryly. "Because it sounded like the latter."

"*I get to play with my two friends and see my precious solnishko. Of course I'll come! What's the job?*"

"Knowles," Carter answered. He could not believe it was this easy to hire all three of these men. He'd expected days of negotiations, not this instant response. Especially as Eidolon had been refusing jobs lately. "Specifically, we're to retrieve Monet's *Bridge Over a Pond of Water Lilies* and restore it to the Met."

"*Tricksy stole it for Knowles; we're undoing her work,*" K threw in.

Eidolon laughed evilly. "*What a wonderful present. It's not even my birthday. Mr. Harrison, it'll be a delight to work this job. What's the pay?*"

"Client's giving me 10 mil. I'll split it with you guys four ways." Wait, that response made it seem that Eidolon hadn't even heard about the job. Eidolon was too keen on taking it and was ignorant of even the basics. Just what had his broker done to contact the thief? Had he even tried?

"*Excellent. I've done more work for less. When do we start?*"

"Best window to get in that I've found is about a month from now," Carter informed him. He set his curiosity aside to be satisfied later. "But you might see something I didn't. B&E isn't exactly my forte."

"*Hmm. K, I think you and I need to put our heads together and get a firmer idea. For now, are we all meeting up?*"

"*You three can. I'll mostly be working remote on this. I'll be nearby if I need to jump in, though.*"

Ari nodded as if this didn't surprise him. "Fair enough. We need a safehouse for Harrison, K. You got something in this area we can use? Rem's not out of school just yet so I'd prefer to stay here a little longer until we're ready to move."

"*Not really.*"

"*He can stay with me,*" Eidolon volunteered readily. "*I have enough room for a guest.*"

"*Yeah, that's more feasible,*" K agreed without giving Carter a chance to get a word in edgewise. "*Harrison, I'll text you the address.*"

Carter stared suspiciously at the phone. "You don't have my number."

"*You're adorable. Talk with you later.*" K abruptly hung up.

Ari snickered at Carter's expression. "Just assume K knows everything."

"*Faster that way,*" Eidolon agreed equably. "*I was bored; this is good timing. See you soon, solnishko!*"

8

ARI

Ari waited until later that night to call Kyou again. He was fairly sure he'd made the right judgement call, but it never hurt to double check. Remi was in a massive bubble bath, singing at the top of her lungs, so it was safe to do some business. A light wind rustled through the trees, taking the edge off the humidity, which he appreciated. It was a typical southern night, light on the heat and bugs, although he kept the screen door closed on his back porch. No sense taking chances. They were at the far edge of a subdivision, hovering on that edge of having good internet connection and yet some privacy at the same time. He sat in a chair on the patio, enjoying the night breeze and a beer, and called up his friend.

"*Speak,*" Kyou deadpanned.

"That joke never gets old for you, does it?"

"*Is it my fault that your childhood was so lacking you don't know* The Addam's Family? *What's up?*"

"You'd tell me if I needed to shoot Harrison, right?"

"*Dude. That is quite possibly the stupidest question you've ever asked me, and you've asked some really stupid questions over the past fifteen years. Unless he's done something that's made you uneasy?*"

"No. No, he hasn't. He's reassured me he won't breathe a word about Remi. It's just..." Ari trailed off, not sure how to explain his fears and make it sound rational. He'd never envisioned, back when he decided to take Remi in, that he'd be seized with irrational urges where she was concerned. That just the thought of her being harmed would constrict the breath in his chest so hard it hurt.

"You know we won't let anyone touch the princess. I've got multiple alerts on her. If anyone even looks at her funny, I'll know. I wouldn't have accepted the job if I had any doubts about Harrison anyway. He's been in this business almost as long as we have, and he's never once double crossed anyone. And he's careful with kids."

"I know. It's why I didn't shoot him on sight. He wasn't even packing when he came to talk to me. I think he ditched the gun before stepping in. He didn't want to scare Remi."

"Yeah, that fits with what I know of the man. You're just rattled someone aside from us can ID her."

Ari took a swig of beer rather than answer because that was it exactly. The fear ran strong enough he was half-tempted to shoot Harrison regardless. But he'd promised he wouldn't do that, and he didn't want to become a man who let his fears rule over him. "You coming in to stay with us for this job?"

Squawking, Kyou protested, *"I can work remote!"*

"Really? You of all people know how much Ivan has to be babysat with tech. You really think you can walk him through it remotely? And you know good and well Remi will need to sit with you when we go in. I can't leave her on her own."

Kyou whined, *"But the outernet is scary."*

"Getting away from your computer monitors will be healthy for you. Not to mention taking a break from your stalking."

"Excuse you very much, I am not stalking him. I am looking out for his interests."

"For two years. Without pay. Suuure, that's not stalking." Ari was mostly teasing. Mostly. Kyou really had been cyberstalking one man in particular. He claimed it was to repay a debt but wouldn't give Ari or Ivan any real details about it. They weren't even sure who the man was. "Your love life aside—"

Kyou squawked again, sounding like a parrot choking on a cracker.

"—you need to come. You know you do."

There was a lot of grumbling on the other end of the line

and not much agreement.

"Kyou. You know that if you don't have Remi with you, she'll get into something. She wants to be part of what we're doing."

"*Yeah. She's cute that way. And it's true, I wouldn't mind another set of eyes while dealing with Knowles. At least she knows some of what I'm doing. The rest of you are clueless.*"

Ari would protest, but it would not help his case. "So when do you get here?"

Sighing as if the world was coming to an end, Kyou grudgingly answered, "*Gimme a few days. I have some loose ends to tie up, and I need to pack my equipment before I can come.*"

Ari pumped his fist in the air in victory. Getting Kyou out of his lair took a lot of baiting/bribery/threats these days. The computer hacker preferred to be safely tucked away from the world with a monitor between himself and society. Remi was the most reliable way to draw him out, but not always. "She's really excited to be working with you again, you know."

"*I know. Ari...can I level with you?*"

"That doesn't sound foreboding or anything."

"*It's just, I know the rising generation is good with tech. They seem to be born with the know-how. But Remi's...Remi's really good with it. She instinctively understands what needs to be done. I know she's all set to be an assassin, like Black Widow, but do you really want her to do that?*"

"In all honesty, not really. I'm good at what I do, but it's come at a cost. And I don't want her to pay the same price. She'd be safer as a hacker. You willing to train her?"

"*I already have been. Which is why we're having this conversation. We need to find ways to leave her with me more often, is all I'm saying. Open her mind to the possibility. She's only eight, it's not like she should be deciding on a career anyway at this point.*"

"I wholeheartedly agree with you, man. And look at you, being a good uncle and shit."

"*How I became an uncle when I'm not even related to you is my question.*"

"It's because she's adorable."

"*Lethal is what she is. Alright, I'll be there in about three days, okay? Maybe two. And I'll keep an eye on Harrison. I don't think I need to, but better safe than sorry."*

"Yeah. Thanks, man. I'll see you in a few days." Ari hung up and let the phone drop onto the round, glass table at his side. He took another swig of beer and relaxed a bit further. He felt better with having someone on hand for this job to look after Remi.

Kyou and Ivan, as it turned out, were a godsend. They always pitch-hit when he needed a babysitter, which was fairly often. Six months ago, when he'd taken his daughter in, Ari hadn't envisioned how much help he'd need to raise her. But the old saying was true. It really did take a village to raise a child. His village happened to be his lawyer brother, a professional hacker, and a Russian thief. Probably not what most people would advise, but Remi was happy and thriving, and that's all he cared about.

Speak of the devil. She came out in her Batman pajamas, hair still dripping wet from the bath. Remi climbed into his lap without any invitation, a bit heedless where her limbs went.

"Elbows," Ari gasped out, flinching as one hit him dead in a place an acupuncturist would not suggest putting pressure.

She giggled, as if he were teasing. Ari had not been able to convince her that her elbows were in fact deadly, even for him. But she got comfortable, butt on his thigh, delicate hands resting on his chest and arm. "Daddy. Is Uncle Kyou coming too?"

"He sure is. I just talked to him. He said he has some stuff to wrap up, then he'll be here. Three days, more or less. He wants your help on this one," Ari added, planting the idea early on in her brain to prevent arguments later. "Knowles is going to be tough. The more eyes he has on the cameras, the better."

Remi perked up at this possibility. "Really? He said that?"

"He did. You don't mind helping him, do you? You're the only one who can. You know his systems better than we do."

She nodded, accepting this as truth. Which it was. (That time Ivan attempted to help Kyou was a thing best buried and forgotten.)

"Daddy. I like Mr. Harrison."

"Yeah?"

A little worried, she asked, "You're not going to shoot him, are you?"

So she'd caught his worry, had she? Damn, this kid was sharp. "I don't want to, sweetie. And I won't, unless he gives me very good reason to. But I don't think he will. Uncle Kyou and I, we know his rep. He doesn't double-cross people, he's honest about any contract he takes, and he's careful with innocents. Kids especially. I don't think I have to worry about him with you."

"But you're going to keep an eye on him anyway." She said this as a foregone fact.

"Yeah. Going off first impressions gets you killed. Besides, it's not a hardship. He's a beautiful man." Shiiit he should not have said that. Ari had fallen into the habit of just talking to Remi, telling her whatever, as she was a good listener. And he wanted good communication lines between them. But that, that he should not have said.

Remi's face lit up hopefully. "Will you ask him out?"

"Honey." Ari dropped his head to the back of the patio chair. Dammit. This question about dating kept cropping up in different ways since their first conversation about him being gay. Like now.

"But you said, if you find a guy you think is beautiful, and knows about your real job, you'd be able to date him. It's just that not many nice men know about you." Her mouth twisted up in something dangerously close to a pout.

"I said all of that, yeah. But honey, Harrison is just here for a job. In a month, he'll be gone on to the next job."

Her expression closed off and she shrank in on herself. "I don't think that's it. It's because of me."

Shit. And this was why he didn't want to talk about dating. Ari wrapped an arm around her, hugging her into him and kissing her forehead. How to get this through to her? "No, Rems, it really isn't. I promise you, it isn't."

"It's harder to date when you have kids. Mo—she always said so."

Any oblique references to the woman who'd given birth to Remi inevitably ended up in conversations he really, really didn't want to have. "That may be true, but honey, I was single long before I found you. I promise you, it's not because I'm a dad that makes dating hard. I'm just hard to date."

She didn't look at all convinced.

Ari had no idea why Remi was fixated on this point. It might be fear, that if she stood in his way, he'd grow tired enough of it and get rid of her. It might be that she wanted him happy too. It could be something else entirely, something he hadn't thought of. Ari had lost his mother at eight, so he didn't really remember what it was like to have a parent—his crappy foster parents didn't count—and he couldn't really put himself in her shoes and figure it out. His memories of his mother were murky, to say the least. It would likely take a child psychologist to unravel the mystery, and he had too many secrets to keep to make that a viable option.

All he could do was reassure her, time and again, that it was alright. That everything was fine. Ari had never for one second regretted rescuing her. "Rems, odds are he's straight. And straight men don't always react well when another man flirts with them. I don't want to make him uncomfortable, okay?"

Her shoulders dropped as she deflated. "Okay. But if he likes you, will you ask?"

Ari gave that a fat chance, so the promise was easy to make. "Sure. I'll ask. In the meantime, off to bed with you."

"It's early," she pointed out, not budging. "And I don't have school tomorrow."

Arching an eyebrow at her, he challenged, "And I'd thought you'd want to go play with Ivan. Didn't he say he wanted to teach you safe cracking next time? We've got three days before Kyou gets here, don't you think he'll want to teach you while we're waiting?"

Her eyes widened and she was off his lap in a flash, sprinting back inside. "Night, Daddy!"

So easy. He chuckled as he lifted the beer back to his lips. "Night, sweetie!"

As the door slammed shut behind her, his smile faded. He'd bluffed Remi that he wasn't interested, but in fact, something about Carter had caught his attention. Ari didn't really notice men, not like that. He could visually find someone appealing and not be at all tempted to touch. Something about Carter looked touchable though, and damned if he understood why. Even if he figured it out, he didn't think Carter would be around long enough for him to even consider an approach.

Taking another swig of beer, he shrugged off his strange attraction to the man. It was a moot point, anyway. Carter was clearly not comfortable around him, and that was assuming the man would be interested in the first place. Remi's hopes were dashed on this. Oh well.

Finishing his beer, he got up and went to bed. There was plenty to do and not much time to do it in. If he were smart, he'd get some good shut eye while he could.

9

CARTER

In the normal course of events, Carter found the idea of sharing a roof with another criminal to be, well, normal. Sharing one with Ivan Azarov made him wish for a safe room. The man had been welcoming enough when Carter drove up into his driveway, even introducing himself by his real name, but that didn't squash any of the butterflies duking it out in Carter's stomach. Rumor had it that Ivan held ties with the Russian mafia. No one was clear on how, just that he'd left the mother country twelve years ago and chose to work primarily in the US. Sometimes Europe. The tattoo on the man's chest that peeked out from underneath his shirt collar hinted he was part of *something*, so Carter was inclined to give that rumor some truth.

Normally, he wouldn't have given staying near the man another thought. He often teamed up with other criminals to get a job done. Mercs weren't really lone wolves by nature. They liked teams, it was how they operated, and Carter was more sociable than most. But the way Ivan had immediately greeted Remi with a warm and affectionate *solnishko!* (which if Carter's Russian was correct, meant little sun) stank of potential trouble. The thief clearly adored Remi, and he would not look on Carter favorably because of it. Carter's knowledge of her would land him on the wrong side of Azarov's good will.

So he was on guard when he wandered down into the

kitchen of the huge, two-story house he'd bunked in last night. He had no idea where Ivan was, and he wanted to properly scope the place out, as it had been late when he'd gotten in. Ivan had given Carter a quick tour, turned on the security system, and then they'd both gone to bed. Carter had slept with a gun in his hand, but that was just to be expected.

Today, he wanted to properly see the aircraft hangar in the backyard and scope out the property some, but he wouldn't. Not until he knew where a certain thief was.

The smell of pancakes and coffee wafted out into the hallway. His nose twitched, mouth salivating in appreciation, and he stepped through the wide doorway and into a kitchen that'd likely seen its last renovation in the late '90s. All the beige and brown were a good clue.

Ivan stood at the stove without either a shirt or apron on, flipping pancakes. He was a tall figure of a man, whipcord lithe and with the grace of an MMA fighter. A couple years younger than Carter's own thirty-five, perhaps, with just a hint of crow's feet. He wore dark wash jeans, setting off his pale skin and short, ruffled acorn brown hair. The thief looked...dangerous, to sum it up in a single word. The Glock riding in a holster at the man's waist might have something to do with that impression, too. He glanced over his shoulder as Carter entered and gave him a nod, grey eyes friendly enough on the surface. "Morning, Harrison."

"Morning, Azarov," Carter returned in the same manner. "That smells good."

"There's enough for you as well," Ivan assured him.

"Oh? Thanks." Carter went and fetched a mug. As he did, he got a better look at Ivan's chest and the interesting collection of tattoos on the man's collarbone. An eight-pointed star was dominant in the space, with two smaller stars and a sun below it. The eight-pointed star was Russian mafia lingo for a professional thief. Carter knew that much, but he'd never seen the combination of three stars and a sun before. What the hell did that mean? He wanted to ask but thought it safer to let it ride, and instead poured himself a coffee, noting Ivan had indeed made enough for both of them. He was certainly thoughtful. Or buttering Carter up for the kill.

Ivan must've been a mind reader, as he paused before putting more batter in the pan, eyeing Carter sideways. "You worried about me?"

Dammit. Carter had a better poker face than this, he knew he did. "Can you blame me? I went looking for Malvagio. Instead I find his daughter, who happens to be adored and protected by three of the toughest men in the industry. If you decide I'm a threat to her, I'll never see you coming."

"Keep that attitude, and you'll live." Ivan had the audacity to wink before going back to the pancakes.

The man sucked at reassurances. Well, maybe he should take the pancakes as a sign that Ivan didn't expect to kill him later. Unless, of course, the pancakes were poisoned. Or the coffee. Just what the hell had he walked into, anyway?

"You say the best opening is a month from now?" Ivan asked casually, shifting a done stack of pancakes over in Carter's direction.

He eyed them with a sort of paranoid resignation. He didn't dare turn those down. And really, he didn't expect Ivan to kill him now. Carter was the one who'd accepted the contract. The one who knew who to return the painting to. It would be *after* the job was over that his life would be in imminent danger. He took the pancakes.

"That's my take on it. Knowles is scheduled to have an upgrade in about a month—software and cameras. It will take a straight week for them to do everything. If we don't hit them before that upgrade, we'll have a very narrow window of two and a half weeks to scope the place out, plan our entrance, and pull the job off."

Ivan let out a low whistle, grey eyes narrowed thoughtfully. "Instead of the four weeks we have now. Tight, either way."

"Trust me, I know. I spent a month looking for Malvagio, and I could feel time ticking away in the back of my head the whole time." The pancakes were actually rather good. Light and fluffy. Carter stood with the plate in his hand, his hip leaning against the counter's edge, balancing both words and food. He shifted a bit more to avoid leaning against the gun at his back. "But he's the only one I knew of who'd successfully gotten in and out. I didn't even want to attempt the job without him."

"I don't blame you. I'd not want to attempt it alone, either."
A quick grin crossed over Ivan's face, making him look friendly
for a second. "In fact, I didn't. Last time, we came out with a
diamond ring. It was hard enough with a small object in hand.
With a painting? That much harder."

"Not to mention we'll need into the vault." Just thinking
about it gave Carter a headache.

Ivan's head canted in question, studying him. "Why did you
take the job?"

"Honestly? They came to me. And they were frank about
the fact they'd tried to reach you first and couldn't find you.
They thought maybe I could do it. I gave them no promises but
said if I couldn't crack into Knowles inside of a month, I'd tell
them. Give someone else a shot at it."

"Fair."

Carter debated the wisdom of asking. Curiosity won out.
"You're normally reachable for jobs. I was surprised they
couldn't get you for this one."

"Got injured six months ago," Ivan answered smoothly.
"Took a month off to heal. Then Ari came in with Remi, and I
stayed dark a little longer, helping him."

That made sense. No, wait, it didn't. "Ah..."

Ivan shot him a look.

No, his curiosity wasn't worth getting stabbed. And stabbing
was in his near future if he asked why Malvagio only had Remi
as of a few months ago. He covered his curiosity with a different
question. "So, I take it Remi typically hangs out with you guys
while you're planning a job?"

"Normally. She's in school for a few more weeks now." Ivan
turned back to the pan to flip the pancake.

"She's suspended this week, actually."

Ivan's head came around sharply in surprise. "Suspended?"

"A boy at school tried to put his hand up her shirt," Carter
explained, the words strange in his mouth. It felt surreal to
know something about Remi that Ivan didn't. "She flattened
him."

Ivan snickered evilly. "That's my solnishko."

"Is she really that good? I mean, she's in elementary school."

"She trains every day. And she wants to be good. That

attitude makes her focus." Ivan's gaze turned distant for a moment. "She likes to connect with us. She wants to be part of what we're doing. We often teach her things, share with her what we know. It will help safeguard her, if trouble comes."

He had that right. Carter had no idea why Remi was with her assassin father instead of her mother, but if she was? Then there had to be a damn good reason for it.

Ivan finished up his stack and flicked the stove off, turning and also leaning against the counter in order to eat. As his fork cut into the stack, he asked casually, "You have some information about Knowles, I assume?"

"Yeah, a little. I dug into it while searching for Mal—Ari. I wasn't able to get a lot." Carter shrugged because that more or less went without saying. Knowles was worse than Area 51. "But I can pull up my laptop and let you read what I do have."

"Da, do that. And I will give you K's email, you can send the information to him. Save him a little time."

"Yeah, sure."

Ivan had to swallow his mouthful before answering. "Forgot to mention, K will join us. We'll need him on hand for this."

Wow. He'd actually get to meet the man behind the legend? Carter was one part intrigued two parts unnerved. If this went sideways, he was so in over his head. "Gotcha."

The front door opened and both men went tense, hands on guns, their manner alert.

"We're here!" Ari called out.

Ah, good. Carter relaxed again and went back to eating, watching as Remi came through the kitchen door first.

A brilliant smile lit her face as she went straight to Ivan, tackling him around the thighs. "Uncle Ivan!"

Ivan dropped a hand to rest on the back of her head, smiling at her in turn. It softened the man's expression, which was an interesting effect. He looked less I-am-the-shadow-you'll-never-see-coming and more doting uncle. "There's my solnishko. I hear you flattened a stupid boy who tried to put his hands on you?"

She grinned up at him impishly. "Widow's combo."

Clearly, the thief knew what that meant, and he cackled. "Ah, my solnishko, you are a joy. I'm sorry I missed it. Do you need pancakes?"

She batted large chocolate brown eyes up at him, looking plaintive and pitiful. "Pancakes?"

"Don't let her give you that." Ari glared down at his daughter. "I fed her this morning."

"Yogurt." She made a face.

"And toast," he reminded her.

Remi ignored that completely and went back to making puppy eyes at Ivan. Who, predictably, caved and started feeding her bites off his own plate. Carter got the impression this was an ongoing scene and it had absolutely nothing to do with whether Remi was full or not. It was a subtle sense of something not quite right, although he couldn't put his finger on why he felt that way.

The byplay distracted him for a moment but he couldn't really ignore Ari for more than two seconds. The man was like the elephant in the room. He'd been skating on thin ice with this man all day yesterday and confusedly attracted—and those two feelings did not mix well. It left Carter with a sort of sour feeling in his gut. Today, apparently, Ari was more inclined to be amiable. Or at least, he no longer looked a breath away from shooting Carter between the eyes. The assassin even managed a civil nod good morning, which Carter returned.

"Kids are bottomless pits," Ari groused to Carter. "They should come with warning labels. She's constantly stealing bites from people's plates. Harrison, K said he'll be here in about three days. Maybe two. He's got some loose ends to tie up first. I thought we could walk through what we know of Knowles, maybe do some preliminary scouting while waiting on him."

"Outer perimeter scouting, at least," Ivan agreed while hand-feeding Remi another bite. "I don't want to go inside without him."

"Yeah, me neither. But a good look at the outer perimeter won't hurt. You down for that, Harrison?"

"Sure." So they were going to start on a professional footing? He could work with that. Carter swallowed a mouthful of coffee before adding, "I do have some intel on me. You want to go through that first?"

"Yeah, that'd be good."

It took a few minutes for them to get situated around the worn-in kitchen table. Carter grabbed his laptop, then pulled up the schedule for the security changes, as well as the upcoming timeline of events. It made for a tight squeeze, all three men pressed next to each other so they could read the screen, with Remi balanced on Ivan's knee. Carter ended up with his thigh and hip smack against Ari's which…wasn't helpful.

Swallowing the impulse to flirt down, he focused on the screen. "So here we have it. There's six events over the next six months, most of them in the next two. They're moving inventory around, changing out which art pieces they're going to show. They've got new purchases coming in for the museum upstairs. They've got two gala thingies I expect will be a major blowout, at least a thousand in attendance for each one. I don't know if it'll be easier to hit them during a party?"

"Tougher," Ari and Ivan denied in unison. Ari waved for Ivan to explain.

"They double, sometimes triple, security during such events." Ivan's nose scrunched up in disgruntlement. "We used a party last time because the cover of more people allowed Ari in close to the mark. But in our case, it will not be good. Zanuda. Njet, not a good idea."

"Let's get K on the phone real quick. I want to run through the basics before we figure out our next step. He might know something we don't," Ari added to Ivan. "You know what an information hoarder he is."

Ivan grunted agreement. "A magpie, that one. Alright."

Without prompting, Remi pulled a tablet from her backpack and punched in a video call. Carter was rather impressed with how competently she did so, and on a program he didn't recognize. Then again, it was probably something of K's creation. He couldn't imagine a professional hacker using box store apps. When the call connected, she smiled. "Hi, Uncle K!"

Carter blinked at the screen. With only a single letter code name, he'd not known what to expect of the hacker. K, apparently, was of Asian descent. Those eyes were pitch dark, his face oval in shape with a paler skin tone, no doubt from staying indoors all the time. His blue-black hair was cut in a low fade, the longer, textured strands brushing his forehead in a ruffled sort of way. K the hacker was rather cute, actually, in a geeky way. And if he were older than thirty, Carter would turn straight.

"*Hey, princess. What's up?*"

Ari tilted sideways in his chair to be seen on the screen. He braced himself against the table, no part of him touching, but it made him basically tilt over into Carter's lap which also was very unhelpful. "We want to run through the job and the basics of Knowles. Thought we might do some setup and a perimeter sweep while waiting on you."

"*Sure, not a bad idea. Harrison, let's start with job specifics. Who's your broker on this one?*"

"Emura," Carter answered. He got four blank looks in response. Granted, brokers popped in and out of this business, but it didn't bode well that these three hadn't heard of him. "Ah...you don't know who that is."

K frowned and shook his head slowly. "*No, I don't. You worked with him before?*"

"No, actually; this is the first contact I've had with him."

"What were the terms, exactly?" Ivan inquired.

"He handled all money and contact with the client. Takes one percent fee. I thought it was fairly standard, except the fee, as it is a rather large payout."

"Even one percent would be a good chunk of change and not much work on his end," Ari agreed, but he was still frowning. "Still, almost every million-plus job I've taken had a ten percent broker's fee."

"*Remi,*" K requested, "*Look this guy up for us.*"

Remi seemed all too happy to participate, and she promptly minimized the screen and shuffled it off to the side. With the smooth expertise of a criminal, she had the job site up and logged into, searching under the broker's page. Carter was more than a little impressed. She did stuff like this often?

His attention was pulled from her by Ivan's next question.

"If we're going to be doing this stealthy?" He waited for Carter's nod of confirmation before continuing. "Then the painting will need to be switched out. Who is the forger?"

"Emura said he's got Lansky working on it."

Ivan, K, and Ari all groaned. Ivan actually flopped halfway

across the table.

Carter did not like that reaction. "Why? Is Lansky no good?"

"Lansky is exceptionally talented," Ivan denied, still sighing like doom had just knocked on his door. "But he's the slowest painter I've ever seen."

"He's a perfectionist," Ari explained, and he too looked like doom was kicking the door down. "He won't surrender a painting until it's absolutely perfect. It takes months, sometimes a full year, to get a forgery from him. For a quick job like this, he's not a good choice."

That uneasy feeling from before doubled and settled uneasily in his gut like bad sushi. "Honestly, I felt like something was a little off when Emura contacted me. Why hire a merc? This isn't really in my field."

Ari's brows arched. "But you took it."

"Well, yeah, 'cause that's a pretty paycheck, and I had this crazy notion that if I found you, I might be able to pull a team together and get it done."

Ari spread a hand and canted his head in acknowledgement. After all, Carter had managed just that.

"Found him," Remi announced. "Emura, no last name. Registered six months ago as a broker. Has only seven jobs on his resume. Here, Uncle K, I'm sharing screens."

Ari and Ivan leaned over her shoulder to get a look. The reaction was pretty much instantaneous and simultaneous.

"Chert svoloch."

"Figlio di puttana."

"*This bastard again?*"

Carter's head swiveled between them, alarm climbing. "Just how bad is this guy?"

"That is Derek Collins. Last job I took from him, he gave me bad intel," Ivan filled in with a growl. "Got shot. Ari had to come save my hide. *And* he didn't pay me."

"*I had to hack his account to get the payment,*" K threw in, still growling like a wounded bear. "*We reported him to the site and they revoked his access. He should not be back on here, even with a fake name and photo. Damn him for aging that photo—that's no doubt how he got around the security filters. Dammit. Good job, Rems. I'll flag this guy and get him*" *booted again. This time, it better take. This bastard is not trustworthy.*"

To say Carter was dismayed was a vast understatement. "Well, shit. Now what?"

"*I can find a way to contact our client directly,*" K offered. "*No reason to ditch the job just because of this bastard. Although the question of the painting is...I don't know, guys. Do we really need a perfect forgery for this?*"

Ivan's head waffled back and forth. "Njet. I do not think so. We need a painting only to fool security cameras, right? Just long enough for us to get out and clear? It doesn't have to be forgery to do that."

Carter nodded slowly, his mind taking hold of this idea. "That's true. A security camera won't be able to tell the difference between a painting and a high-quality print of a painting. As long as it's the right size, and on a canvas, does it matter?"

"As much as Lansky drives us crazy, he does pull through. Let's not step on toes. Maybe contact him, tell him Emura's a bad broker. Let him know we don't need the painting," Ari suggested.

Carter was always for preserving good will in the industry. "I can do that. I have his phone number. You all okay with this plan?"

"*Yeah, only thing that makes sense. I guarantee you Lansky isn't anywhere near done with the forgery. A Monet? He'll still be at it a year later.*" K laced his fingers together and stretched them before settling them on the keyboard and typing like a madman. "*I'm contacting the site admin now and reporting Emura. They're slow, though, the job might be done before they get their acts together. Let's assume we'll have to work around Emura for now.*"

Carter nodded. "Okay."

"*Harrison, what do you know about Knowles?*"

"Very little, but enough to know I don't want to tackle it alone. Knowles is ostensibly a showcase for the Knox family. They don't actually live there most of the time, although the mansion can house about fifty people. The top three floors are bedrooms, pools, tennis courts, ballrooms, and a massive gallery to showcase their art and jewelry collection. There's a vault somewhere on the property that stores anything they're not interested in displaying. They've got their own private security company made up of a lot of mean men with guns, and they're not rent-a-cops. These guys are pros. They can more or less be gotten around, I think. Here's the problem." Carter faltered. "Actually, you know the problem better than I do."

Ari snorted in wry agreement. "That we do."

"Tell me, tell me," Remi encouraged, bouncing in place.

Turning her a little in his lap, Ivan faced her, ticking things off on his fingers as he listed their problems. "Solnishko, it's like this: the place is a fortress. The vault has walls two feet thick, made with steel reinforced concrete. The doors are blast doors with lockdown bolts—"

"What are those?" she interrupted, paying rapt attention.

"When the alarm sounds, the bolt slams into the door and can only be manually reset. It has a thousand pounds of pressure on it. It's not possible to cut, hack, or blast our way through without damaging what's inside."

"*Worse, getting to the vault is a challenge in and of itself. The place is riddled with motion detectors, heat sensors, and ground sensors along the perimeter. All of this with a state-of-the-art security system to protect the area. And the cameras are dumb, they go straight to the server. I can't hack any of it remotely.*" K looked very put out about this, as if such a design was a personal affront.

Carter was actually dismayed by this litany of security. He'd known some of it, but not all, and that list was disheartening, to say the least. "How on earth did you get in last time?"

"I posed as a guest and went in to tour the art gallery on the top floors," Ari answered. He had his head tilted back to stare thoughtfully at the ceiling. "What I was after ended up actually being on the owner himself. There wasn't a need to go into the vault, thankfully."

"Even then I had to slip in with him and create enough of a distraction for him to get out again," Ivan pitched in. "And it took three tries to put in a signal booster thingy so that K could get into their systems."

K gave him a pained look. "*Wireless bridge is the term you're looking for, Ivan. But good try.*"

The Russian thief waved this off as unimportant.

"I'm sure they've upgraded their systems since we last tried this," K added thoughtfully. *"It's a rule of thumb in the tech world. Anything running is obsolete. And the Knox family is obsessed about being cutting edge. I'd have to double check, but I'll bet my eye teeth they've upgraded their hardware at the very least. The cameras were on the edge of being outclassed when we were in there."*

Carter interpreted this without any issues. "So you're saying it's gotten harder."

K tipped his hand back and forth. *"Maybe harder. Maybe easier. It depends. Most cameras these days work off a wireless signal. Even if it only has an ethernet port for network connectivity, and it's hardwired via Cat-5 cables, it'll have wireless capability. Maybe not in use, but it'll be there. If we can tap into just one camera, I can access the rest, using it as an access point."*

Seeing the problem, Carter groaned. "But we have to find a way to access one?"

"And that won't be easy. Especially as we're not going to be going into the mansion this time. The mansion cameras and vault cameras run to separate servers. And both are under the same security system, and cracking it last time gave me a migraine. It was running a Brenner, last I was in there."

"Brenner?" Carter had no idea what the hell that meant but it sounded problematic.

Remi, strangely enough, went "Ooooh" and winced. "That's not good, Uncle K."

"Tell me about it, princess."

It felt a little strange, but Carter asked the eight-year-old seriously, "Brief me."

"A Brenner is one of the toughest security systems," she explained, face scrunched up in a perfectly adorable manner. "It's smart and it learns from your mistakes. Uncle K said it's got a heuristic algorithm."

K pointed to Remi. *"See? She remembers the right technical terms."*

Not bothered by this, Ivan returned blandly, "She's also smarter than me."

Grinning at her uncles, Remi continued, "Think of it like a really mean hunting dog. It will shut doors on you, herd you into a room, and trap you in it until the security team retrieves you. It's not fun to hack. Uncle K has a dummy he let me try on." Hard resolve flitted over her face. "I haven't gotten through yet but I *will*."

"*You have to train up to Brenner level,*" K said supportively. "*Don't worry, you'll get it.*"

"So you can get in?" Carter asked him hopefully.

"*Eh...maybe. We're assuming it still has a Brenner. It's a bad/worse case scenario. It's bad if they've replaced the security software with something else, something I'm not familiar with. It's worse if they've kept it because the Brenner system learns from previous attempts to crack it. It'll remember me, and my methods, is what I'm saying. I won't be able to attack it the same way I did last time.*"

Carter's dismay must have been written all over his face as Ivan gave him a bracing pat on the back. "No worries, my friend. We got in last time, didn't we? We just have to figure out how to do it again."

"Yeah," Carter responded faintly. "Piece of cake."

10

ARI

The more Ari thought about it, the more it didn't make sense to stay home. Sure, Remi had another two weeks of school left, but she was suspended for one of them. It was kinda a wash at this point. He ducked out of the house, leaving Remi with Ivan for a minute, and made another call to Kyou.

"*Now what?*"

"You sound a little irritated."

"*It's because you guys keep calling me. I can't focus and get crap done.*" The sound of keys clattering told Ari he didn't have Kyou's full attention. It sounded like a herd of elephants stampeding.

"Last call for the day, promise," Ari soothed. "It just occurred to me that it makes no sense to stay here and wait for you to arrive. We might as well get up to DC and start scoping the place out."

The typing abruptly stopped. "*Wait, I thought Remi had another two weeks of school.*"

"She's already suspended for one of them."

"*Oh. Ah, I see. No point in staying for that one week? Gotcha. Honestly, man, the timing on this is so tight, we need every day we can get on it. It'll be better to move now. And it's, what, a three-and-a-half-hour drive to DC from where you're at?*"

"In good traffic, yeah."

"Which DC is not known for. Better to just get up there. Not waste a lot of time going back and forth on the road. I've found a safehouse for us in Mitchellville."

Ari wasn't as familiar with DC as Kyou, but he thought he knew where that was. "Isn't that east of Capitol Hill?"

"By about twenty minutes or so. In good traffic. It's a townhome, five bedrooms. I can get furniture moved into it in three days, so we should be set."

With that location, the ability to scope out Knowles became that much easier. Knowles sat just north of Capitol Hill, enjoying both the prestige of its location and the social atmosphere. "I like it. Should we head in tonight, then?"

"If you want to play tourist, stay at a hotel, you can."

"I think we will. The timing is just so tight. I don't want to waste a day if I can help it."

"I hear you. Talk it over with the other two, let me know."

"Will do. Later." Ari hung up, then stayed on the porch for a moment longer, thinking. He'd never promised Remi any sort of stability when it came to school. It wasn't possible, not in his line of work. Still, he'd wanted her to have that experience of normality to start out with. A base of sorts. It bothered him they'd not managed it for more than four months. He couldn't say why, it just did.

With a shake of his head, he went back in, not at all surprised to find Remi sitting on the couch with a combination lock in her hands, Ivan coaching her on how to unlock it. This one seemed to be more than a cheap combination lock, as it gave her trouble. Harrison was in the loveseat nearby, laptop on the coffee table, frowning at something on the screen. He glanced up as Ari came in, then straightened altogether, as if sensing Ari had something to say.

He really didn't know quite what to do with Harrison. His possible danger to Remi aside, Ari found him rather attractive. It was hard to know which instinct to follow when it came to Harrison. For all that the man was a mercenary, there was something soothing about him. Calming. He didn't rattle easily, he handled things serenely, and used politeness like a charm. Ari had a weakness for gentlemen, he knew he did, but he found them impossible to approach because that type was horrified by his line of work. Was his libido taking an interest because it recognized Harrison was an interesting blend of gentleman-criminal?

Ari really didn't have time for this. He gave himself a good mental shake and put himself back on task. "I think we need to go."

Ivan immediately snapped around, his hand falling to Remi's shoulder, prepared to move her in a second. "Why?"

"We need every minute we can get to crack Knowles. Another week of school for Remi isn't worth it in the long run. K's safehouse will be set up in three days. Let's pack up, head in. Stay at a hotel, pretend we're tourists, and start scoping the place out."

Remi started bouncing, ponytail swinging, brown eyes bright with excitement. "Can I help on this one? Please, Daddy, *please.*"

"Of course you're helping on this one," he retorted, grinning at her. She was such an excellent little criminal in the making. "You'll help with our cover of playing tourist, and I expect you to count guards. And street cameras. You know Uncle K's going to quiz you later."

A shark-like smile graced her features. "What do I get if I'm right?"

"I'll raise your allowance by five dollars."

Hopping off the couch, she came to him and extended her hand. "Shake on it."

Biting back a smile, he solemnly shook on it, his hand engulfing hers. He caught the expression on Harrison's face at this byplay. The man looked amused but also something else, something Ari couldn't quite put a finger on. Perhaps he found it strange Ari would say something like this to Remi. Admittedly, it might seem odd, that they were training an eight-year-old. That they included her in all of the planning and prep for a heist. Ari didn't know how to do anything else. He needed Remi to be alert, to know how to look for security cameras and guards, how to avoid them. He needed her to understand what the stakes were, how to go to ground. There was no one else he could trust her with except Ivan and Kyou, not without sending her to his brother, which...he didn't really want to do. Luca might not give her back. And if something happened to him? Then Kyou and Ivan were likely with him.

Ari had rarely been caught in his career but it *had* happened. If something went sideways, Remi would likely be on her own, and that idea terrified him. He needed her to have the skills to fend for herself until he could get back to her. Fortunately, Remi was street savvy and smart as a whip. She picked up on things quickly. If he could just pound into her the basic skills necessary to survive, maybe he'd be able to sleep at night.

Also another thought for another time. "Alright, we all in agreement on this?"

Harrison closed the lid to the laptop with a soft snick. "I feel better about moving, personally. How much time do you need to pack?"

"An hour. I'll meet you guys back here. Come on, Rems."

Each man had their own vehicle, so it was something of a caravan driving into DC. Remi chose to ride with Ivan, as she wanted to catch up with him. They hadn't seen each other in a week, and frankly, Ivan was more trustworthy when he had a small child to look after. Otherwise he got bored and sidetracked. Ari wasn't sure which was more problematic to the safety of the world: nuclear weapons or a bored Ivan Azarov.

It made for a very quiet ride in, but Ari needed the quiet. He was still adjusting to his nightmare of someone in his profession learning about Remi. Even sleeping on it hadn't helped much. Thank ever-loving Christ it was Harrison who'd found her. Ari wouldn't be able to sleep at all if it had been someone of a more evil nature. Well, okay, he would have. Because the fucker would be six feet under with a bullet in his head.

His mind revisited the scene in the kitchen. Harrison had looked tense for a minute, as if he wasn't sure which way Ari would jump. Had he really been that off? So fidgety the mercenary had picked up on it? His mental state was only partially because of Remi. Mostly, being near the man made Ari's nerves dance a merry tune. Especially when he'd sat next to him at the table, leaning in so close without touching—that had really sent him for an emotional tailspin for a second. He'd felt like one live wire of sensation. If Harrison had touched him, even lightly, Ari would have embarrassed himself by coming right out of his skin.

And he really, really needed his instincts to settle one way or another. Flirting with Harrison seemed a bad idea all around, although his libido didn't think so. Not that it ever made smart decisions, the traitorous bastard. Ari blamed his spotty track record for getting laid on his libido's uppitiness. It was just so hard to relax his guard around other men that it was difficult to get into the mood. He hadn't been mincing words with Remi about it being impossible for him to date. And it definitely predated her.

Dating aside, this was the first time he'd taken Remi into a job with him. It was the third job he'd done since adopting her—and she'd spent most of her time with Kyou—it was just that this was Knowles. Knowles was a whole different ballgame in many respects. Part of him felt like it was a bad idea, but he didn't have many other options.

Well, to be honest, he had precisely one.

Unease sat on him like a lead blanket, and he pressed the bluetooth button on his steering wheel. "Call Luca."

The phone rang three times before his brother's voice came on. "*Hey, Ari. Tell me this isn't an emergency.*"

"Not an emergency," Ari promised faithfully. "Just a head's up. I'm going on a job."

Luca paused for a long moment. His response came very carefully worded. "*Yeah? Where you heading, little brother?*"

"DC. Remi's with me. Look, I'm...with my friends too. So there's not really anyone to watch her. She'll be with her computer-loving uncle for the majority of the job, but if something goes wrong, I want her to be able to reach you. Keep your phone on you, yeah?"

"*Shit, Ari. Don't do this to me. I haven't even had a chance to properly meet her, just talk to her over the phone. You know how much I hate that? I have a niece I haven't even met face to face. A niece who might need me to help her if something happens to you.*"

And that was definitely part of the problem. Guilt squirmed

greasily in his gut. "It's hard on you when we meet up, though."

"For this, I'll find a way to make it work. Remi needs at least one staying force in her life that isn't...that."

He blew out a breath, feeling relieved. It would be so much easier on them all if Luca at least met her once. If she knew she could go to her uncle. Even though it was hard for the brothers to share the same space for any amount of time, they'd manage for a day or two. For Remi. "Yeah. Yeah, okay. After this job. We'll work out the logistics."

"Any chance you can do it now?"

Ari hesitated strongly. Would it be safer? Yes. Undoubtedly. But... "I really don't want to do that if I don't have to. She's so looking forward to being with everyone. You know that doesn't happen often. And her computer-loving uncle wants to show her more of the ropes. She's got real talent with computers. We're hoping to encourage her to go that direction."

For a long moment, Luca digested that. *"It would be safer all around. And it would tie in well with normal life, if I can convince her away from the dark side."*

Ari gave that a heaping helping of not happening. But Luca could dream. "If it looks dicey, or if my gut starts throwing up signals, I'll put her on a plane to you. Okay?"

"Alright. I'd rather you just send her to me now, but alright. You put a ticket and some cash on her, okay? And make sure her cell is charged, just in case."

"Yeah. I mean, she has half that always on her anyway. She knows the exit protocol if it comes down to that."

Not for the first time, Luca said in heavy exasperation, *"Ari, why the hell did you adopt a little girl? I know you love her to pieces, but she really does complicate your life and it would be safer all around if I had her."*

"Not on your life are you getting my daughter." Ari glared at the phone, wishing his brother was close enough to smack.

"You stubborn son of a bitch. I thought you didn't want kids."

"And I don't want kids. I want Remi. That's it."

"I love how you feel those two things are separate."

And this was why he and Luca didn't do well in person. They inevitably ended up arguing. "Just stop it. I'll have Remi call you if things go wrong. I don't really expect them to, I've got pros with me, this is just a better-safe-than-sorry phone call."

Luca's voice turned soft and sad. "*One day, brother, you're going to call me not because I'm the last resort, but because you honestly miss me.*"

That sent a sharp pain through his chest. He kept his eyes on the road, because the traffic rather demanded that of him, but his hands tightened around the wheel. "Who says I don't miss you?"

"*We see each other three times a year, Ari. Our birthday. Christmas. The anniversary of our mother's death. You barely call or email me in between those days. If not for Remi, you wouldn't be calling me even now. You're worried about what will happen to her if you go down. You know what that does to me? That you could disappear on some fucking job, and I'd never know, not until my niece calls me. And that situation is an improvement because at least now I'll get a fucking phone call telling me you're in trouble. Before, no one even knew who I was.*"

True. He'd kept silent about Luca for years before he trusted Ivan and Kyou enough to share. Even then, he hadn't given them any last name or way to contact Luca. He didn't realize how much that had hurt his twin up until this moment. "You know why."

"*To keep me safe,*" Luca responded in a weary voice. "*To supposedly keep you safe, so that I can't be used against you. I know. I thought, I hoped, that Remi might change you. Might influence you to clean up your life entirely.*"

"I'm in too deep for that." Ari swallowed around the hard ball in his throat and wondered, not for the first time, why the two of them were so different. Twins were supposed to be alike, weren't they? "I love you, brother. I just don't know how to walk any other road than the one I'm on."

Luca sounded exhausted and heart sore. "*I know. I wish to hell I knew how to change that, for all our sakes. Let me do one thing.*"

He felt guilty enough that he almost promised anything. "What?"

"*Let me put my name next to Remi's. Give me joint custody*

of her. If shit hits the fan, give me the legal power to protect her so she's not yanked into the system."

For Remi's sake, that would be perfect. Ari hesitated for another reason altogether. "That's traceable, Luca. Your name will be linked with mine in the system that way."

"And that's my choice. I'm not leaving my niece to the wolves if something happens to you."

Shit. There was that. "Alright. I won't argue with you, if you want to do that. But I'll make sure you have a way to reach K. If something really happens, odds are he won't be in the line of fire. And you'll likely need his help."

He expected an argument on that, but Luca seemed to recognize the compromise for what it was. *"Okay. I'll take that. You have Remi call me tonight, and walk me through her exit protocol for DC. So I know exactly what she's doing."*

So they both knew what to do, he meant. "I will. Luca— sorry."

"You always are. Next time, try to call me for a happy reason, okay?"

"Yeah." Ari hung up, as he didn't know what else to say after a conversation like that one. Why did life have to be so damn complicated? Or maybe it was more his relationships with other people were complicated. Maybe Ari needed to compromise a bit more. Come up with some way of keeping his brother safely in the loop. Because now that he knew what it was like, to worry to the point of pain, he felt guilty for consistently putting his twin through it. It was a delicate balancing act. He'd have to think of a safe way to do it.

It was also probably just as well he hadn't mentioned someone else knew about Remi. Luca would have lost his shit hearing that a black mercenary knew Remi.

Yeah, that was definitely a conversation for never.

11

CARTER

Carter didn't know what happened on the drive in, but something clearly had, as Ari looked unsettled. Unsettled and unhappy. He didn't want to pry unduly because whatever the man's personal business, it wasn't Carter's. Still, if something had gone wrong, he'd like to know about it. As they unloaded from their cars in the hotel parking lot, he came in close, trailing light fingertips along the back of Ari's arm to get his attention. Ari flinched, head coming around sharply, torso twisting so he was out of immediate range of Carter's touch. Shit, he hadn't meant to startle him. Was he that locked in his head? Carter went still, body language as non-threatening as he could make it, as he murmured lowly, "Everything alright?"

"Yeah." Ari almost left it at that, Carter could see it on his face. But something made him continue. His body language became more relaxed, hands unclenching at his sides as he spoke. "I'm just second-guessing my decision to keep Rems with us on this. Knowles isn't easy."

That was perfectly understandable. "But you don't have a safe place to send her."

"I do," Ari admitted, face twisting up in a grimace. "And I talked to that safe place on the way in and got an earful for not putting her on a plane already. It's just...she's so excited to work with us. And K wants to teach her more hacking, and she doesn't get to see him face to face all that often. I don't want to send her off just because I'm afraid something might go wrong."

Carter was surprised Ari did have a safe place for Remi. He was even more astonished Ari would tell him about it, even obliquely. It said something about how much the man trusted him. He appreciated his frankness and tried to return the favor in kind. "Then don't. We'll put together an exit strategy for her. Ari, I sympathize with your fear, I do. But keeping Remi completely in the dark doesn't help her. You know that."

"Better to give her the knowledge and tools to deal with crap than to shut her out." He looked up, a half smile on his face as Remi popped out of the car, still chattering a mile a minute to Ivan. "I know. My instincts are at war, is all."

Carter had the strongest urge to wrap the man up in a hug. It would probably end in multiple contusions and a splintered skull if he tried it, but still. The urge was there. Ari needed a hug just then. Carter was very touchy-feely by nature, and it had taken time for him to understand that not everyone was like him, or appreciated his hands-on approach. Ari was Italian, though, or at least the phrases he used gave that impression. He was certainly hands-on enough with Remi and Ivan—he didn't seem to have a concept of personal space with them. He oscillated between being in Carter's space or across the room from him. Maybe he wouldn't mind as much?

Did he want to run the risk of pissing off an assassin?

Carter thought better of his instincts and kept his hands carefully to himself. "Come on. Let's check in, get dinner, and I'll work up different ways for Remi to get safely out of the city. If we don't just teach her a specific route, but how to adapt on the fly, she'll have a much better chance of getting out of a sticky situation."

Ari gave him an odd look, head tilting, shoulders tightening imperceptibly. "You'd do that?"

That expression made his hugging instincts clamor louder. Carter ruthlessly squashed them under a mental heel. "Of course. I like Remi. I don't want her hurt. And you've already done me the favor of leaving my head attached to my shoulders—"

The assassin snorted a laugh, dark eyes dancing merrily. The defensiveness of his posture eased and his shoulders relaxed as he leaned his back against the car.

"—which I appreciate very much, thank you, so if this eases your mind about her? Sure, I'm happy to help."

"Harrison. You're really a team player, aren't you?"

"Always have been."

"Why are you not still in the military?"

So it was that obvious he'd been military? Or Ari knew something of his history via K. Probably both. "My CO gave me a bullshit order I refused to follow through on. Got me dishonorably discharged."

Ari's dark brows winged up into his hairline. He looked good in the late afternoon sun, casual and ruffled, touchable. Carter curled his fingers into his palm to keep himself from running them through Ari's soft looking, sexy bed-head waves. Ari considered Carter for a long moment before his head slowly dipped down into a nod. "I can see you doing that."

"Most people say the same thing." And Carter wasn't quite sure why. Did he look rebellious?

Remi bounced up to them, automatically taking her father's hand in both of hers, a wide smile on her face. Carter adored her shirt, although he hadn't found a chance to tell her that yet. Above her jean shorts she wore a black tank that read: *I am beauty, I am grace, I will punch you in the face.*

"Daddy, let's get pasta. I'm hungry. Uncle Ivan says there's a place not far from here that's really good, and their breadsticks are super yummy, and the owner owes him a favor so there's always lots of breadsticks and sometimes dessert."

Ari looked up at his friend with a bland expression. "Antonio is still feeding you?"

"He loves me." Ivan's accent thickened a mite as he spoke, mischief rolling visibly off him in waves.

Carter debated for a split second, then decided he didn't really want to know. He might know too much about this group already.

They took ten minutes to check in under various aliases, threw suitcases into their rooms, then walked the three blocks down to the restaurant with Ari and Remi leading. That left Carter and Ivan strolling side by side, but since the man had fed him pancakes, Carter was less inclined to think his life was in danger. Plus, it was a nice view from back here, too.

Ari possessed a nice ass, and watching him and Remi swing their joined hands together and chat was a sight too cute to miss. Carter had a good relationship with his parents, but he couldn't remember ever holding hands with one of them and just chatting. They'd focused most of his life on him behaving and doing things on schedule. He wasn't sure if he'd ever been as close to his father as Ari was with Remi. Ari, surprisingly, was an awesome father.

Even mid-afternoon the nation's capital was very lively, to no one's surprise. The traffic flowed thick even at this midday hour, the humidity and heat enough to make his shirt stick unpleasantly to him. Ari had sensibly ditched his jacket before leaving, and Ivan bemoaned his own choice of jeans. They passed all manner of pedestrians, mostly people walking in a great hurry to some other destination, but there weren't many on the sidewalks. Cars, subways, and buses were the main ways of transportation in this city. Walking was done by tourists around sites, mostly.

Since the thief seemed to be in a relaxed mood, Carter decided to press his luck a little. "How did the three of you meet?"

Ivan spared him a glance, his expression going reminiscent. "It was K, really. About, oh, five years ago I was bored. Walking through New York, in between jobs, and not sure what to do with myself. I started picking pockets, just for something to keep my hands occupied. I got through three wallets when I realized the one I'd just picked had nothing much in it. Just a twenty and a note that read: Meet me at the Rockefeller Center at eight o'clock. I have a job you might be interested in. Bring my wallet with you."

"He was auditioning for a thief?" Carter snorted in amusement. "And you did, I take it."

Ivan shrugged, still amused at the memory. Carter preferred him with a half-smile. It softened the angles of his face, made him look less hardened. "As I said, I was bored and in between jobs. I don't think he believed he'd catch such a big fish with his lure, but he wasn't upset about it, either. Ari he already knew."

"We were both in foster care," Ari explained over his shoulder. "We ran into each other a few times, stayed in the same house once for about six months. We didn't keep track of each other, but once we got into the business, he looked me up for a job. I almost backed out of it, because he had this idiot lined up for it."

"Wait, both of you for the same job?"

"All three of us, really. K's not much for hands-on, he prefers to work his magic remote." Ivan shrugged. "For the job, I needed another set of hands. I do not know many thieves I trust to work alongside, and the two I do know were busy on their own jobs. But an assassin's skillset overlaps with a thief's well enough—we both have to quietly get in and out of places to reach a target. K knew of Ari, and when offered, I was amiable to at least trying."

Ari's tone turned fond. "Turns out we're a formidable team. And we don't get on each other's nerves, which is a rare thing."

That explained why Ari had so easily pulled in the other two. Neither man said as much, but the implication was clear enough. Given a choice, they preferred to work with each other. This made things easier and conversely harder for Carter. Unlike other team-ups with criminals, these guys were already accustomed to working together. That was the easy part. The hard part was finding his own way to slot into an established team dynamic.

"It's great to have a dedicated team to back you up," Carter responded honestly. Not to mention a little wistfully.

Ivan gave him a sharp, weighing look from the corner of his eye. "You don't have that?"

"Not for lack of trying. Usually my team-ups go okay, but no one's really interested in repeating the experience. And sometimes, it goes so pear-shaped that I refuse to work with them again. My last job was that way." Carter made a face. "Sometimes I totally understand why Batman worked alone."

The conversation stalled there as Ivan went ahead, opening the door to a hole-in-the-wall restaurant. It looked very established, everything from the aging red paint around the door, to the worn-in dark green carpet on the floor. The inside smelled heavenly—full of baking bread, cheese, and simmering sauce that hit Carter's taste buds with a sledgehammer of promised delights. Really, nothing advertised a restaurant better than scent.

"Ivan!" A happy man roared out over the customers' heads, barreling straight for them. He was nearly as wide as he was tall, dark hair so thin on top that the mellow lighting of the room gleamed off his head.

Ivan smiled in return, grin stretched from ear to ear, arms held out in an anticipated hug. "Antonio! You haven't aged a day, I swear it."

Antonio came straight to him—as much as he could with tables blocking his way—grabbed the man by both shoulders and kissed him on either cheek like an old friend. His Italian accent was thick as he scolded, "I haven't seen you in a good year, at least, and now you just pop onto my doorstep without even a call ahead. Shame on you, I would have given you my best table."

"We didn't actually know we'd be here until four hours ago," Ivan said by way of explanation. "Here, come meet my friends and my solnishko. This is Carter, Ari, and his daughter, Remi."

Antonio greeted them politely enough but his eyes kept going back to Remi. "Such a beautiful girl you are, Remi. Did your uncle tell you how we met?"

"Only that he helped you once," she denied, eyes wide with curiosity.

Leaning in, Antonio whispered the story like a secret. "Ten years ago, I was just starting out. I made the mistake of borrowing money from the wrong loan sharks. Your Uncle Ivan, he ate here regularly at the time, and when he learned about it? He told me off for being so stupid. The interest rate was insane, I was barely treading water, and then the ovens shorted out. I had to replace them, but didn't have the money to do it. But without them, I couldn't keep the restaurant going. I was faced with broken knee caps for defaulting on a loan. It was terrifying. But Ivan, he stepped in. Bought me new ovens, re-worked the loan so he carried it instead of the company. I paid him off steadily, at a much lower interest rate, and stayed open. Really, it's all thanks to him."

Aaaand that confirmed Ivan really had been part of the mafia at some point. Carter still didn't know whether it was Ukrainian or Russian. Either way it was bad news.

"Best investment I ever made," Ivan swore with that wide smile still in place.

Antonio grinned back at him, practically vibrating with his joy. "Come, I shouldn't keep you standing here. Sit, sit, order whatever you like. I'll bring you wine. Remi, what would you like to drink?"

"Coke," she responded hopefully.

Ari made a sound like a buzzer on a game show, the one for the wrong answer. "Uh, no, missy. You do not get caffeine. You're worse than the Energizer Bunny. Try again."

"Sprite," she amended with a sigh and a frown at her father.

Antonio patted the top of her head, amused. "I'll bring it out. And menus."

Carter debated the wisdom of saying they shouldn't be drinking on the job. But technically they weren't on the job yet, and it wouldn't hurt to have a glass. Half a glass might be safer.

Someone's phone beeped and Ari and Ivan both pulled theirs out to check. It must have been the same message, as they grunted before putting it away again.

"K will meet us at the house in a few days," Ari relayed to Carter and Remi. "He'll need help lugging all of his computer equipment in and setting it up."

Remi immediately brightened and thrust an arm into the air. "I'll do that."

"I'm sure you will, honey, but you can't lug it all upstairs. We'll need to help him too."

It stood to reason K would bring his own system with him. It was something Carter had learned from one of his first jobs. A hacker needed their own equipment, their own software, and it wasn't something that could be acquired from a box store. One hacker he'd met claimed he'd spent three weeks building and perfecting his system. Seeing how many CPUs the man used, Carter believed him. If K's setup was anything like that man's, they'd definitely need to help him carry it all in.

They sat at a corner table, something allowing them to see both the front and back door. Carter had his back to the wall, giving him clear line of sight. Remi was the only one with her back to the room, but that was fine. Asking either Ivan or Ari to sit like that would have likely fried their synapses. Their table sat far enough away from the other patrons that it gave them a bubble of semi-privacy. Enough to talk in, at least.

Carter leaned in a touch anyway before asking, "Who's taking lead on this?"

"I am," Ivan informed him. "This falls under my expertise."

He had no problem with that. "Okay."

"Harrison." Ivan eyed him thoughtfully, grey eyes dark in the lighting. "I don't really know your skillset."

That would be a problem. "Yeah, 'merc' doesn't really tell you much, does it? I'm sorta a jack-of-all-trades. I can do basic hacking, override electronic locks, that sort of thing. I'm a demolitions expert. I'm comfortable with handguns, sniping, and hand-to-hand. If you need requisition, I'm your man. That was one of my jobs while still in uniform. People know me as a retrieval expert. Hence, you know, the current contract for the job we have."

Ivan gave him a slow nod, absorbing this. "You really are jack-of-all-trades. Horosho, that's useful. You can cover bases if one of us needs a hand. How known is your face?"

"Not very. I operate on the down low. Anyone searching for me will come up with my military history, basics of my childhood, that's about it. I've got one of those generic everyman faces anyway, it's hard to find me off a description."

"I'll have K scrub you from the system just in case. You'll be more infamous after this job, trust me."

Carter didn't doubt that for a second. "I'd appreciate his help. I know we shouldn't really tackle the job without him on site, but we still planning for a drive by and lookie-lou after dinner?"

"Da," Ivan confirmed easily.

He accepted this with a nod. "Then let's focus on something else over dinner. Remi." Her attention focused on him. "Quiz time. How many ways of transport are there in DC, and which ones can you board without raising suspicion?"

Remi's mouth pursed in a little bow before she answered, "Cabs, metro, buses, walking. Do planes count?"

"For you, yes. Which ones can you take?"

"Metro and buses. Maybe planes?"

As he walked her through the possible ins and outs out

of the city, Carter couldn't help but observe that as he talked Remi through the basics, Ari stared at him hard. Ivan seemed intrigued as well, but something about Ari's expression...it wasn't irritation. Or seemingly any sort of negative emotion, although Carter could understand if it was. He might be stepping on toes. But really, he was following through on an earlier promise, to help Remi come up with an exit strategy. To ease Ari's mind about having her here.

No, it wasn't irritation. Or worry. Or anything like that. It was something else, something Carter couldn't quite read. He did know it made his skin a little too tight and hot, his mouth a touch dry. And god, as agitated as it made Carter feel, he wouldn't mind if Ari stared at him like that for a few more hours.

12

ARI

This should not be sexy. Or a turn-on. Harrison leaned towards Remi, seriously listening to her, giving her all of the attention people normally reserved for other adults. Remi responded in kind, oriented towards Harrison, and if someone didn't know better, a third-party observer would think it was uncle and niece talking. Or perhaps even father and daughter. Remi had no reserves with him, and how the hell was Harrison charming her so thoroughly as to manage that?

Watching and listening as a mercenary walked his daughter through all of the escape routes of the city shouldn't be alluring. But damn if Ari didn't want to drag the man into a backroom somewhere and blow him. Harrison was clearly very good with kids. Which was somehow surprising, although Ari wasn't sure why. He oscillated between being hopeful, to being confused at being hopeful, and slapping his libido down. Was this a thing now? Had being a father changed his perceptions so much that he found Harrison's attitude toward his daughter attractive?

Being a parent really should come with warning labels.

Fortunately, no one seemed to realize his head had gone straight into the gutter. Well, maybe Ivan. But Ivan was good at reading people. They finished dinner and set out once again, this time doing some of the necessary shopping.

Anyone going through DC would tell you that the two fastest ways to get anywhere were by bus or metro. Cars might come with more freedom but it meant being stuck in traffic most of the time. People opted for the metro for that reason—it was just faster. The first thing they did was stop by a station and buy metro passes for all of them, including Kyou. They picked up maps of the stations as well. This would be one of Remi's tasks—to memorize where every station was.

After they had the passes, they immediately used them, going towards their target. As they waited for their train to come in, Ari bent down to Remi's level. With the crowds on the platform, and the noise of the trains coming and going through the tunnels, he had to speak a touch louder than he wanted to make sure she heard him. Even with her standing in between his knees. "Rems, you keep that with your phone, okay? We'll use it a lot."

Her cellphone case had a pocket for a debit card, which she also already had tucked in there. It was strictly for emergencies, in case she needed to get out quickly. Ari had been surprised at how well she obeyed that rule. She never touched the card without his permission.

Nodding, she slotted the metro card on top of her debit card before putting the phone back into the Black Widow backpack on her back. "Daddy, Uncle Luca texted me just now. He said if I wanted, I could come stay with him during the job."

She didn't voice the question, but her eyes asked, *Do you want me to*? Ari phrased the words carefully before speaking. "Rems, I think you can stay with us. Uncle K's really excited to have you here. He wants to teach you more computer stuff. Uncle Luca's worried about you being here while we're working. It's up to you, though. If you want to go stay with him for a month, you can."

Remi chewed on her bottom lip, obviously torn. "I do want to meet him. But I want to stay, too."

That was more or less the answer he'd expected. "I guarantee we're going to meet him soon. Our birthday is coming up. I told you about how we always celebrate that together."

"Yeah. And that's August 21st."

Remembered that, had she? "Yup, sure is. So you're going to meet him sooner or later. Up to you, gattina. You want to stay with us or go?"

"Stay," she said decisively.

Also the answer he'd expected. Still, he found himself grinning at her. "I figured. If things get hot, though, you call him. You go directly to him, tu capisci?"

"Lo capisco."

"Okay. Uncle K will be relieved you're staying. He's counting on you to be another set of eyes on the cameras. And you know how bad Uncle Ivan is with the electronics. I expect you to watch him."

She didn't quite salute, but her body language was right for it. She gave him a serious nod. "Okay."

The train arrived, an announcement blaring out over the speakers in a detached female voice. The passengers on board shuffled off, then the ones on the platform shuffled on. Ari kept a tight grip on Remi. He'd learned that lesson the hard way. Finding a panicked eight-year-old in the New York metro system had *not* been fun.

Remi apparently remembered that as well, as she kept a firm grip on his hand, although she couldn't do much more than comfortably cling onto three fingers.

They got a bit battered on all sides as they loaded. It was nearing rush hour, and Ari kicked himself for not planning ahead. Benches lined the walls, all of them full, and the standing room quickly filled up with people, all with hands latched onto the various offered handholds. Ari took one look at the situation and grimaced. "Whose bright idea was it to go anywhere at four o'clock in DC?"

"Chert, zanuda," Ivan grumbled crossly. "We should have considered that."

"Here." Harrison touched the small of Ari's back and Remi's shoulder, subtly guiding them more towards the cavity of the doors.

Ari went, as that was the only sensible option to stand and block Remi from being crushed by everyone else. He grabbed the handrail near the benches, bracing himself, Remi tucked against the door in front of him. Then he nearly leapt out of his skin when he felt Harrison close in from the right side. His head came up sharply, and it was then he realized Harrison's extra two inches of height over him put their heads uncomfortably close together. (A bit more of a tilt and they could actually kiss. Not that Ari was thinking about that. At all.) Fortunately, Harrison's attention wasn't on him, but on the passengers crowding in from behind. He had a hand braced against the door above Remi's shoulder, his other hand wrapped around Ari's back and holding onto the rail. Ari recognized that stance all too well—it was something he'd done a time or two himself in the army. It was a protect-the-citizen stance and done so smoothly he didn't think Harrison had made a conscious decision to use it.

What? Why? Huh?

It had been a dog's age since anyone had tried to protect him. Even from something as casual as the crush of rush hour traffic on a subway. It did funny things to his heart, speeding it up and twisting it a bit in his chest.

He's doing it to protect Remi, Ari kept telling himself. Harrison was flanking on the right side to keep the girl from being crushed, that was all. The fact that his arm was pressed up against the small of Ari's back, and that their shoulders overlapped, that was just coincidence. Happenstance. Unavoidable in these close quarters, really. So, he really shouldn't be fixated on the obvious strength of that warm body pressed close, or stubble framing Harrison's mouth. His heart shouldn't be skipping a beat every time the rocking of the train pressed Harrison just that bit closer. His instincts were currently at war between relaxing into the cradle of Harrison's arm around him or keeping rigidly upright. The vote was currently: 1 for leaning in, 0 for keeping distance.

Damn, he smelled good. Like warm skin and musk. Was that cologne?

Ari stared into Remi's innocent eyes, by far the safest thing to look at, and swore at his libido. He really needed to do something about easing all of this sexual tension. Clearly, if having a man step on his shadow had this sort of effect on him, he'd gone too long without. Although really, when had his brain decided to trust Carter Harrison? Up until this morning, Ari had been debating putting a bullet in him.

The turning point might have been the conversation over dinner. Or maybe not. Ari couldn't pinpoint it cleanly. He just knew the man's proximity was causing havoc on him now.

It might have been fifteen minutes. Or a small eternity. Really, anyone's guess, but eventually they reached the right stop. Ari had never been so relieved to leave a subway car. They either weaved or bulldozed their way through the crowds to get up the stairs and onto the sidewalks once again. Then it was another ten-minute walk to their actual destination.

Ari leaned down and scooped Remi up, setting her on his shoulders as they moved. "Okay, Rems. You now have better vantage than we do. I need you to count guards and security cameras, okay?"

He didn't, really, but it was good practice for her. And there was the possibility she could see something from his shoulders they couldn't. The fence along the perimeter was nine feet of wrought iron, spaced so that a man could slip his hand through easily, but nothing larger than that. Most of the view to the mansion was blocked not by the fence, but the line of trees just inside. It meant she would only be able to see snatches of what was going on inside, in between the leaves and the branches, which was frustrating now but would come in handy later.

Her hands settled on his head and he felt her nod. "Okay. Should I tell you now?"

"Yeah, no one's going to be paying much attention to us."

"Take a good look, solnishko," Ivan requested softly, closing in on his left side. "You can stare that direction without issue. We stare too long, the guards get nervous."

"That's cause you're scary, Uncle Ivan."

Ivan chuckled and Harrison snickered. "Ah, solnishko, you always say such sweet things to me."

"Everything inside the big black fence?" Remi double checked.

"Yup. We'll focus on this side of the street." Ari kept his walk casual, more a stroll than anything. Million-dollar homes, restaurants, and those elite stores only the truly wealthy could frequent lined the street. One bank as well, on the corner. It looked picturesque, with planter boxes and landscaping in full bloom, the trees trimmed to within an inch of their lives. Picturesque, but not without its security measures. Everything had cameras, as far as Ari could tell. Most of them faced the front doors, which only made sense. That's what the owners were interested in protecting.

"How is it?" Ari murmured to Ivan.

"I think some of the cameras are problematic," he returned in the same low tone. "They've got enough of an angle to catch across the street as well. Not all, though. K can work his magic here."

"Assuming they're not all dumb, on their own servers."

Harrison cleared his throat meaningfully. "You two do remember this is a covert operation? We need to switch it all out without anyone realizing we were there."

Ari made a face. "That's the optimistic result. I'm planning for pessimistic everything-goes-wrong first."

"Besides, it still counts as a covert operation if no one lives to tell about it," Ivan observed absently, his eyes still studying cameras.

Harrison gave him a worried look, not sure if Ivan jested or not.

Trying to assure him, Ari muttered from the side of his mouth, "He's joking. Mostly."

"Mostly," Harrison said blandly. "Right."

"It's like the Hilton job in LA. 2008. Good times," Ivan reminisced.

Harrison startled visibly. "The Zoe Diamond? You stole that?"

Remi thankfully interrupted before the conversation could further go off the rails. "Daddy, I see two guards walking along the grounds. There's two more on the front door of the house."

"Okay, that's four. Keep an eye on them, see if they switch out with someone else."

They turned the corner and kept walking, all the world like tourists out to see the sights.

"Ground sensors," Harrison muttered while making a face. "Those are going to make jumping the fence a no-go. At least they don't have dogs."

"Dogs are hard to get around," Ivan agreed in the same disgruntled tone.

Ari waggled his eyebrows at both of them. "Something you two want to share with the class?"

"Long story." "Bad story." They said in near unison in a

quelling don't-ask manner.

It took another ten minutes to walk to the end of the block, and the property line. Knowles was less a house and more like an estate, eating up very pricey real estate in an obvious show of wealth. The perimeter fence stayed steady and true all the way, with a distinct, if low-grade, hum. If that thing wasn't wired for shock, Ari would become a cop. After all, it had been last time.

They kept walking, this time crossing the street to make it less obvious they were casing the joint. A street vendor sold ice cream cones, and they all stopped to get one, Remi opting for a popsicle. She didn't get back on his shoulders for which he was grateful. Ari had experienced sticky gooiness in his hair before. It was a pleasure he could live without.

"Only the one entrance," Ivan noted. "Still."

"It did initially surprise me they didn't have a side entrance for deliveries and such," Harrison pitched in, licking at his Rocky Road. "But it really does make sense from a security perspective. Easier to guard one entrance."

"They were smart about how they set up security." Ari glared at the extensive, well-manicured grounds as if they were an insult to his mother. "Bastards. Remi, what's your guard count?"

"Six," she answered promptly.

"There were ten last time we came in." Ivan didn't look at the grounds again, keeping his attention on Remi. "Of course, some of them are on vault and house duty, we won't see them out here. K will need to find the roster, double check if things have changed."

Ari would personally bet they had. They'd already been robbed once, after all. "Either way, we've done what we can today. Let's get back to the hotel. Remi's got a date with the pool."

Elated, she bounced once in place. *"Yes."*

"But first, swimsuits," Carter added practically. "Because I don't know about any of you, but I certainly didn't pack one."

That was a good point. "Quick shopping trip, then pool."

Remi was fine with going to the pool, excited even, right up until it came time to get into the water. She hesitated strongly at the pool's edge, staring down at it with open trepidation. Ari didn't initially understand why, as they were at the shallow end, and even with her shortness it wouldn't go over her head. Then it hit him—had she even been in a body of water before that was bigger than a bathtub?

Kneeling next to her, Ari asked softly, "Gattina, you know how to swim?"

Shaking her head, she kept staring at the water as if it might reach up and bite her.

Well, this was a problem. Ari wasn't that strong of a swimmer, himself. He'd not been in a pool that many times in his life. Normally, if he was in water, he was fighting for his life. It hadn't endeared him to large bodies of water. (He largely blamed Africa for that. But then, Ari blamed Africa for a lot of things. His fear of snakes, for one.)

Carter hopped in and then came around, wading easily. "Remi, you coming in?"

She didn't so much as even dip in a pinky toe, just shook her head.

Proving the man wasn't just a pretty face, Harrison cocked his head and asked, "You not comfortable swimming?"

"Don't know how," she said, barely above a whisper.

"Well, that ain't good, kiddo. I can tell you point blank, you need to be comfortable swimming. You don't know what life's going to throw at you. How about this. If your dad's okay with it, I'll drown-proof you." Harrison eyed him askance even as he made the offer.

Ari nodded encouragement, as he really didn't know how to approach this one. Harrison exuded confidence, so he clearly did. "Yeah, that's fine by me."

"Remi, sit on the side for now, let me show you a few things. Ari, can you assist?"

"Sure." Ari had no idea what the man was up to, but willingly went along with it. He didn't want Remi to hold onto this fear. Bad enough he had trouble with water.

Harrison flopped onto his back, easy and comfortable with the water lapping over his chest. He was beautifully muscled with a hint of padding around his stomach. "Now, first thing. The trick to staying afloat is your chin and hips. All your body weight takes its cue from the head, believe it or not. Here, watch. Ari, take my head and turn it any way you wish."

That sounded like an odd request. Ari wasn't sure how he felt about deliberately touching Harrison, either. He was a little hesitant to do so, keenly aware of Ivan lounging next to the pool in the hot tub and watching this play out. He gently grasped the sides of Harrison's head, his slick hair soft against his palms. Ari liked being able to touch, and he had to clamp down on his expression before he gave too much away. He kept his grip gentle and turned Harrison's head slightly to either side. Harrison's body stayed loose and his body rotated with his head, a beat behind. Ari couldn't seem to tear his eyes away from the sway of Harrison's up-thrusted hips, the way his black trunks clung to the top of his thighs and dick, shifting with every eddy of water.

"You see?" Harrison asked Remi, still being maneuvered and with no apparent concern. "The head dictates where you go. If you want to stay afloat, you keep your head straight and your chin and hips up, and you'll be okay. Chin, hips, and toes."

Ari let go of Harrison, a little quicker than he should have, as he wasn't sure what to do with his body's reaction to any of this. His hands still tingled from touching Harrison's warm skin. His lower body was starting to react and even the coolness of the water wasn't helping much. Why was he reacting this strongly to Harrison?

At Harrison's coaxing, Remi came into the pool. She went up into the same position and floated, Harrison's hands under her back supportively. Then he slipped his hands free and she stayed afloat. The slow smile that dawned over his daughter's face was worth every bit of Ari's discomfort.

Harrison, it seemed, was a natural teacher. He taught Remi how to swim next, and she did laps in the shallow side of the pool, gaining confidence with every lap. Ari swam alongside her, especially as she ventured slightly deeper into the pool. Ivan wouldn't budge from the hot tub nearby, although he stayed angled so he could watch the show. Remi stayed in over an hour, tired but pleased when she finally agreed to come out.

Pulling up a folded towel, Ari slung it around her, not

wanting her to catch a chill or some pervert's attention in her swimsuit. He nearly jumped out of his skin when he felt a towel being draped around his shoulders too, the brush of Harrison's fingers against his bare shoulders jolting through him. The only thing that saved Harrison from a punch in the throat was the man talking to him as he did it, alerting Ari to his presence.

"Don't you catch a chill either. It's kinda cold in here."

Ari gave him an odd look. Was Harrison just oblivious to the effect he had on Ari? The man kept coming in close, as if he didn't realize the contradicting tailspin it put Ari into every time. Hell, was the man even gay? Ari honestly couldn't tell if he was or just one of those touchy-feely people who didn't know what personal space meant.

Passing them, Ivan threw over his shoulder, "I'm ordering in pie. Who wants some?"

"Apple pie!" Remi cheered, following him immediately out the door.

Ari shook it off and followed as well, flip flops lightly smacking as he went down the hallway to their room. He stayed hyper aware of Harrison following, but of course he followed—his room was across from theirs. Ari went through the motions of getting the chlorine washed out of his and Remi's hair and them both into dry clothes before going next door to Ivan's room.

The thief was already ensconced in the king-sized bed, munching on a plate of pie, the TV on the wall cued and ready. Ari took one look at the screen and grinned. "Nice. New competition?"

"As of yesterday. Kyou sent it to me." Ivan shot him a sharp, questioning eyebrow. "Is Harrison going to be alright with this?"

"I mean, all wrestling is a little gay. I guess we'll see." Ari was curious about it himself.

Remi was not a fan, so she gave the TV a disgruntled frown, lip curling up, before she took her pie and settled in with a book at the only table in the room. It left the bed to the adults. Ari piled on next to Ivan, a pillow propping him up against the headboard, with enough space that Harrison could sit on his other side. He was of two minds about that but really, there wasn't any other place for Harrison to sit.

Harrison came in a minute later, although he had popcorn in hand. Wasn't in the mood for pie, eh? He sauntered to the bed and slung himself into it, the bed bouncing a little with the impact. Traitorous mattress that it was, it bounced Harrison *closer* so that once again he was casually encroaching on Ari's space as their shoulders brushed together. It was all Ari could do to not move and not react. Part of him really wanted to react. Although whether he'd punch Harrison for confusing his libido or kiss him was still up in the air. He rather wanted to do both at the moment.

"What are we watching?" Harrison inquired, snagging a handful of popcorn from the bowl in his lap. "Wrestling?"

"Turkish wrestling." Ivan hit play. "Only sport the three of us can agree on. For obvious reason."

"What obvious—" Harrison stopped dead and watched for a minute. "Is his hand seriously under that guy's waistband?"

"Yup." Ivan popped the *p*.

Ari watched Harrison carefully from the corner of his eye. The mercenary's eyes stayed glued to the screen, jaw dropping steadily as the two (rather attractive) men wrestled on screen.

"His hand has to be on that guy's—" Harrison shot Remi a look before modifying, "junk. Has to be. That's not illegal?"

"Not in Turkish wrestling," Ari said.

"It's why we all like to watch it," Ivan threw in, still cheerful.

Harrison whistled, grin spreading over his face in a rakish way. "I just found a new favorite sport. How the hell did I miss this one?"

"It's too gay for most Americans." Ivan's voice radiated severe disapproval.

Harrison snorted. "There's no such thing as too gay. Oh man, oh man, I can't believe that's legal. I mean, he's literally grabbing his ass, you know he is."

"Oh yeah," Ivan agreed dreamily.

Well. Harrison, it appeared, had no problem with anything queer. If he was straight, he was at least comfortable around it, which was just as well. Ari was unquestionably gay. So was Kyou. Ivan was technically bisexual but leaned so close to his own gender that he'd only ever had two female lovers. And considering his track record, that was a very small minority.

"I did not bring enough popcorn for this," Harrison mourned. "Tell me there's lots of footage."

"Lots and lots," Ari promised him, relaxing a hair. Seeing Harrison's enthusiasm eased one of his concerns and sparked something Ari cautiously labelled as hope. He didn't feel the need to be as defensive since Harrison wasn't the type to be homophobic. He still wasn't sure how to react to having the man's shoulder pressed against his, but it was rather nice. He'd not had full on contact like this with a man in...god...he couldn't actually remember. Ari found himself alright with the possibility of Harrison sitting like this for a while. Maybe, by the time the match was over, he'd have figured out what his instincts wanted to do with the man.

13

CARTER

Carter had a towel around his waist when his sister decided to call him. Her timing was always perfect that way. He grimaced, staring at the phone distrustfully, because it was late and for once they were in the same time zone. So if she was calling near ten o'clock? It couldn't be good.

Resigned to his fate, he answered blithely. "'Sup, sis."

"Carter. I need a favor."

"Well, I hope it can wait a few weeks, cause I'm in the middle of a job."

Maddison sighed, aggravated. *"Well, cancel it. I need you."*

"Funny how I might be the black sheep of the family but when shit gets real, I'm the one you call." Carter couldn't help but get the dig in. Their last family gathering, Maddison had screamed at him about being the only one in the family she was embarrassed by. (She'd also been completely wasted and coming out of a bad marriage, so he didn't really hold it against her.)

"Look, I really am sorry about that, alright? I don't even remember saying it, that's how drunk I was."

"Oh trust me, I am in no doubt about how drunk you were." Carter found himself forgiving her, a little. Maddison was his only sister. He tended to cut her a lot of slack because of it. "Alright, maybe I can help you out long distance. Whatcha need?"

"That bastard of an ex-husband threw me out of the house. I have the clothes on my back, my purse, and my car and nothing else. I literally can't function like this, and he's changed the locks. I can't get back in."

Carter let his head hang for a second. "Are you sure I can't shoot this sonovabitch?"

"Don't fucking tempt me," Maddison growled. *"The only reason why I'm staying as patient as I am is that my lawyer swears we have him dead to rights. And doing crap like this is only hurting him. But it does leave me in a sticky situation. Can I stay with you?"*

He let the towel drop, pulled on boxers, pulled up a pillow, and stretched out comfortably on the bed. He had a feeling this would take a while. "I'm not in Florida right now. But tell you what, I'll give you the code to the garage. That'll let you into the house; you can stay in my guest room until you've got it sorted."

"Thank you, thank you, thank you. I didn't want to tell Mom and Dad. They're already planning his funeral arrangements. I don't want them in legal trouble."

This amused Carter. Mostly because it was true—he could see his parents taking that fight, but also for what she didn't say. "But it's fine if I'm in legal trouble?"

"You do quasi-legal stuff all the time, don't give me that. So...are you even in country right now?"

"I am, but I shouldn't tell you where or what I'm doing. It's one of those quasi-legal things."

"Ah." A pregnant pause. *"Do I need to worry?"*

"Not this time. This time, I've got really professional guys I'm working with. Some of the best, actually. I kinda started off on the wrong foot with one of them—accidentally stumbled across one of his secrets—but he's left my head attached. I think he's forgiven me, since he agreed to work the job." And he'd handled Remi several times under Ari's eyes and neither Ari nor Ivan had taken offense. That alone told Carter a great deal. The men had apparently decided to trust Carter with Remi. He was honestly glad. Relieved, mostly, but glad too.

"Wait. I'm hearing this little note in your voice. Is one of these guys hot?"

This, at least, he could talk to his sister about. His brothers didn't mind that he was gay. They just didn't want to hear details. Maddison adored talking boys with him. It was one of the reasons why Maddy was secretly his favorite sibling.

"Smoking hot. The other guy is good looking too, but super intimidating. I wouldn't cross him in a dark alley. But the guy I'm talking about has that tall, dark, and handsome look."

"*Yeah? Can you give me a name?*"

"Probably not. Call him Sexy."

"*And is Sexy interested?*"

"I don't...know? I find him hard to read. Some guys in my line of work, they have trigger reflexes. He initially struck me as that way, but I've seen him interact with his inner circle, and he doesn't react with them."

"*But he reacts with you?*"

"Has every time I've stepped in a little too close. It's interesting body language I'm getting from him. Like, I'm seeing these little tells that he's interested, and when I do come in close, he never moves first. It's just that he initially flinches, then forces himself to relax. It's totally instinctual on his part, that initial flinch. And it tells me he's been hurt, and hurt often enough when a man comes in close, his first instinct is to throw his guard up."

It pissed Carter off, actually. Not towards Ari, but at how ingrained the reaction seemed to be. He hated that Ari had been hurt so many times, he felt threatened by another man in his personal space. Had no one properly watched this man's back? Was there no one to shield him when Ari needed it? He forced his hand to relax before he accidentally broke his phone.

Maddison sighed. "*Oh god, I can hear it now. You've just flipped into protective mode.*"

"Excuse you, I have not."

"*You totally, totally have. You really don't get how much your tone gives away, do you? But I can tell. You like this guy, it upsets you he's reacting like this to you, and you want to win him over.*"

Carter tried denial for a full second. It failed utterly. "How come you know me so well?"

"*You aren't complicated, little brother. The reason why you're good at retrieval jobs with kids is because your protective streak is legendary. I should somehow warn this guy about you. He needs to brace himself.*"

"Shut it, I'm not that bad. And it's not like he needs protection, not really. He's formidable in his own right. It's just, I don't think anyone's really watched his back before. Even his friends seem to operate on the opinion he can handle himself alone."

"*You don't agree?*"

"Of course I agree he can. But no one should have to. Life's hard enough, you don't need to do it alone, without any backup or support. And I hate the way he flinches. Seriously hate it."

"*Yup. Really should find a way to warn him. It's probably too late now, though. He's got your attention.*"

"Well, yeah," Carter confessed sheepishly. "Although really, I don't know how viable it is for me to try dating him."

"*Whoa! Who said anything about dating?*"

"Maddy, I don't like hookups, you know that. And this guy... he's seriously worth so much more than a one-night stand. Anyone who wants a quick fuck with him needs their head examined. He's more than that."

Maddison breathed for a few seconds. "*Carter. Are you falling for this guy?*"

"No? I've only known him for two days, it's too soon for that! I just really like him. I wish I could explain it better to you, but if I tried, I'd spill the beans about the secret I uncovered. And then he'd really be forced to kill me."

"*That bad?*"

"That important," Carter corrected. "I won't risk either my relationship with him or what he's protecting by talking casually. Not even to you, sis."

"*Fair enough.*" Maddison hummed, the sound she made when she was thinking hard. "*If this goes the way you want it to, do you think you can bring him home and introduce him to the family? Is he that kind of guy?*"

Carter thought about it. Thought about Ari and Remi in his parents' home. It was strangely easy to picture and emotionally satisfying in a way that was hard to grasp. "Strangely, yeah. He's family oriented. It's part of what's drawn my attention. Whether he'd ever relax his guard enough to be okay doing that is another question entirely. But you're jumping way ahead of the curve, Maddy. I have to figure out if he'll even be willing to date first. And I'm a little leery of pushing my agenda there, considering the job we're doing. Tensions are running kinda high on this one."

"You'll have to tell me about it later, when the job is done. For now, though, I need to go. Text me that code, yeah? And keep me updated on this situation. I haven't heard you this interested in a man in years. It'd be nice if you could snag a boyfriend who would understand you and your insane ways."

Carter snorted. He'd protest the 'insane' part but unfortunately he really didn't have a leg to stand on when it came to sanity. "Yeah, I'll keep you in the loop. And tell me if things get worse. I'll come down and help you with the ex if you need me to."

"See, you say 'help' but I hear 'bury.'"

"Your hearing has always been exceptional."

Maddison snorted a laugh. *"Love you, Carter. Thanks, bye!"*

Hanging up, he texted her the code, then stayed in that sprawled position awhile and stared at the phone thoughtfully. He hadn't realized how much of all this he'd decided on until he got it out in the open like that. Talking with Maddison always helped him sort things out and put it into prospective. But apparently Ari really had caught his interest. Wanting to shield him so the man stopped flinching was only part of it.

Staring upwards at the bland white ceiling, Carter considered his options. Just how should he approach this?

He wasn't really firm on any sort of game plan by the next morning. They more or less met in the dining room for a continental breakfast. Carter wasn't really that hungry this morning so settled for toast and coffee. Remi already sat at the table with pancakes and orange juice, her father and uncle in line and filling up their plates.

Settling in, he gave Remi a smile. "Morning."

"Morning, Mr. Harrison," she responded happily. Then she

paused and stared at him doubtfully. "I don't know your call sign."

"Ah, that's because I don't have one. Mercenaries don't really do call signs most of the time. We might make something up on a job so we can talk to each other over comms without giving away our identities, but we don't take nicknames like your father does."

She hummed, thinking about this. "Hmm, okay."

Carter assumed that to be the only question she had this morning but she surprised him by staring at him hard. "You okay?"

He stared back at her, not sure why she was asking. "Do I not look okay?"

"You look confused."

This kid really was sharp. She must keep Ari on his toes. "I think I make your dad nervous sometimes. I'm trying to figure out how to reassure him."

"Oh." Shaking her head, she corrected seriously, "He likes you. It made him happy you watched Turkish wrestling with him. He said you weren't homo—homo—"

"Homophobic?" Carter guessed.

Her frustrated expression cleared up. "Yeah, that. It made him and Uncle Ivan happy."

Carter had more or less figured out the other two men were either gay or bisexual or something along those lines. The way they'd kept drooling while watching the wrestling match had more or less told him all he needed to know on that subject. But it was nice to have another confirmation. "Yeah, honey, I'm not. I'm gay myself."

Remi nodded, not surprised. "Figured. You want to be friends with Daddy and Uncle Ivan?"

"I do. They're nice guys."

She beamed at him, pleased, and returned to her pancakes.

This kid was seriously so frank. It tickled Carter's funny bone badly because he was never able to predict what she was going to say next. And what did she mean, it 'figured' he was gay? Was she merely going off what the adults around her were saying?

Ari returned to the table and settled, eyes automatically

sweeping over Remi and her plate. "Well, seems like we have an open day today while we're waiting on the house and K. Ivan wants to stalk Knowles some more. Harrison, what do you want to do?"

He'd thought about ways to tap into Ari's trust last night and had a good answer at the ready. "I thought I'd help you and Remi walk through an exit strategy."

The assassin's espresso eyes came up to meet his in a sharp cut. "Who says we were doing that?"

"Come on, Ari, I'm not an idiot. It's all well and good to talk her through it, but she doesn't know the city. And she's never had to travel on her own before. Of course it makes sense to do a few dry runs with us following her."

"Us?" Ari parroted the word, both questioning and suspicious.

"Why do it alone if you don't have to?" Carter responded reasonably. "Another pair of eyes can't hurt. You okay with that game plan, honey?"

Remi nodded, her eyes trained on her sire. "I'd like to practice it, just in case. Daddy?"

He stared at Carter a little longer before tearing his eyes away and giving Remi a smile. "Sure. Let's do that after breakfast."

14

ARI

Remi might know, intellectually, how to get out of the city. But she didn't really know the city or how to avoid the cameras. Hard to avoid something when you didn't know where it was. For that matter, Ari had flown in and out of DC before, but he really didn't know the city either.

For their benefit (and sanity), they decided to do a mock run with Remi. Ivan went to scope out Knowles a little more, see if he couldn't get a better head count of how many guards were on day roster. Harrison and Ari followed Remi at a ten-foot distance, letting her go first as they headed into the metro.

At nine in the morning on a Sunday, it wasn't too crowded. They didn't speak to each other as Remi led the way into the first metro car. She flashed them a triumphant look, pleased with herself for navigating this far.

"She's surprisingly good about retaining instructions," Harrison mentioned, and he sounded downright pleased. "I've worked with adults who would have screwed it up by now."

"Tell me about it. It's my one saving grace with her. She's a show-once kind of person. If she was anything else, I'd be in trouble." Ari held onto the pole above his head, feet braced as the train car gently rocked him side to side.

"Are you really encouraging her to be an assassin?"

Harrison didn't sound judgey, mostly curious. Ari took the question in stride and shrugged. "I'm not the kind of parent who makes decisions for their kids. Between you and me, though, I'm hoping she becomes a hacker. K's been teaching her and says she's got a gift for tech. We're all trying to encourage her in that direction."

"It would mean she's shot at less often."

"Yup. I'd rather she not be in the line of fire most of her adult life. Up to her, though."

The conversation stalled as they got off that subway and went back out of the station, still following Remi. She stopped at a map, got her bearings, and then headed off. No one stopped her. No one asked any questions of her. It hurt Ari's heart in a way he wasn't sure how to explain. Was a child that invisible to most adults? Was she someone else's problem?

Harrison's thoughts must have run along the same line, since he muttered, "I know I told her she could do this, but it's pissing me off in a way that it is working. You'd think at least one adult would stop her and ask why she's alone."

"Yeah, non va bene. But good for us she can do it if she needs to." It frankly gave Ari chills, though. He couldn't help but think about that night, six months ago, when Remi had first approached him. If he'd not paid attention to her and just left, what would have happened? His imagination provided nothing good.

Random rain drops fell and Ari grimaced up at the sky. It had felt humid and heavy all morning but he'd hoped the rain would hold off for a little longer until they were back under cover.

"Figured this would happen." Harrison reached into the messenger bag over his shoulder and pulled out an umbrella. With a press of the switch, he popped it up over their heads, then took a step closer so they were both under its cover. It meant their shoulders overlapped, as two grown men didn't really fit under an umbrella well. Harrison seemed to be eyeing him sideways, making sure this was alright. Ari forced a smile and deliberately relaxed his shoulders. It was fine. This was fine.

Okay, it wasn't, the touches were still playing havoc with his instincts, but part of him was honest enough to admit the attraction. Carter Harrison was a ruggedly beautiful man. He was good natured. Kind. Competent. Great with kids. Patient.

The combination of all that slipped underneath Ari's guard and ambushed him.

Harrison may or may not prove to be the exception to Ari's dating issues. He couldn't really say one way or another at this point, as he didn't know the man well enough to predict him. He felt torn about the opportunity Harrison presented, though. Did he even want to try?

Shaking the thought off, Ari focused back on the here and now. Remi was his priority. He didn't want to lose her on this crowded sidewalk. He could think about vexing and attractive mercenaries later.

Remi's three dry runs getting safely to the airport and booking a ticket were a success. She found the best and most efficient method during the third run, and Ari breathed easier knowing she had it down. If it all went to shit, at least she'd get out fine.

All of the walking and thinking had worn her out. Remi lay sound asleep in her bed, snoring a little. Ari took the opportunity to slip out, heading for Ivan's room next door. He gave a soft rap on the door, not surprised when Ivan opened it within seconds. There was a knowing look on his friend's face as he gestured him inside.

"Vodka?" Ivan offered with a smug tilt to his mouth that spoke of trouble.

Not sure if he wanted to know, Ari tried deflecting as he settled on the end of the king-sized bed. The bland hotel room had gained a little personality because Ivan had apparently bought a street artist's work. The bold sunset picture of a beach was at odds with the blank white walls and bland khaki colored carpet of the room. "Isn't that a bad idea this time of night?"

The thief scoffed, already pouring a shot for him from the mini bar. "Vodka is medicine."

"How very Russian of you." Shaking his head, Ari took the glass and downed it in one go, as frankly, he needed something to settle him. And it was good vodka.

Ivan grabbed the single wooden chair in the room,

straddling it so that his arms could rest on the back, watching him steadily. "Something eats at you. Not Remi."

"No, I'm...good with how we've got things worked out. Even if it all goes to shit, she'll be able to get out and to Luca." Ari opened his mouth, froze, then closed it with a frown. He really had no idea how to express the emotions swirling through him. It wasn't that he felt embarrassed about doing so either. A real man expressed his feelings and didn't shy from his own emotions.

"Carter Harrison." Ivan said his name like it was the answer to a complicated word problem.

Blowing out a breath, Ari stared at the glass in his hands, finding it easier. "Yeah. I don't know what to do about this. At first, I was ready to take him out just because he knew about Remi. But he's been so...reassuring, I think is the word. He swore he wouldn't breathe a word about her to anyone, and I believe him. And that's a very strange feeling, believing someone other than you guys."

Ivan nodded. "Da, I see what you mean. But I feel the same, that he can be trusted."

Relief coursed through Ari. So it wasn't just him feeling that way? "Is it his reputation? Or the way he's been responding to Remi?"

"Both, I think." The smug tilt to Ivan's mouth came back with a vengeance. "But is that why you're attracted to him?"

Ari wished he had another shot of vodka in his hands with fierce longing. "This stays between me and you, okay?"

"Da," Ivan agreed immediately.

"I have no idea why the fuck he's affecting me like this." Ari ran a hand roughly through his hair, his mind a whirling dervish that wouldn't settle. "You know me, I'm not attracted to men all that often. I'm a take it or leave it kinda guy most of the time. But something about him makes my nerves light on fire whenever he gets near me. The man's pushing buttons I didn't know I had."

"This is not bad thing," Ivan pointed out, taking his glass and pouring him another shot.

Ari took it gratefully as Ivan settled back into his chair. He didn't drink it just yet, though. "Isn't it? My life wasn't conducive to romance before Remi. Having an eight-year-old to keep track of makes it even harder. And you know as well as I do, she's too soft a target."

"You think Harrison would not protect her?"

As much as he'd like to argue, Ari didn't want to lie. Shaking his head, his hand tightened on the glass until his knuckles shone white with strain. "We both know if shit hit the fan, Harrison would protect her automatically. It's one of those buttons he's pushing. I didn't know 'protective' was sexy until yesterday. That whole thing on the train about turned me into goo."

"I saw you melting." Ivan winked at him. "Do not be alarmed. It takes one who knows you well to read the expression. I don't think he realized. Ari. What are you really scared of? It's alright to date, you know. Or even hookup, if you want to try that. If he does something stupid, I'll kill him for you later."

That actually did make Ari feel better. "Is it really that easy? Can I just blindly try? You know I suck at hookups."

Ivan shrugged. "Not all men can relax their guard enough to be intimate with a stranger. Your guard is higher than most. Date, then."

"The only time I've really been on a date was to get close to a mark, though."

Ivan pursed his lips. "I would not think I had more dating history than you. This makes me worry about Kyou."

Snorting a laugh, Ari tossed back his vodka before snarking, "You really think he leaves his batcave for any length of time? He's more attached to his computers than a man with a new mistress."

Grimacing, Ivan didn't disagree. "Da, you have good point there. We need to drag him outside more often."

"That's what Remi's for. She's our lure."

Ivan lifted his glass, still undrunk, in a toast for a good idea.

As much as Ari felt better about airing all of this, he didn't feel inspired to actually do anything about it. Quite the opposite, really. It was all well and good to admit to being attracted, but did he really want to act on said attraction? And knowing how he operated, it would mean easing into a physical relationship, which Harrison might not be interested in. Dating seemed even more impossible of an option. Ari absolutely did not want to upset the balance by trying for something he wasn't sure Harrison was even interested in. The man was touchy-feely, sure, but that didn't make him gay. Or bi. Or anything else, really.

Ivan sighed gustily. "You just talked yourself out of it, didn't you? Chert durak, why do you do this? Life will give you only so many chances, you know."

"While we're trying to tackle Knowles, you want me to date?" Ari objected, a touch defensively. "While we're trying to tackle Knowles in *four weeks*?"

His friend didn't budge an inch. "There will always be good reasons for not taking that leap. Just like there will always be good reasons for trying. Decisions made by fear are never good ones."

"I know that, but I can't risk Remi."

Ivan sighed the sigh of a very exasperated man who wanted to pound sense into someone and was exercising virtuous restraint in not giving into the compulsion. "Then I hope, for both your sakes, Carter Harrison knows how to make a move."

15

CARTER

Carter arrived at the townhome later the next morning with no fanfare. Two furniture moving trucks were unloading, mostly beds, Carter noted. A table, chairs, desk, and some couches as well, but mostly beds. It made sense. They only needed the essentials for the next four weeks and this place would likely be abandoned after that. Although it did beg the question: who covered the costs for expenses on this project?

The townhome was a typical red brick, two-story building matching with all of the others around it. Anonymous in the best sense and Carter approved. The side of the house had white siding and a two-car attached garage, which he also approved of. Being able to keep the vehicles out of sight while they prepped would be important. K apparently knew how to set up a safehouse. The parking spaces in the front would work for the four vehicles they needed to park, as of course each man had driven his own car in.

He slipped in behind two of the furniture movers, following the dulcet tones of an irate man's voice. Mid-western dialect twined through the words the louder he got. Carter got a good look at the place as he moved. It was so neutral in tone and color, he found it bland. Beige carpet, off-white walls, no personality whatsoever. At least it was perfectly clean and in good condition. He'd stayed in worse places. Although somehow Carter got the impression that if Remi hadn't been with them, the accommodations wouldn't have been nearly so nice.

The speaker was in the kitchen, leaning against a granite-topped island, his free hand gesturing in the air as he spoke. He wasn't much taller than Carter's five-ten, slim and wiry, his messy, shortish-textured black hair not styled. He looked pale, the sort of pale stemming from too much time spent indoors. He was in loose jeans, flipflops, and a t-shirt faded to grey from many, many washings.

The hacker, K, had arrived. As he turned, Carter blinked. Huh. He was actually cuter in person. He reminded Carter of those K-pop idols his sister liked to drool over. He had that pretty-boy look to him.

K gave him a quick smile and held up a finger, asking for a minute. Then his face hardened as he practically snarled into the phone, "I'm not mad you called me that. I'm sad you lack the creativity to call me anything else, you knuckle dragging, inbred swamp twat. You listen to me; I have to go dark for a month or so. I can't watch your back during that time, and I can't help you unravel this current problem more than I have. Use the brain your daddy gave you, and the painstaking intel *I* gave you, and watch your back, you hear me? What? No, I'm not in trouble. Brannigan. Bran, quit it. I'm just on a job, it's not something you can help me with. Oh you're *so sweet*," K's tone made it clear he thought the opposite, "but I have my criminal friends to help me, and I don't need your hot ass in the middle of this. You focus on your own problem, hmm? Don't give me that lip, you ingrate. You have a hacker as your guardian angel, you don't get to make that argument. Shut up."

Carter's eyebrows rested in his hairline at this point. Just who was K talking to?!

Something that might have been a blush crossed that pale skin before K muttered more gently, "Watch your back, okay? I'll be back in a month." K hung up the phone and slid it into his pocket before offering a hand. "Sorry for that. I'm Kyou, nice to meet you."

Carter shook his hand and found it firmer than he expected. "Nice to meet you. Thanks for taking this on. I know it was very last minute."

Kyou canted his head, looking intrigued. "I'm amazed you

found Ari at all, frankly. Walk me through step by step how you did so later, when I have the computer up."

"So you can wipe any electronic footprint they have? Sure. I'd rather no one else put the pieces together about Remi."

"Good, thank you. And we're always up for a challenge. Just live up to your reputation and don't do anything stupid."

That sounded like a warning. Carter gave him a game smile. "I'll do my best. What can I help you with?"

He got another funny look and this time Kyou was slower to respond. "I've got my gear in the car. A lot of it's too delicate to trust to movers. If you want to help me with that?"

"Sure. And I meant to ask, who's in charge of expenses on this trip?"

"I've been keeping a record of it. I figured we'd split costs evenly at the end."

"If you want me to take that on, I can. I have to report expenses when the job is over anyway."

Kyou stopped and scrutinized him again. "Huh. Ivan's right, you're really a nice guy. No wonder Ari hasn't killed you yet."

"I'm actually a little surprised by that myself." More like, he was astonished the assassin hadn't already done so and instead seemed to be steadily thawing towards him. At least, he'd come into contact with Ari several times over the past few days and every time, instead of flinching, Ari seemed to lean into the contact. Carter wasn't quite sure what to make of the body language he was reading. Either Ari was touch starved (possible), was attracted to him (doubtful, but still possible), or buttering him up to kill him later (most likely).

"I've got a corner in the living room reserved for setting everything up," Kyou informed him, leading the way through the kitchen and into the attached garage. "For now, let's set the boxes in the kitchen. I think the desk will need some assembling. There's five bedrooms in the house, so when we're done, just pick one and throw your stuff in. If you don't mind, let Ivan or I have the master downstairs. Ari will sleep better if Remi's within a short distance of him."

"Sure." There wasn't much else to discuss. They went back and forth, unloading the many, many boxes in Kyou's Jeep Wrangler. Heeding the hacker's warning, Carter was careful in setting them down. He absolutely did not want to break anything. For one thing, Kyou might murder him in his sleep. For another, they might not have the necessary time to replace broken equipment.

The rest of the gang arrived while he was unloading things. Remi went straight for her Uncle Kyou and got a hug in, her smile wide on her face. She kept a hand on the hacker even as Ivan called to her, switching hands to respond to Ivan's request so she held onto the thief instead. Carter took an unobserved moment to really watch her reactions to the men and felt his instincts stir once again. There was something...off. Not wrong, just subtly off, like a picture out of focus. It took him a minute to see it.

Remi stayed in constant physical contact.

He'd never seen a child do this. All children liked to be picked up, hugged, held. But they were also independent. They wanted to go explore, get into things, play. Especially in a new house, like this, why wasn't she running up and down the stairs, exploring? Claiming a bedroom? Remi demonstrated none of that behavior. If she wasn't holding onto her father, she was in Ivan's lap, or pressed up against Kyou's leg. She acted as if she'd spent years starved of affection, only to now be offered a constant feast. Even knowing she'd have access later, she couldn't stop indulging.

He might be wrong, but Carter trusted his instincts and observational skills to keep him alive. He didn't think he was wrong. It raised even more questions, questions he'd likely never get an answer to. Why had Remi recently gone to her father instead of her mother? Likely because it was safer with her father. Despite his profession. Remi had the air of a formerly neglected child. She was definitely getting all of the love and attention a child deserved now, no question, but she clearly was still overcoming a darker period of her life. If Carter were smart, he'd make allowances for that.

The observations whirled in his head as he went about setting things up. He chose a bedroom upstairs, made his bed up with new sheets and a comforter, listened as Ari and Remi did the same in their own rooms. Then he wandered back down, coming to Kyou's side as the man screwed the glass and metal desk together. "Want a hand?"

"Sure. And I talked it over with the others. If you want to start tracking expenses, go for it. One less thing for me to worry about. Food is on our own heads, but that's it."

Carter felt like he'd finally been accepted with this responsibility. He grinned without really meaning to. "Okay. After we get you set up, hand all the receipts over to me."

"Can do." Kyou offered him a table leg.

He took it, and they silently screwed in brackets and lifted things into place.

Ivan came out of the back bedroom, trailing over to stand nearby and watch. "I want pizza. Anyone else hungry?"

A little girl voice called down the stairwell, "Me!"

Turning his head, Ivan called back, "I did not ask the bottomless pit!"

Remi giggled.

"Seriously, that kid," Kyou groused in an affectionate manner. "Is she in a growth spurt? She's constantly hungry."

That's not it, Carter couldn't help but think. That wasn't it at all. She was proving, time and again, that these men were invested enough in her to feed her. Did they realize? Were they just playing along?

Ivan was already on his phone, looking up restaurants. "Harrison, what do you like on yours?"

"Huh? Oh, anything but anchovies and olives."

Kyou gasped and feigned horror. "You don't like olives? What's *wrong* with you?"

"Says the man who puts pineapple on his pizza," Ivan mocked, still scrolling, not even looking up from the screen.

"Screw you, pineapple on pizza is delicious."

"No pineapple!" Ari called down the stairs.

Ivan raised a hand as if voting. "Motion carried. Three larges?"

"And breadsticks," Kyou insisted. Was that a pout on his face? "Garlic."

Shrugging good naturedly, Ivan put in the order before calling up the stairs, "Solnishko, you want Sprite?"

She sounded resigned as she answered. "Yeah."

The rule about not getting caffeine was apparently rather

firm. It made Carter wonder, did she get that hyper?

Ivan settled on the new couch, legs tucked off to the side, chin on his fist. He had an expression on his face that was part thoughtful, part worried. It in turn made Carter worry, and he paused what he was doing to ask, "What?"

With the desk in place, Kyou looked around as well, studying his friend's face and groaning. "Uh-oh. I know that look. What now?"

"I think this is not a job where we can make assumptions," Ivan said carefully, as if weighing each word.

Staring at him, Kyou's eyes narrowed to mere slits. "I'm not going to like this, am I?"

"No," Ivan admitted cheerfully. "I am, though."

"That's what I was afraid of. Ari! Get down here!" Kyou waited the three seconds it took for the assassin to join them before he said, "Ivan's plotting shit again."

"I object to the word plot! I just think we may have made an assumption we should not have."

Ari crossed both arms over his chest and glared at Ivan. "It's when you use this oh-so-reasonable tone that we know you're actually plotting trouble. Alright, out with it."

Ivan paused only long enough for Remi to join them, pulling her in to sit on his lap as he asked, "How do we know the painting is in the vault?"

Carter blinked at him because actually, that was a very valid question. They'd all assumed it must be, because openly displaying it in the gallery would be impossible. Not when a painting that well known and famous should be at the Met. But....

"Come to think of it, they might have hung it elsewhere in the house. Like a bedroom or a study, a place most of their guests wouldn't go. And anyone who saw it in the house would assume it a reproduction and nothing more. Not many people have the expertise to know a reproduction from the original to begin with."

The thief gave him a gracious nod. "Exactly the point I make, da? How do we know it's in the vault? It could be inside the house."

"You just want to go play." Kyou shook a finger at him in

accusation.

Ivan splayed a hand over his heart, a pout forming. "You wound me."

"That can be so arranged," Ari growled at him. "Ivan, seriously, do you actually believe the painting is in the house and not the vault? Or are you just bored and want to go poke at the viper's nest?"

"We need to do a dry run to test if Harrison's intel is accurate," Ivan pointed out, maintaining that oh-so-reasonable tone of his.

It formed a tic at the corner of Ari's eye, which Carter carefully didn't show any amusement about. He had a feeling Ivan routinely pulled stunts that prematurely aged his friends.

Ari held his breath, skin turning red, then blew it out in a huff. Turning to him and Kyou, he growled, "I hate it when he makes a good point."

"It's what makes arguing with him so fun," Kyou agreed in the same tone. "You're really that sure you can get into the house with no trouble?"

"We'll need to do some prep for it. But if I can't even get into the house, then the vault is a lost cause." Ivan's raised brows dared them to disagree.

Carter hated to admit it, but... "I really can't disagree with that logic. And my intel is now a month old, things could have changed since then."

"Mine's not much more up to date," Kyou grumbled, staring blackly at his computer, still in various boxes, waiting to be assembled. "Okay, Ivan, fine. We'll prep for a dry run first. I'll need a few days to get ready on my end. You're not going in there blind."

Ivan did pout this time, and the expression just looked *wrong* on a former Russian mafioso's face. "You suck all joy from life."

"The phrase you're looking for is 'you take all the fun out of things' but good try." Kyou ran a hand roughly through his hair, looking as stressed now as he had been on the phone earlier. "Alright. There's a few things we need to tackle, and we don't have a lot of time to do them in. First thing: because this job has the potential to go to shit very quickly, I've got panic buttons for all of you. It looks like a wristwatch, and it's easy to engage. Slap it quickly three times, and it engages a GPS alert beacon. I'll be able to follow you wherever you are."

Carter had the distinct impression the watches were less for their sakes and more for Remi's but had the sense to not say so. The little girl was far more likely to keep hers on if they all wore one. That and he was realistic enough to admit he'd prefer a panic button for this job, as Kyou was unfortunately correct. It could go wrong very quickly.

"Harrison, where did that red hard case get off to?"

He had to think for a second, as he'd carried a lot in from the car. "Island, I think, near the sink."

Kyou went to fetch it, still talking as he went. "There's a function on the watch that allows you to track everyone else, too. I'll teach you how to use it while we're waiting on the pizza. After lunch, I'll need to put my system back together. What are you three going to be doing?"

"We'll need to get a fake Monet to switch out for the real one," Carter answered, watching curiously as Kyou unzipped the red case, revealing a selection of masculine watches that looked like those smart watches or calorie counters people wore. "I figured it would be good to start there, have it on hand."

"And drones," Ivan added.

Taking the watch Kyou handed him, Carter looked askance at Ivan. Drones? They hadn't talked about drones at all for this job. Or was this a carryover from the first time they'd done Knowles?

"Drones?" Ari repeated in confusion.

Okay, obviously not.

"I had an idea last time we were here," Ivan explained with all the excitement of a child before Christmas. "I'll need a drone. Airborne distraction."

"And at some point today, we need to sit down and actually discuss the plan," Kyou added as if he were merely continuing from his own original thread. "Because obviously people have ideas to share. Okay, Princess, give me your wrist."

Remi promptly did so and beamed as a Black Widow watch fit over her thin wrist. "You got me Black Widow!"

"Of course I did, what kind of uncle do you take me for,

anyway?" Kyou seemed pleased by her reaction. Then again, the man had bought that particular band in mind for the little girl who loved the superhero.

Carter watched them together, the ease of their affection, the way they teased and worked, and a pang of envy settled in his chest. He'd always liked being part of a team dynamic. It was where he felt most at home. Most of his adult life, however, he'd been outside of one. No matter what he tried, he seemed to just miss having the connection he sought. He looked at these men, and the darling little girl they doted on, and wondered.

Maybe he could try again?

The thought lingered in his mind as he went to the unused dining room. It had nothing but a card table in it and his gear. Carter went through his duffle bag, double checking what he had, doing an inventory on ammunition. This wasn't supposed to be a shootout at any point, but...well, it never hurt to be prepared. And it gave his hands something to do so he could think. Right now, he really needed a minute to think.

Remi appeared out of nowhere and looked at the display of guns curiously. "You need all of this?"

"Need? Probably not. Want? Yes." He grinned down at her. "You know what it's like. The man who dies with the most toys wins."

She nodded sagely back at him. "Daddy's the same way. You're a lot alike."

Her last statement had not been innocent. Carter eyed her suspiciously. "What are you driving at, kid?"

"You know," Remi said seriously, "People say 'I love you' in a lot of different ways."

Carter hunkered down to her level, regarding her curiously. He literally never knew what this kid was going to say next. "Yeah? How?"

Ticking them off on her fingers, she starting quoting: "Have you eaten? Get some sleep. Buckle up, kiddo. Be safe. You can have the last slice. Are you tired?"

Throat tightening, Carter felt tears burning at the back of his eyes. Those common questions really meant that much to her? "To you, all of those words mean 'I love you?'"

"Yeah. 'Cause no one ever said them to me before. Daddy

was the first to say them to me. Then Uncle Ivan, and Uncle Kyou. Now you. You have to care about the person to think of them."

Damn, she was going to make him start bawling any minute. Which was ridiculous, he was a street-tough mercenary. Eight-year-olds should not be able to break him this easily. In self-defense, he hugged her to him for a second. She threw her arms around his neck and settled into the hug for a moment with a satisfied sigh. For all of her dynamic personality, she felt entirely fragile in his arms. Carter felt his protective instincts kick into higher gear, and it was with reluctance he let her ease back.

Remi kept her hands on his chest, keeping them physically connected. With that same earnest expression, she encouraged, "Daddy says those things to you. You say them back. You like each other."

Rubbing the back of his neck, Carter looked away for a second, wondering how to explain the difference between liking someone and being attracted to them.

"And he thinks you're beautiful," she tacked on hopefully. "But he said he wouldn't flirt with you because it would make you uncomfortable."

Carter froze, staring at her from the corner of his eye. "Bullshit. He did not say that."

Sensing victory already, she grinned at him. "You could ask him out."

Heaven help him. He was being matched by a child with an agenda. "Wait, Remi—"

Getting a belligerent look on her face, she stuck her bottom lip out in a pout. "You *do* like him."

"Well, yeah, I do—"

"And he likes you and says you're beautiful."

"You're not making that part up, are you?"

A hair's breadth from stomping her foot, Remi pointed a finger toward her father's direction. "Stop being chicken. Go ask him out."

"Can you explain to me why you want me to ask him out? Aside from what you just said."

She opened her mouth, paused, and stared at him

thoughtfully for a moment, weighing her words. Finally, she confessed, "He says dating's hard. He told me that finding a man he liked who he could trust with me was pretty impossible. But he trusts me with you."

That was quite possibly the bluntest answer he'd ever been given for dating. Logically, it made sense, too. But when had his love life fallen to the point it took an eight-year-old to kick him in the right direction? "Okay, Rems, let's pause here and consider. Say you're right, and we do start dating, you realize what that means for you?"

She patted him on the shoulder reassuringly. "It's fine. I like you too. And when you want to do adult things, I can go stay with Uncle Ivan or Uncle Kyou."

Carter gave up. For his sanity, he didn't want to continue this conversation. "Right. I'm going to go talk to your father."

"Okay," she agreed brightly. With a skip in her step, she went off to the kitchen table, picking up the variety of locks there.

He watched her go. Carter had been thinking about this for two days, but this conversation made it more real to him, somehow. Dating an assassin, having a little girl in his life. Carter squinted at her as he tried to picture it. Did so quite successfully. Had to stop.

Damn. Maybe he was crazy after all, because that had to be the best idea he'd had all year. He could see them so clearly, taking jobs together, doing school and dance classes and family vacations. His imagination happily supplied images of them on a beach, at a dance recital, at Carter's family's house for the holidays. It was not only stupidly easy to envision but it filled him with longing. If he daydreamed about it much more, he'd turn into sappy goo on the spot.

The desire to have them was certainly strong. Now the question stood: how did he successfully approach Ari without getting the man's guard up?

16

ARI

Ari had no idea what Harrison was up to, but if the man didn't stop soon, he'd...he'd...do something, at any rate. Harrison was driving him straight up the wall and didn't even seem to be aware of it. It wasn't even so much when the mercenary had stopped him to tuck Ari's collar's tag back in, then let his hand linger in a warm sweep down Ari's back. He'd had to repress a shiver from the heat of Harrison's hand spread out between his shoulder blades. And it wasn't when he'd slid the chain of Ari's necklace around so the clasp lay hidden away without a single comment, fingers drifting across skin. Or even the way he'd helped Ari into the light windbreaker before they left the house, going to pick up breakfast for everyone. It certainly wasn't the way he'd topped off Ari's coffee over breakfast without asking, or that he'd given Remi the last piece of bacon with a warm smile. It wasn't any of that. Alright, fine, it was partially that. But mostly it was the other thing.

It was that the man was fucking beautiful doing nothing at all.

It was the half-alluring little movements Harrison made as he worked. The cute furrow between his brows as he flipped through receipts, the way he balanced his pen between his nose and upper lip to get Remi to laugh. The pattern of how he shifted in his seat, little huffs when something vexed him, and that one full body stretch that actually made his mouth go dry as Harrison's muscular strength went on display.

He just found the man insanely attractive and oddly trustworthy, and the combination of those two things were throwing him seriously out of whack. It made him want to try things that had never worked well for him in the past. Libido, maybe let's learn from past experience, yeah? Not repeat mistakes.

The libido was not listening.

He needed a breath of fresh air, away from all of them, but especially Harrison. He needed to get his head on straight before he messed things up entirely. But he also had to play it cool because if either Ivan or Kyou realized how bad Harrison shook him up, they'd tease him mercilessly about it. Worse than brothers, those two. And he should know.

Ari finished up the breakfast dishes, cleared his throat to get Kyou's attention and said, "I'll go do a little scouting around, see if I can't get us a good Monet fake and a portfolio to carry the real deal in."

Kyou popped off his headphones, turning in his chair to look at him directly. A great many screens populated the three monitors taking up the new desk, and none of it meant anything to Ari. It could have been Greek for all he could decipher it. "Great idea. I'll watch the squirt. Take Harrison with you."

He was alright with the first, but not the second. "Why do I need to take Harrison?"

"He's got the credit card we're using for expenses," Kyou answered, already turning around. His attention remained only half on Ari now, the other half on whatever he was doing on the screens.

For this, Ari would gladly pay for it out of pocket, but he sensed that if he did, he'd give his friends an opening to pry. And it was the prying he was most anxious to avoid. Ivan was already amused at his hesitancy. Dammit. "Fine. Where is he?"

"Playing hide and seek with Ivan and Remi, I think."

Ari blinked. "Why?"

"Because he's a nice guy and for some reason likes your daughter?" Kyou tilted his head against the back of the computer chair to give him a smirk entirely too knowing. "I understand from Ivan that turns you on."

"Hey train wreck, this isn't your station." Ari frowned at him as menacingly as possible.

Unfortunately, Kyou had known him long enough he was fairly immune to that glare. "What are you making a fuss for? Harrison's trustworthy. I wouldn't let him near the princess if he wasn't. He's hot. He's hot for you. You're hot for him. Make a move, man."

Ari wasn't going anywhere near that statement. It was an undetonated landmine. "You're only pushing 'cause your love-life is even more pathetic than mine. You want to live vicariously through me."

Sighing woefully, Kyou lamented, "I wish someone would take me out."

"Are we talking on a date or with a sniper rifle?"

"Surprise me."

Rolling his eyes, Ari extricated himself from this conversation and went to bellow up the stairs, "Harrison! I'm going shopping! Either come with or throw me the card!"

The man came out of the main floor's stairwell closet/cubby thing. Ari blinked in surprise. A grown man could fit in there? Was Harrison part cat? He folded up rather well.

"Shopping?" Harrison brushed his shoulders off. "I thought you went out already this morning."

"Not for food," Ari corrected him, struggling to keep a neutral expression on his face. It kept trying to break out into something besotted and entirely un-assassin like. "For the painting and a portfolio to protect the real deal when we get it."

"Oh. Yeah, it'd be best to get that sooner rather than later. Ivan wants specific drones; we can pick those up while we're out. We didn't get them yesterday, like we planned."

The trip out had gotten sidetracked by their research into the security company protecting Knowles. And how to get around said security company. They wanted to pose as employees and bypass security that way, but the logistics of creating employee records proved tricky. Kyou was positive he could hack the company and get them some IDs, but he wasn't certain he could do it quickly enough to make it feasible for them to use it as cover. The security company was—gasp, surprise!—rather secure. Their firewalls weren't something easily toppled.

They'd spent hours tossing out ideas back and forth, not sure which would work best. They hadn't come to any firm conclusions, but it was best to make as many preparations as possible while they had the time instead of cramming it all in last minute.

As he juggled the SUV's keys in his hand, he asked Kyou, "You need anything?"

"Sanity," Kyou sighed, sagging sideways in his chair. "This security company is seriously driving me insane. They've got a rotating encryption system that's giving me a migraine to hack remotely. It might be easier to send Ivan in with a flash drive at the rate I'm going."

"Now I know you're desperate." Ari couldn't resist leaning in to murmur for Harrison's benefit, "Ivan and tech don't get along. He's not really that good with it. He can handle electronic locks, but anything with an actual computer attached gets dicey. He's old school."

"Successful old school," Harrison observed. "Which is an interesting mix."

"Isn't it, though." Kyou levered himself back up and reached for a small plastic box on the desk. "I've got these set up on a frequency channel now. One for each. And yes, I've got one for Remi too. That way she's abreast of things. She's already got one in her ear."

Ari understood what he meant when Kyou opened the lid and extended it toward them. Inside were small earbuds, compact enough that they'd pass for hearing aids. Ari picked up one and stared at the translucent tech, whistling low. "I'm impressed. The last version we had wasn't this small. What's the range on this thing?"

"About twenty miles. Battery power lasts eighteen hours. I've got a wireless charger for them, so turn them in when you're not using them. They are waterproof, but not EMP proof, so don't lean up against things magnetized or supercharged."

"So, avoid the things that normally kill people, and the buds will be fine," Harrison drawled. "Got it."

Kyou grinned at him. "So sarcastic. Ah, do a drive by of the security company, get me a picture of what vehicles they drive and their uniforms. Nothing on their website shows that."

"Roger." Ari put his earbud carefully in. He'd once jammed one in too far, and his ear had ached for a day afterwards. When he felt it was situated snugly inside, he tried shaking his head a bit, but it didn't budge. Satisfied, he looked to Harrison. "Ready?"

"Sure, let's roll."

They went out through the garage, with Ari taking the driver's wheel. He didn't ask if Harrison knew DC better than he did. He needed the excuse of not looking at the man.

"National Gallery of Art will probably have a print," Harrison mentioned casually. "A good quality print, I mean. It's on 6th and Constitution Avenue."

"Did you look that up or did you just know it off the top of your head?"

"I may have looked it up this morning with Kyou. That man's googling ability is supersonic."

Ari snorted in amusement. "Understatement."

"*I can hear you guys, you know,*" Kyou pitched in.

"You hush and go hack something," Ari shot back.

"*Oooh, salty. Want some fries with that salt?*"

Ari ignored him. Sometimes, that was the safest option.

They drove without much being said between them. Ari kept his eyes firmly on the road, not only because it was the sanest course of action in DC traffic, but to keep himself from staring at Harrison. The silence grew and thickened between them, and while it wasn't tension, it wasn't comfortable. His skin felt charged and he was hyper aware of the man in the seat next to his. Ari felt like fidgeting right out of his skin, he was so antsy, and would have, if it didn't mean giving a major signal to the other man he wasn't comfortable.

"*Hey, Daddy? Can you hear me?*"

"I sure can, gattina, what is it?" Right, he could talk to Remi to cut the silence. Thank god for daughters. Ari couldn't take much more of the atmosphere in this car.

"*Can you get me a laptop? I want to help Uncle Kyou. He's swearing and listening to that Mong Metal music again.*"

Both not good signs. Kyou considered Mongolian metal music his 'fight music,' so if he had that blasting? Then he wasn't making the progress he wanted to.

Before Ari could get a word out, Kyou interjected in true horror, "*You want to use store bought*?! *Princess, no, that's so many levels of wrong! If you want a computer, I'll build one for you, okay?*"

"You don't have time to build one," Ari pointed out. "It's fine. Next job, Rems, we'll plan ahead, okay? Get you a computer so you can help him."

His daughter's voice held an audible pout. "*Fine.*"

Harrison pointed out the turn they needed to make, and Ari shifted lanes to reach it.

The painting and portfolio proved to be a quick in-and-out. The print would not in any way, shape, or form fool a close look, but it would a quick glance, and a quick glance was all they needed. This was a stalling tactic to fool the security cameras and nothing more.

They were back in the SUV in fifteen minutes, stashing their purchases in the back seat. Harrison took the wheel this time, as he knew where to go, and they took to the streets again in search of the security company's office building. It resided in the spiffier part of downtown—a noticeable statement of wealth to afford a four-story building in this section of town.

It also boasted plentiful cameras and two guards at the front entrance, encouraging people to not loiter. They couldn't just pop up, take pictures, and walk on. Not without attracting attention.

Harrison slowed a tad as they passed the building, not enough to draw attention, but to give them more than a glance. "They've got a sidewalk in front. Pose as a couple, walk it, get some footage? I can stick my camera in my front pocket, no one would suspect it."

It was a viable enough plan and Ari nodded. Being able to touch Harrison without raising suspicions had nothing to do with his quick agreement. (Bullshit, but he sometimes tried lying to himself to see if it would stick. Despite his many warnings to himself, he did want to at least touch. Casual touching should be fine, right? It wouldn't get him into any trouble.) "Let's try it."

Pulling off a minor miracle, Harrison found a place two blocks down to park along the street, and they got out there. It was a meter parking, so Ari fed the machine a quarter for thirty minutes of parking while Harrison got the camera started on his phone and slid it into the breast pocket of his light-weight jacket. It sat well, the top of it just tall enough for the camera lens to not be blocked.

Joining him at the meter, Harrison gestured toward the street, "I'll walk on your left to give the camera the best angle. Should we just lap the block, or cross the street and walk back?"

Harrison's hand came up as he spoke, fingers finding Ari's shirt collar and flipping it, straightening it out so it lay straight. Part of Ari leaned in, enjoying the brush of warm skin, part of him stalled, not sure how to respond. The dual responses fought for dominance. Carter's eyes met his for a second, and Ari felt very exposed.

Harrison caught the conflict—of course he did, as he was an observant man. He stopped with his fingers barely touching Ari's shoulder and slowly withdrew, slate blue eyes searching Ari's. "Sorry. I'm making you uncomfortable when I touch you, aren't I."

"No. Yes. No, it's..." Ari bit back a growl of frustration, the words tangled in his head.

Harrison's mouth quirked up in a wry manner. "Well, that was definite."

"I don't understand why you keep doing that," Ari burst out, the frustration finally getting the better of him. "You don't touch either Ivan or Kyou like this."

"Well, I'm not attracted to them, either." Harrison held his gaze, part challenge, part question.

Ari's jaw just about hit pavement. Had he suspected Harrison's interest in him? Sure, he'd wondered. But the last thing he'd expected was for Harrison to just put those cards on the table and see what Ari would do with them. Dumbfounded, he said the first thing that popped into his head without thinking to check it. "You're such a straight shooter."

"I don't know how to be anything else," Harrison admitted frankly. "But if you don't want me flirting with you, I'll stop—"

"Whoa, whoa, who said anything about stopping?" Ari flushed and mentally cursed himself. Smooth, man, real smooth. Clearing his throat, he couldn't meet Harrison's smug grin. "I just didn't know your intentions. I'm good now."

"Yeah?" Harrison murmured and shifted in a half foot, his hands coming up to rest on Ari's hips. It pressed his chest up against Ari's lightly, putting them in kissing distance, which was as nerve-wracking as it was nice.

Ari suddenly developed a slight problem where it became hard to swallow. His skin felt too tight and stretched over his bones. He really wanted to lean into Harrison the last couple inches, take that mobile mouth with his and kiss him until they were both dizzy. Something held him back. Even he wasn't sure what. He just wasn't comfortable doing so right in this moment.

"You're not comfortable enough with me." Harrison said it like a statement instead of a question.

Dammit. The man did read him too well. "It's not you. I'm... it's hard for me to let another man in my space."

"Hey, man, I get it. In your line of work, if someone's this close, they likely have a knife in their hands."

Ari just about melted in relief. Harrison really did understand. "Yeah."

The mercenary let go and leaned back, giving them a few inches of space. He evaluated Ari for a moment, in a manner suggesting he did high levels of calculus in his head. It felt absurdly flattering he did so over Ari.

"Alright, let's clear the air. Remi said you liked me, that you're attracted to me."

Ari had the sudden, burning desire to have a little heart-to-heart with his eight-year-old. He cleared his throat and forced himself to meet the man's eyes levelly. "I am."

"You've got to understand something about me, Ari. I don't like sleeping around. So if I'm pursuing a man, it's because I really want to date him. You're not the type to sleep around either."

It hadn't been a question, but Ari nodded anyway in confirmation. "Harrison, are you really suggesting dating? Honest to god dating?"

"It's a perfectly normal thing to do, you know." Harrison's eyes crinkled up into crow's feet in a silent grin.

Well, yes, he knew that but...it wasn't like Ari had actually ever done it. Not for just himself. The idea tantalized him. What would it be like, to have Harrison—Carter—that way? To have an actual relationship with the man? He looked into those slate blue eyes and saw endless possibilities. It was scary, thinking about trusting someone else to that degree. Like free falling. With all of the stomach-swooping, terror, and adrenaline of a heist. Ari reviewed all the reasons he'd talked himself out of this very thing, all the things he'd told Ivan, and found them to be excuses. He'd never let fear stop him before, not when his life was on the line. He couldn't let himself do it when his heart was on the line instead. As terrifying as this was for him on one level, he was equally excited by it, because dammit, he liked the man. Ari apparently liked the man well enough to step out of his comfort zone and try. A smile tugged his mouth up, an unconscious decision. "Dating sounds good."

"Yeah?" One of Carter's hands shifted to his arm, trailing heat and tingles along the skin to his wrist before Carter pressed his hand lightly against Ari's. "Then let's date. Starting now."

Ari laughed soundlessly, and it was him who tangled their fingers together. He felt strangely relieved, as if the concerns and worries he'd been harboring over this very thing were suddenly lifted off his shoulders. Strange, how Carter's straightforward approach had done that. Excitement bubbled in and mixed with the feeling, leaving him intoxicated and giddy in a way he'd not ever felt before. "Now, huh. Sure, let's start now. Just...don't jump me."

"I won't approach you from behind or to the side, not until you get used to this," Carter promised seriously. "I know your reflexes, and I don't want to get on the wrong side of those. I'll end up with a hole in my throat before you even realize it's me. Which doesn't lead to sexy times."

A wave of relief swept over him. That was exactly why he couldn't date civilians. They didn't understand his reflexes, and he couldn't explain them accurately either, which led to problems. Very, very occasionally he was able to orchestrate something so he was comfortable enough, in control enough, to enjoy a bit of rough sex. But it took some doing and most of the time, he didn't feel the effort worth it. It was novel, really, the idea of dating someone who he didn't have to explain anything to. Who got it. Who lived a similar life. It made him impulsive, and for the first time in his life, he gave into impulse without considering how much the action would draw attention to himself. He tilted his head just so and kissed Carter, quick and chaste.

Carter wasn't content with that and leaned in, the kiss still chaste, but lingering, giving them both a firmer impression and sweet heat. He pulled back a bare inch to murmur above Ari's mouth, "Later, when Remi's in bed, you and I are going to spend a little time together."

"Sounds perfect." And maybe in the next six hours or so, the idea of dating Carter would settle better and let Ari relax enough to let the man in his space. Just doing this was hard, but that could be because they were in a public area. He couldn't really relax out here.

"*Hey, love birds,*" Kyou's voice suddenly popped into his right ear.

Ari almost jumped a foot, and he swore mentally. He'd honestly forgotten for a minute the earbud was in. From the disgruntled look on Carter's face, he'd forgotten too.

"*You two are being cute and all, but you do remember van and uniforms?*"

"K, one day, you're going to find someone, and I will take great delight in turning these tables," Ari growled the promise lowly, meaning every word of it.

Kyou laughed, not at all concerned. "*You can be kissy-kissy with each other later. We've got a narrow window to get the stuff.*"

Carter, being more patient, just sighed and got a move on. He did not, however, let go of Ari's hand. Ari found himself highly reluctant to break that contact. They were in public, yes, but for the first time in his life he was honestly dating someone and dammit, he wanted to linger in that high for a minute.

There was a soft female giggle and Ari cursed himself all over again. Right. Remi had an earbud in as well. He and Carter shared a somewhat horrified look, although the crooked lift of Carter's lips suggested he found the situation humorous as well. Which was fine for him as *he* didn't have to have a little talk with an eight-year-old after this.

Ari groaned and kicked himself mentally. Why hadn't he turned the earbud off? Had Carter seriously affected him so much he'd forgotten it?

Vans and uniforms. Focus on vans and uniforms. Little girls could wait another hour.

17

ARI

Ari had every intention of talking to his little girl the second he got back but was sidetracked by an argument in progress. Ivan and Kyou stood nearly nose to nose in the living room, which was comical in the extreme, as the Russian thief tried to loom over the hacker with his three inches of superior height. Kyou was not fazed by Ivan's looming and repeatedly stabbed a finger into Ivan's chest, yelling at full volume, "—stupid even for you! You're not going to just waltz in there!"

"Who said anything about waltzing?" Ivan retorted and oh shit. He wore his mile-wide smile, the one that flashed a hint of his gold tooth, and that meant he planned something dangerous and stupid and would enjoy every second of it.

Carter cleared his throat and asked in concern, "What are you talking about?"

Kyou didn't even turn his head while he explained, still glaring up at Ivan. "I can't hack the security company remotely, not without a lot more time. Time we don't have. Ivan wants to just walk in and get his head blown off."

Putting a wounded hand over his heart, Ivan retorted with that shit-eating grin still firmly in place, "Your lack of faith hurts me, comrade. I can get in fine. I've had worse challenges."

Kyou ignored him. "I caught him sneaking out with nothing more than a baseball cap, latex gloves, and the flash drive I need plugged in their system."

"I have a bed sheet too," Ivan added indignantly, as if this was a vital part of his plan.

Carter gave Ari a look of bemusement, eyebrows twisted up in an eloquent, *He's kidding, right?*

Leaning into his side, Ari muttered, "That unfortunately sounds about par for the course. Ivan's idea of thief tools do not match most of the known world. The crazy thing is, most of the time he's right and it works fine. It's an ongoing argument between Kyou and Ivan, though. Ivan deliberately picks borderline insane things just to get a rise out of Kyou."

"Ah. Got it." Carter stepped in closer and placed a gentle hand on each of their shoulders. The touch strangely seemed to settle both men, grounding them. "Let's do this. Put a body cam on, Ivan, so we can see if you get in trouble. I'll be backup nearby."

Kyou studied Carter for a long moment before apparently deciding this was an acceptable compromise. "Fine. But you're going in tonight, Ivan, not right now."

Ivan shook his head in immediate disagreement. "That's when most of their personnel are on high alert. They're more concerned with night attacks. Better to go during lunch break, which is in the next hour and a half."

It was a valid point, really. Security companies were aware most thieves liked to operate under the cover of darkness. And while not all thefts occurred at night, the majority did, and a security company would have more on staff at night than during the day. "He's right, Kyou."

Kyou groaned. "Dammit. I was hoping for another six hours. I haven't gotten control of all the CCTV cameras on that street yet."

Waving this concern off, Ivan assured him, "Show me which ones you do have. I can avoid the rest."

"Fine, alright. You madman. You deliberately do stuff like this to give me an ulcer."

"I never," Ivan said, his face splitting in a broad grin.

"And that's a lie," Ari retorted, shaking his head in amusement. "You absolutely have."

"True," Ivan agreed, sounding proud of himself. "I have, I enjoyed it, and I'm likely to do it again."

Kyou gave him a glare and stomped back for the safety of his computer. Ivan bounced along at his heels like a puppy looking forward to a treat.

It left Ari staring at the man he was now dating, the observation whirling in his head. Carter had stepped in so naturally and acted the part of a peacemaker, he hadn't ruffled any feathers. Interesting. He didn't quite know what to do with the information, but it was something to keep in mind.

Remi bounced up to Carter and lifted her hand up for a high-five. "Good job."

Grinning from ear to ear, Carter smacked his palm lightly against hers. "Yeah, yeah, you were right. Thanks for the tip."

Reminded, Ari went and scooped up his daughter, trying his best to maintain a frown when really, he felt like rewarding her. "Rems."

She completely jumped half-way into the argument and protested, "But he likes you too!"

Highly aware Carter listened avidly to every word, Ari kept his attention focused on Remi. "Gattina, I realize you're happy because this worked out like you wanted. But prodding people because *you* want something is non va bene, yeah?"

An indignant pout formed on her face. She quite clearly did not agree. "Fine. I won't do it again."

Ari gave that a flying fat chance. But saying anything more would just be beating a dead horse and wouldn't get anywhere. He'd have to find a way to subtly reinforce this later. He let her down again and she immediately went to Kyou, clambering up into his lap. The hacker made room for her even as he continued to walk Ivan through which cameras to avoid.

Shaking his head, he went to help prep. Job now, complicated little girls later.

Forty-five minutes later, Ivan slithered out of the SUV and headed in. Ari was driving so Carter could peel out and head directly in if Ivan needed the backup. Normally Ari would be the one to go in. They'd let Carter be backup for two reasons: one, he'd been the one to offer. Two, it was a good way to test how Carter would work with them under pressure, although everyone had carefully not said so. Carter kept his eyes on the laptop in his lap, watching the body cam feedback as Ivan casually strolled toward the back of the building.

Ari looped around the block, trying to find a good place to park that would give them a quick and easy out. He might as well be hunting for a unicorn while he was at it, because such parking spaces absolutely did not exist in DC. Especially at this noon hour of traffic. Everyone was out on their lunch break and traffic became a touch more insane because of it. Yeah, he'd just play Mario Kart and keep looping.

"Eidolon, I'm curious, what's your game plan?" Carter asked.

"*I walk in, plug in the flash drive, walk out.*"

"Wow. That's a stunning plan, man, I'm not sure if I followed. Walk me through it again?"

Ivan snickered. "*I hear that sarcasm.*"

"I'd hope so."

"*The thing is, if you're sneaking, people notice. You're acting strange, you draw their attention, da? But if you just walk in, people don't really pay attention to you. Especially if you act like you belong there. Why should they question someone who is obviously on his own business? I do not sneak into buildings. I walk in.*"

Carter caught Ari's eye and mouthed, *Seriously?*

Shrugging, Ari nodded. As insane as it sounded, it actually did work. He'd seen it in action too many times. Ivan didn't even look like a businessman, really, but put him in a suit and he could walk through any corporate building without being stopped. It was crazy how little attention people really paid their surroundings.

"And you think that'll work even in a security building?" Carter's question dripped dubiousness.

"*Most of the building should be empty right now. Most people go out for lunch. And me, I'm not going anywhere really secure, like their server room. No need. Right, K?*"

"*Literally any computer not on the main floor will work. All of that is admin stuff, mostly receptionists and they won't have the access I need. Accounting, HR, something like that will get us the access we need."*

"Da, da, see? No problem."

Carter clearly saw many problems but didn't say so. Ari let a smile play over his mouth. Wait until he saw Ivan in action. Then he'd understand.

Ivan found a back door with a thumbprint lock on it. Ari of course couldn't really watch the live feed and drive, although he kept sneaking glances. He heard the snap of a latex glove as Ivan put one on, and then Carter's bemused huff.

"Eidolon. Did you just lick the glove—"

There was an audible beep as the lock disengaged.

"What. The. Hell." Carter stared at the screen, spluttering. "Seriously?! All of those fancy gadgets meant to hack a fingerprint lock and you can just lick a latex glove and it'll let you in?!"

Ivan snickered like the demented soul he was and sailed through the door.

"It's stupid, right?" Ari commiserated. "First time I saw him do that, I about flipped my lid. I couldn't believe it'd worked. I still don't know how he even figured it out to begin with. I mean, who tries that?"

"Crazy Russian thieves, that's who tries it." Kyou paused a beat before adding, *"Although in all fairness, if you think about it, it makes sense. The sensor doesn't just read a thumbprint, but body heat too. By licking his thumb like that, he's applying both heat and moisture to the previous print scanned and reactivating it."*

"I'm so remembering that trick," Carter swore.

"It's a good trick," Ivan agreed cheerfully. *"As good as the bedsheet trick. Not sure if I need that one today, though. Haven't seen a motion sensor yet."*

"A bedsheet. Thwarts a motion sensor? Now that I've got to see in action."

Teasing a little, Ari asked, "You feel like you're in a practical for Thieving 101?"

Carter flashed him a grin. "Yeah, actually."

"Where is he now?"

"He's past the main floor—he was right, only the receptionist is still at her desk—and he's up the stairs now. No locks on the stairs, and he's through to the second story. Eidolon, I'm just curious, what is your story if you get caught by someone?"

Ivan just laughed.

"I take it that was a stupid question."

"You *do* get caught occasionally, Eidolon," Ari couldn't help but point out. "Remember Tulsa, 2016?"

Ivan said something in Russian he probably shouldn't have with a young child's ears still listening in.

"*Oooh, I see an Accounting sign near an office door. That do for you, K?*"

"*Won't know until you plug the drive in. But yeah, probably.*"

"He's in the office," Carter picked up the narration for Ari's benefit, "and drive is in. It working, K?"

"*Working. I can do what I need to now. Eidolon, give it another minute and then you can unplug and leave.*"

"*Sure, I'll sit here and look decorative.*"

Ari kept his eyes firmly on the road, constantly evaluating the best way to get back to the building if things went abruptly south. Which, even with the best team and planning, sometimes happened. The minute passed in taut silence, only interrupted by the frantic typing on Kyou's end.

"*Alright, we're good. Go.*"

Ari assumed Ivan immediately pulled the drive and made tracks back out. He took a right at the next light, looping around to the back of the building. "Eidolon, I'm coming up on 20th in thirty seconds."

"*I'll meet you at the corner.*"

There was no huffing for breath, no rapid footsteps. Ivan maintained the same casual walk on the way out as he'd used for the way in. That was another mistake amateurs made. Nerves got the better of them and they started hurrying. Hurrying led to mistakes every time.

Ari saw no place to pull over, and the streets were crowded enough that trying to stop would be a problem. Still, the traffic was at a crawl and it was easy for Ivan to pop open the back door and slide in. He tossed his messenger bag to the side while he got comfortable and beamed at them. "See? Easy."

Carter twisted in the chair to face him. "I still can't believe you just did that. Any other team I'd been on would have planned for a week straight before even trying to get in, and they would have used a lot of gadgets and guns to do the job. Where did you learn to lick a glove, seriously."

"It's the Golden Rule, da? If all else fails, lick it."

Ari rolled his eyes. "Pretty sure that isn't the Golden Rule, you nut job. Alright, K, how are we now?"

"*I've got profiles for you and Carter in the system. You're now techs. Now all we need is to print up IDs, get shirts embroidered with your fake names, and get a van, and you can drive right onto Knowles property without a hitch.*"

Remi piped up, "*Does that mean Stage 1 is cleared?*"

"Almost, gattina," Ari responded, taking a left and heading back toward the house. "We still need to verify the painting is in the vault, like we think it is. Which means Ivan gets to sneak into one more place."

Ivan cackled in the back seat. "This will be so much fun."

18

CARTER

Carter was very aware he was being observed.

Some would say trying to date an assassin while his two criminal partners looked on was the height of insanity. Carter would agree with them. Then again, he wasn't really known for making sane decisions. This situation wasn't even the craziest thing he'd done in recent memory.

The only thing he could say in his defense was that Ari did something to him, something he hadn't felt in years. Decades, maybe. Dangerous men with sexy vibes wasn't something new for him. He'd been working with men like that for decades. It was the mix of hard and gentle that had snuck under Carter's guard and ambushed him. He was frankly amazed (excited, thrilled, smug, and a few other dozen emotions) he'd gotten Ari to agree to date. From Ari's initial reactions to him, he'd not been sure of his success. But now that he'd gotten a better read on the man, he had to wonder if nerves held Ari back.

No one should be so anxious about having someone come in close. Ari's flinches bothered Carter on a primary level, and it honestly made him want to murder someone most of the time. Worse, he sometimes saw Remi react in a way that signaled she'd been abused at one point, too. The way she clung to the men indicated she was constantly searching for a safe harbor, someone to protect her. Carter swore to make it his personal mission to ensure those two understood he would protect them.

Anyone who knew Carter could have warned Ari that the fastest way to get the man's attention was to tap into his protective instincts. After that, it was all downhill. He wasn't blind to how Ari acted the slightest bit nervous with him, either. The man was clearly not accustomed to dating, and while he liked it when Carter touched him, it always took him a second to settle.

Patience was required here. Fortunately, Carter had an abundance.

He practiced little touches with Ari through the rest of the day. Brushes against his shoulder, light squeezes of the hand, warm smiles. He knew he was getting somewhere when Ari paused in what he was doing to accept a fresh cup of coffee and give Carter a bone melting smile in return. God, this man was going to ruin him.

In between all the flirting, they bought uniform shirts, made sure the size fit, then dropped them off at an embroidery shop. Ivan came back with a van and a stencil kit. Remi had fun helping him rub the letters onto the side of the van. For some reason, the project required a lot of giggling.

After all the excitement of the day, it took a while for the house to settle. Kyou stayed up at his computer, typing away at something or other. Ivan went to bed at the same time Remi did. It gave them a bubble of quiet and semi-privacy, and Carter took immediate advantage of it.

As Ari came out of Remi's room, he caught the man's hand. Those pianist's fingers were warm, the calluses brushing in a rough rasp against his own as Carter silently drew him toward his room, at the end of the hallway. Ari swallowed hard but followed, his eyes never leaving Carter's as they walked slowly into the room. Carter made careful, broadcasted movements as he backed into the wall near the door. Pinning Ari against the wall was absolutely out. Ari would come out of his own skin if Carter tried to cage him like that. He'd let the other man choose if he wanted the door closed or not. Right now, this moment was less about catching a little cuddle time and more about laying down a foundation. *You can trust me.* That's what he needed to get through Ari's head.

Smooth sheetrock hit his back and Carter stayed there, his

hand in Ari's, drawing him gently forward. He wouldn't press this, just ask. Ari's lips slightly parted, his espresso eyes almost black with desire. Still, he hesitated. Neither man said a word but the tension between them grew steadily tauter.

Ari deliberately relaxed his shoulders and stepped in between Carter's spread legs, pressing their hips together. A rush of heat flashed through Carter's body, and he swallowed around a dry mouth. Ari didn't hesitate the rest of the distance, angling slightly for a kiss, and Carter met him halfway. Their lips brushed against each other's gently, searching and learning each other. Warm lips, hot breath, hands trailing gently as they searched for a better hold. He angled his head a little further, felt the rasp of a five o'clock shadow against his skin, and nearly purred. Yes. Damn, yes, this was perfect. While Carter was perfectly willing to tug the man toward the bed, all he really needed was now, this moment. This sweet moment.

Drawing back an inch, Ari breathed, "You're smiling."

Was he? Probably. "I like kissing you."

"You deliberately put your back to the wall instead of caging me against it."

"It didn't seem a good idea to crowd you."

Ari dropped his head against Carter's shoulder, and Carter let his arms enfold Ari in a loose embrace. "You really have the patience of a saint, don't you?"

"I haven't needed to be all that patient with you?" It came out as a question because Carter really couldn't understand why Ari had said that. Or rather, he suspected other men had demanded things Ari wasn't comfortable with and given him grief. He might need to find those men later and double check they were no longer breathing.

Snorting, Ari muttered against his shoulder, "You're really a different breed. Fortunately for me. But we can have sex tonight, if you want."

No, they clearly couldn't. He was tensing up in Carter's arms even as he made the offer. Carter brushed a hand up and down his spine, trying to get him to relax again, and pressed a kiss against the side of his head. "I think we need a few more days with each other before we're comfortable enough for some naked tango."

The tension eased and Ari relaxed against him, trusting more of his body weight against Carter. "You sure?"

Obviously the right call. Carter made a mental note to trust Ari's body language more than his words. "Yeah. Trust me, you're plenty sexy, hon. I just want to figure us out a bit more before we try hopping into bed."

"Fair enough." Ari lifted his head and kissed him, this time with a languid heat that hit Carter right in the gut.

Making out like teenagers for a while was absolutely fine with him. Carter sank into the moment and enjoyed.

He didn't expect Ari to stay, and the assassin didn't. It would be a while before Ari relaxed his guard enough to sleep next to Carter. Carter was fine with that and didn't make a fuss when Ari retreated to his room. He'd expected to wake up alone but instead when he opened his eyes, he found a little girl's chocolate brown eyes staring right back at him. Carter jolted—seriously, how did she get on the bed without waking him?!—and blinked several times to clear the sleep out of his vision. "Morning?"

"Good morning," she greeted with a gamine grin. "Daddy's making eggs and pancakes. He's singing too. You must have made him happy."

Now that he was awake, Carter could hear some sort of Italian pop song being sung at full volume downstairs. That was Ari? He had a rather nice voice. He blinked back to the child inquisitively poking at him. It pleased him she felt comfortable enough to tease, so he poked her back in the stomach. Remi giggled and squirmed, a happy grin on her face. Carter wasn't a fool—these two came as a package set. A wise man would act accordingly. "Well, I'm certainly trying to. I know you pushed me to ask him out, Remi, but how are you feeling about all of this?"

She regarded him thoughtfully for a long moment, something undecipherable whirling behind her eyes. Then she waved him in a little closer. "Can I tell you a secret?"

Carter propped himself up on one elbow before he leaned

in playfully. "Sure, what?"

"Daddy's not really my dad. We're not related."

Everything in him froze. Carter never, in a million years, expected to hear that. He searched her face, looking for some hint of deception, and instead found aching truth. His mouth searched for an appropriate response and instead came up with, "I'd never have guessed that. You two adore each other."

That made her smile, although bitterness lingered in the edges. "My mother abandoned me when it got too hard for her. She said no decent guy wanted a woman with a kid already in tow. When she left me, my stepfather started hitting me. It got...bad."

Carter's hands started shaking in rage. He didn't have a lot of buttons, but kids were definitely at the top of his list. Any type of abuse wasn't to be tolerated, and he was quick to stop it if he saw something going on. He grabbed her and hauled her in, holding her tight because right now, he needed to hold her. He needed to hold onto something before he went hunting for a target. Remi didn't utter a peep of protest, snuggling in instantly. God, the idea of this child being beaten on a consistent basis—Carter's vision went red. "Tell me the bastard's been dealt with."

"Daddy killed him. Then he said he couldn't leave me there, and asked me to come with him." She pulled her head free from his chest and that happy smile of hers was back in full force. "I've been with him six months now. It's been the best six months ever."

God, no wonder. The things bothering Carter, the habits he saw of a child who had been abused and neglected, and the way all three men orbited around her. It all made sense with this information. He stroked a hand down her hair. "I'm really glad, Remi."

She patted his shoulder, still watching him like a hawk. "I don't want Daddy to be like her, where she can't find a good man because of me."

Another piece of the puzzle slotted into place. It had seemed strange Remi would act as matchmaker, but if her adoptive father hadn't dated since the day he took her in—and Carter would bet his eye teeth that was the case—then of course she'd leap on the opportunity Carter represented. "I really like him, Remi. But you know, I really like you too. You come as a package set, and I know that, okay? I don't want one of you without the other."

She liked that answer and gave him her smug feline grin again. "Okay. Come downstairs, Daddy sent me to fetch you."

"Roger." She pulled out of his arms, bounced off the bed, and darted out the door. Carter strangely felt like he'd just passed some sort of test. Actually, that was likely exactly it. He had to remember he couldn't look at Remi and think of her as a normal eight-year-old. This was a kid who had grown up rough until an assassin adopted her. She was, by default, much more mature than her years.

Carter ran a hand roughly over his face, facial hair rasping against his palm, and wished he had time for a quick shower before breakfast. He needed a few minutes for all of this new information to settle. Unfortunately, he had the fifteen seconds it would take for him to get downstairs. Which would have to do.

Sighing, he threw the covers back and walked downstairs, straightening his grey checkered pajama pants as he did. They always got a little twisted in his sleep. He didn't bother to put on a shirt, because in this household, he saw no point. Everyone was settled around the breakfast bar, plates in front of them, except Ari who still slaved away over the stove. Ivan wolf-whistled as Carter walked into the kitchen, and even Kyou looked up from the phone in his hand long enough to take in the view. Okay, so maybe he should have put on a shirt after all.

Ari looked up and gave him a once-over, mouth crooked in amusement. "Morning?"

Carter likely didn't look entirely awake yet. He was awake, just a little dazed with information overload. Carter couldn't help but look at Ari and see a different man. A man good enough at his core he not only protected a little girl, but sacrificed his own convenience to raise her. Would Carter have done the same in his shoes? He wasn't entirely sure. Knowing Ari had made the man even sexier, and Carter hadn't thought that possible. It might be challenging right now, them trying to figure each other out, but god. If he could have this man, it would all be worth it.

But that wasn't a conversation to have with an audience, so he set it aside for now. Carter stepped in and pressed a quick, chaste kiss against Ari's plush mouth, lips lingering. "Morning. Some of that for me?"

"Yours is waiting on the bar." Ari smiled and returned the kiss before swatting him on the back, urging him on.

"Damn, they're cute," Ivan sighed happily. "Makes me want to get one too."

"Which?" Kyou asked, not looking up from his phone. "A boyfriend or a mercenary?"

"Boyfriend, of course. I don't appreciate that doubtful look on your face right now, Kyou." Ivan glared at his friend as Carter slid into his seat. "I'm a good boyfriend."

"Sure. You just drive them all crazy because they're going from heart attack to ulcer with you." Kyou passed Carter the maple syrup without prompting and went back to eating through the rest of his pancakes.

Ari flipped off the stove eyes and fixed his own plate before turning and setting it on the bar. They were out of stools, all of them occupied, but Ari seemed content to stand and eat. "Don't you two start. It's too early, and I haven't had enough coffee for that argument."

By which it sounded like they'd argued this point before? Carter bit into his bacon and silently observed. It seemed the right moment to stay out of it and not ask.

"Daddy." Remi's head came up, and she regarded her adoptive father with a cant of the head. "What was your first job?"

Fork paused halfway to his mouth, Ari regarded her in turn. "Where did that question come from?"

She sighed and rolled her eyes. "I just thought of it."

"I swear I don't understand how your mind works...but okay. First job, huh." Ari rocked back on his heels and thought about it. "I think I was ten. The lady next door was going on vacation and she wanted me to come in and feed the fish. I did, followed her instructions exactly, but by the time she came home again, the fish were all dead. I was kinda panicked, I won't lie, but it turned out she didn't like the fish. They were too much hassle, only she couldn't tell her kids that. So she'd turned off the filter and then paid me to come in, cover her tracks. I got twenty dollars, and she was able to get rid of the tank."

Remi giggled. "Fish? Really?"

He winked back at her, dark eyes twinkling. "Gotta start somewhere, sweetheart. Alright, you done? Go shower, then. We've got a full day."

Nodding, she hopped off the barstool and thundered upstairs, sounding more like an elephant than a child.

"Your first contracted murder was fish, huh," Carter said doubtfully, putting air quotation marks around the word 'fish.'

"I know how to make things kid appropriate," Ari protested.

He got a room full of doubtful looks.

Ari glared back and groused, "Your expressions right now are very judgey, and I don't appreciate them. Ivan, eat your breakfast. We have to figure out how to get you into Knowles."

"And if you say one word about a bedsheet, I will jab this fork in your eye," Kyou threatened with a warning shake of the utensil. "A *proper* plan this time."

Ivan sighed gustily. "You take all the joy out of life."

19

ARI

If Ari were being honest with himself—and he tried to avoid that when possible, it was painful—he was a bit nervous. Just a tiiiiny, little, barely measurable, teensy weensy nervous. Normally his dates ended in someone being stabbed or shot, but he liked Carter. He didn't really want to put holes in him. Rather the opposite, really. But Ari was operating out of his norm and his instincts didn't know what to do in this case.

Assassins, if they lived long enough, developed certain instincts about people being in their space. Deadly instincts. Ivan and Kyou didn't register as 'danger' to him and hadn't for years. They'd worked together too long for him to think of them like that. Remi never had. She was too defenseless to be a threat to him. Even with those wicked elbows of hers.

Carter was the weird mix of potentially dangerous but disarming. He had all of the training and lethality to get Ari's guard up, but the past six days had proven he was also very good at disarming Ari's instincts before he could punch a hole in his windpipe. The man deliberately moved in Ari's space in such a way to broadcast no-threat. And every time he came in close, then separated without harm, it disarmed Ari a little further.

Trust. It took time to build, no question. Carter was also very good at laying down the foundation for it. He must be, because Ari hadn't once felt alarmed or instinctively lashed out at him. And that was a miracle, right there. Half the time, things didn't end well when a man approached him the way Carter did.

For the first time in a long while, Ari felt like he actually might have a chance with someone.

Of course, he had no time to really think about it, not when the job demanded his attention. And his curious, smug eight-year-old. She met him in the kitchen, interrupting his thoughts, with a comb and a rubber band in her hands. "Ponytail?"

Ari sighed gustily. "Kiddo, that didn't work out so well the last time I tried it. How about I comb it out and we wait for Uncle Ivan to get out of the shower?"

"Okay," she agreed easily.

Lifting her onto a bar stool, he started at the bottom and carefully combed her hair from the bottom up. Something else he'd learned after acquiring a daughter—hair should be combed from bottom to top. Top to bottom created tangles and crying little girls. He avoided repeating that mistake at all costs.

As he combed, Remi informed him, "I told him this morning."

Ari paused with the comb still in her hair. "Told who what, gattina?"

"Told Mr. Harrison you adopted me."

It took a second to compute, and Ari took the comb out so he could spin her around and have the rest of this conversation face to face. "You did? Why?"

"'Cause he needed to know." Her mouth closed into a stubborn tilt that never boded anything good.

Ari studied her expression carefully. Something in her eyes and body language hinted her motivations went deep. Remi hadn't been casually passing along information to Ari's potential boyfriend. She'd been testing his reactions. If she were telling Ari now, then did that mean Carter passed? "Yeah? How did he take it?"

"He was glad. He didn't like that I was being hurt either. I think," here she spoke like a sage, years older than her actual age, "that if I'd talked to him instead of you? He'd have done the same thing."

"Rems, I'm one hundred percent sure you're right." It factored largely into Ari's attraction. Morals were sexy. Who knew?

"You're not mad I told him?"

Ari suddenly wished he'd had a chance to down a second cup of coffee before he'd been ambushed by this conversation. "No, honey, I'm not mad. Surprised you said anything, but not mad."

She relaxed, the tension bleeding out of her body language. "Okay."

Kyou interrupted them by popping his head into view. "Just got a call that the shirts are ready."

"Alright. I'll go and grab those after I've got Remi's hair done."

Waving him off, Kyou approached. "I'll deal with hair. When you get back, we'll have a proper strategy session. I don't want to use the same tactic to get Ivan in for a looksie. Too many times, and they'll catch onto the breech."

That was Ari's fear as well. "We'll think of something. Be back in a bit, Rems." He pressed a quick kiss to her forehead and went searching for the keys. And Carter. Not that he needed Carter to pick up the shirts, but it'd be nice to steal fifteen minutes and make out in the back seat. Kissing the man last night had proven to be absolutely brilliant. He was definitely up for a repeat.

The keys were not where he expected them to be. Frustrated, he went looking for his windbreaker with the thought he'd possibly left the keys in the pocket. You'd think, with only a duffel of clothes, he wouldn't have to constantly search pockets.

It was soft, barely discernable, but the scuff of a boot against the carpet snagged his ear. Ari whirled on instinct, rolling across the bed and snatching up the gun he had on the nightstand. It was in his hands, aimed at the doorway, finger on the trigger, before he realized who had just snuck up on him.

Carter dodged a half-step back, both hands up in the air in a non-threatening way. "Ari! Just me."

It took a second to realize what he'd almost done. Then Ari sagged back, remorse heavy and sour in his gut. Oh god, he'd nearly shot Carter. "I'm so sorry, I just...it was just instinct, I didn't even realize it was you."

Carter slowly lowered both hands. Even though his eyes were still wide, face flushed, he shook his head in disagreement.

"No, that was my bad. I promised not to sneak up behind you, and here I did just that."

Still feeling shaky from the mental image of the damage he'd almost inflicted, Ari put the gun carefully on the bed. Breathe. Breathe, you didn't shoot him. Breathe.

"Hey," Carter said gently, coming in closer. "Hey, wasn't your fault. My stupid fault, yeah? I need to make noise around you when I'm approaching."

"You're as bad as Ivan, he moves like a damn cat too," Ari tried to joke through a closed throat.

"Occupational hazard. Come here." Carter reached out with gentle hands, enclosing him in a comforting embrace.

Ari went, because even as strange as it felt to be hugged, he needed it. He liked it, too. Nestling his head next to Carter's, he snuggled into the crook of the man's neck, inhaling the warm, clean scent of him. Ari stood there for a long moment and just breathed. It felt good, this embrace. Calming and assuring in a way he'd never felt before. Eventually, his heart stopped beating a crazy rhythm and his breathing wasn't all over the damn map. Now that his initial spike of adrenaline had died down, relief rocked through him. He hadn't shot Carter, despite being startled out of his skin. He'd held in that initial reaction of attack long enough for his brain to get a word in edgewise. It gave him a measure of control—despite all his fears, despite being jumpy, he hadn't actually done anything harmful. Ari was, strangely, proud of himself. Maybe he was getting a handle on this after all.

Against his ear, Carter murmured the question, "You were looking for something?"

"Yeah, the SUV's keys. The shirts are ready, and I was going to pick them up."

"Ah. I think I saw them on the bar downstairs. How about I go with you? I want to talk to you about the revelation Remi dropped on me this morning. Without coffee."

Snorting, Ari pulled back an inch. Carter really was patient. Ari thanked everything he could think of for it. "Yeah, she told me about that. Come with me. I planned to take you with me anyway. If we're lucky, we can steal fifteen minutes in the back seat."

A slow, lazy grin crossed Carter's face, making him look a little foxy. "I'm sure we can manage more than fifteen minutes."

"We're pros, after all," Ari deadpanned back and honestly felt glad to be back on his usual footing with the man. "Come on."

Leaving the house wasn't quite that simple. Something about having a child never made the exit of a house quick and easy. But Carter held all questions until they were safely in the car and driving away.

"You really killed her abusive stepfather and then adopted her? Just like that?" Nothing about Carter's tone indicated judgement, just amazement.

"Yeah. Basically. She stalked me for ten minutes on a bad street, at night, even knowing what I was. Then she hired me to help her with two dollars of pocket change. It still blows my mind she did that. I liked the kid's gumption, really. And I grew up in foster. I know how bad it can be, if you've got crappy guardians. I didn't want that for her." Ari paused at a stop sign and stole a glance at his face. Carter was listening—just listening. No judgements forthcoming there. It opened his mouth and made him confess something he'd never, ever said aloud. "I have no idea what the fuck I'm doing, to be honest. Maybe it's selfish to keep her, I don't know. Maybe she'd do better with a regular family."

"You'd break her heart even offering that. Ari, I've got the regular family background. Grew up in the suburbs with siblings and two loving parents, the full works. Trust me, you're doing fine. You're just as good a father as my own, and my dad's great. Don't think you're not doing right by her. You're just doing it in an unconventional way."

That eased his concerns as nothing else would have. Ari had no idea just how much he'd needed to hear the reassurance until this moment. It also gave him more information about Carter, which was welcome. He really didn't know much about the man aside from Kyou's files. "You really grew up in a normal family?"

"Yup."

"How did you become a mercenary?"

"After I was kicked out of the army, not many places

would hire me. And I really suck at deskwork and retail. I got approached by a slightly sleazy broker for a job and discovered I was rather good at the mercenary thing." Carter shrugged as if he was nothing more than an open and shut case. "But don't get me sidetracked. I have a few more questions about Remi."

Ari didn't mind that. "Shoot."

"Her mom?"

"I'm tempted to hunt the woman down and put a few bullets in her too. Piece of trash didn't even name Remi."

"That bad, huh. Okay. There's...I don't know how to say this without putting your back up."

They pulled up to a stoplight and Ari took advantage to catch Carter's hand and squeeze it once. "I won't take it wrong. What?"

Carter eyed him sideways but spoke. "You realize Remi's behavior isn't entirely healthy right now?"

Honestly surprised, Ari's grip tightened on his hand unwittingly for a second. "I thought she was doing okay. She's so much better now than she was."

"Considering what she told me, I'd believe it. But I realized about a half hour into meeting her something wasn't quite right. She's too clingy with all of you. Kids her age—or at least my nieces and nephews—they're all about getting into things. Exploring new places, wandering into areas they probably shouldn't, crap like that. Remi sticks to you guys like glue. The only time I've seen her willingly separate is if we're playing a game or she's going to bed."

Come to think of it...that wasn't normal, was it? Ari frowned but had to let go as the light was green and it was time to move again. "What else are you seeing?"

"The food thing. Half the time, she's not really hungry. She's reassuring herself, time and again, that you'll feed her. When she talked to me about asking you out, you know what she told me?"

Ari shook his head. "She didn't tell me what she said. Just that she'd talked to you."

"She said people have a lot of ways of saying 'I love you.' Two of the things she mentioned were: You want the last slice? You hungry?"

Ari might need to pull over. He wasn't sure if he was going to rage or cry—the emotions were currently duking it out. Maybe both. "Porca troia."

"Yeah. Hit me in the heartstrings too. Ari, you tell me she's leagues better now than she was in the beginning, and I believe you, but maybe think of a way for her to get some therapy? Love heals a lot, but sometimes you need additional help."

Ari didn't take offense at the suggestion. "I don't know how. Any therapist worth their salt is going to get the full story out of Remi, and that'll paint me as the criminal I am, and then what?"

"Doctor-patient confidentiality should cover you, but... yeah. I see your point. Okay, after this job, let's put our heads together. We'll figure it out."

'We'll' figure it out, eh? The inclusion made Ari smile. He did like the sound of that. "But you think she'll be fine?"

"Girl's got more backup than most kids. She'll be great. I'm not really worried, just wanted you to know what I saw."

"It's good to know. I don't always see her as clearly as I should. Maybe I'm too close, I don't know." Or he just didn't know what normal should look like. None of them did, come to think of it. Kyou had been in foster with him. Ivan refused to talk about his childhood at all.

But his almost-boyfriend did and was steadfastly offering his support. Carter would make up the difference. Ari shot him a smile, caught one in return. Dating Carter might be the smartest decision he'd made this year. Ari mentally gave himself a pat on the back.

The shirts were collected and put away in a closet so they wouldn't wrinkle. It was little details that often gave people away, and this was potentially one of them. The uniform for the security company was very starched shirts, black slacks, and black shoes. Showing up in anything wrinkled would be a tell, and they didn't have the time to spare for those.

Carter had caught him in the garage before they entered the house and spent several minutes kissing him senseless, so Ari miiiight have had some trouble getting his focus to, you know, actually focus. Damn, the man could kiss. Ari's lips still tingled.

A pair of fingers snapped in front of his face and Ari glared at Ivan. "What?"

The thief smirked back at him and said in a tone that made it clear he'd repeated himself, "We're meeting now in the living room to discuss how to get me in. You think you can focus on something aside from hot mercenary?"

He tried to scowl in return but it was a little difficult being upset at anything just now. "Shut it. I can focus just fine."

Ivan's grey eyes twinkled in laughter. "Prove it."

Grumbling a curse in Italian, Ari shoved past him. He felt the pat on his back, though, and knew what Ivan silently meant to say—he was honestly glad. Glad Ari had taken the chance. After their last talk, Ivan probably hadn't expected it. Hell, Ari hadn't expected it. Carter was just charming. He laid all blame for this on the other man's shoulders.

As they walked into the living room, Carter and Remi were on their backs in the middle of the floor, using the space between the two couches and Kyou's desk. Carter was explaining seriously, "—any average coffin has enough air in it for about an hour or two. So don't panic, and definitely don't scream. Just inhale deeply, exhale very slowly."

Remi drew in a breath, her arms crossed over her chest like she was pretending she really was in a coffin, and exhaled slowly. Then did it again.

"Right, just like that," Carter encouraged her with an approving smile. "Now, if someone's burying you quickly, odds are they'll pick a cheap coffin. You can shake the lid up with your hands, maybe even make a hole. Like with a belt, I've done that. But before you do that, cross your arms over your chest, and pull your shirt upwards, then tie a knot at the top of your head to keep the dirt from falling down and suffocating you. Then, when you're secure there, kick the lid with your legs. A lot of the cheap coffins, the lid will already be damaged by the dirt piled up on top of it. So it'll be easy to get it partially up. Any dirt that falls in, push it down towards the bottom, near your feet. More dirt that falls in, the more clear space you have above you. So dirt falling is good, okay?"

Remi followed this all very seriously. "What if it's raining?"

"Then move fast," Carter warned. "Water makes dirt heavy and sticky. But if it's dry, you should be able to get up. Grave dirt is pretty loose, so battling your way up is actually easier than you'd think."

All of the information was interesting to Ari, who hadn't actually known any of this. Kyou was paying close attention too, he noted, and even Ivan seemed to be taking mental notes as he settled into the couch. Ari bent at the waist to regard the two on the floor, leaning over their feet, and couldn't help but ask, "What brought this on?"

"Remi asked me what was the scariest thing I'd ever lived through," Carter explained with a warm smile at the little girl. "First time I was buried alive came to mind."

Everything in Ari froze. "*First* time?"

Carter's eyes snapped back to Ari and honed in. He spoke carefully, each word deliberately phrased. "Yeah. First time was hella scary. I've been buried three times in total."

Later, without the audience, Ari would get the full story on every instance. His curiosity demanded the answer. For now, he asked the most pertinent question. "And are any of those people who stupidly buried you still alive?"

"Aww, are you offering to go settle things for me?" Carter turned his head to whisper loudly to Remi, "He's sexy when he's pissed and protective."

Remi giggled back and nodded in avid agreement.

"Don't worry, hon," Carter assured him cheerfully. "I didn't leave anyone alive in my wake."

There was that, at least. Ari grunted acknowledgement and offered them both a hand. Remi was easy to haul to her feet, Carter more of a challenge. The man was solid and not a lightweight. Remi gave him a quick hug around the leg before bouncing over to sit with Ivan. Carter leaned in to kiss him just under his jaw and whispered huskily, "Thanks."

Ari couldn't quite suppress the shiver. Right then he had a pep talk with his instincts: Look, get over this reaction to having Carter in close. The man was sex on legs. Time to relax and take advantage.

Kyou cleared his throat pointedly and stared at them until

they took their own seats. Ari ended up with Carter pressed up against his side, their hands loosely joined, Carter's thumb idly tracing a circle on his skin. The skinship was nice. Distracting, but nice.

"Right. Let this strategy session now commence. Since we can't use the van and uniforms to sneak Ivan in, how do we do it? I really don't want to assume the painting is in the vault and then go in blind. If we can at least check the house beforehand, make sure it isn't somewhere in a private bedroom, I'd feel better."

"Same," Ari admitted openly. "The house isn't as tightly guarded as the vault. Do you see any weak points?"

"Not really. I mean, you're right, it's not as tightly defended. But it's still locked down pretty well."

Ivan perked up, jostling the child in his lap, an excited smile crossing his face. "I have a solution."

With understandable doubt, Kyou looked at him dubiously. "Really?"

"It involves fire."

"Absolutely not."

Knowing where Ivan headed with this, Ari tacked on, "No explosions, either. We're not going with your usual rule of thumb on this."

Ivan slumped with a noise much like a deflating balloon.

Seeing Carter didn't entirely follow, Kyou explained, "Ivan's usual rule of thumb is everything counts as a stealth mission if no one's alive to talk about it afterwards."

"Ah. No, that rule of thumb doesn't work in this case." Carter actually gave the man a commiserating smile. "Sorry, Ivan."

"It's fine. At least I can play with the drones later." Ivan sighed gustily and let his head fall back onto the couch. "Alright. Let's walk through. One point of entry through the fence. Ground sensors along the perimeter. Cameras throughout. Kyou, how many on roster for night duty?"

"Eight. Four for house, four for vault."

"So slightly larger crew than during the day. And you can't get access to their cameras."

"Not without sending someone in," Kyou said with a shake

of the head. He looked distinctly unhappy, almost pouting. "Something of a catch-22 situation. I hate they were smart enough to wire the cameras straight to the server."

"So I'll have to evade ground sensors, guards, and cameras? What type of cameras?"

"Well, last time they had both motion sensor and infrared. No thermal, but they could have changed that since. I don't have a way of verifying without," Kyou sighed again, this time a groan mixed in, "sending someone or something in. Guys, maybe we should just axe this idea. We risk tipping our hand if Ivan gets caught."

Ivan made an affronted sound and splayed a hand over his chest, aghast Kyou would even suggest such a thing. Remi giggled at the theatrics.

"Knowles is stupidly difficult," Kyou argued with a wild gesture towards his computer. "And we have a very narrow time window. We've got three weeks, meaning we don't have time to let this fully cool off and try again later."

"I can get in," Ivan assured him, then turned his head to assure them all. "Really."

Ari didn't actually doubt this. Kyou was the worry-wart among them. He liked backup plans, and redundancies, and escape routes that didn't involve potentially getting his head blown off. Ari and Ivan both worked a lot closer to the edge. Sometimes, you just had to, in order to get the job done.

"Bedsheets, and licking sensors, and all of that?" Carter tilted forward on the couch so he could see around Ari and look at the thief closely. "You really think you can, or are you bored and want to try it?"

"Little of both," Ivan admitted with a mile-wide smile.

Yes, it was the 'both' worrying Ari. He really believed Ivan could get in, but on the off chance something went wrong? What then?

"I don't want to walk in there blind, working off assumptions," Ari finally said.

Carter nodded agreement. "I don't think that's wise. But I hear what you're saying, Kyou. Let's go through this again. Ivan, tell me how you'd get in. Walk me through it, step by step. If this is doable, then we can at least try it. If it doesn't sound workable to all of us, we'll take a step back and rethink it."

Excited, Ivan shifted Remi to sit next to him, giving him the space to talk with his hands. The more Ari listened, the more he sided with Kyou. Ivan was definitely taking too many chances with this plan. Knowles was difficult, yes, but surely there was a safer way to do a bit of recon.

Surely.

20

CARTER

Carter was woken from a sound sleep by a hand on his arm. He went from dreaming to wide awake, a hand on the gun under his pillow, in mach .02 seconds. Only Ari's scent and voice kept him from attacking in sheer reflex.

"Carter. We've got a problem. Ivan went in."

He took a second to digest the news and then swore, flinging the blankets back. "How far in is he?"

"The house, he says." Ari held out the small earbud.

Slipping it in, Carter demanded, "Eidolon. You good?"

A soft cackle echoed through his ear. *"This is fun. I haven't done something like this in ages."*

Kyou growled, *"He's having the time of his life, the bastard."*

"How did he even get in?" Carter demanded, more bewildered than anything else. After the strategy session spanning most of the afternoon and evening, he hadn't thought it possible. In fact, they'd largely agreed it wasn't possible without tipping their hand.

"I don't even ask anymore," Ari admitted ruefully. "He finds a way, he always does. If you ask him, he'll spin you a story about bedsheets."

Ivan cackled again, not denying this.

Carter twisted to put his legs over the side of the bed. He'd not be able to go back to sleep, and it would behoove them to have a vehicle at the ready to extract Ivan, if he needed that.

"Eidolon, how's it look?"

"*Hmm. Da, horosho.*"

"Yes, good," Ari translated for Carter's benefit. "He always slips into Russian when he's thinking hard."

Ah. That did make sense. Carter did the same even though he was quite comfortable with both Spanish and French. If he was too focused, or startled, English came out every time.

Ari ducked out, no doubt to get dressed, and Carter wasted no time in doing the same, reaching for clothes he'd discarded only a few hours ago. Years of having to move with little notice made it easy for him to fully wake up and function even though he was tired enough to want to roll back into the bed and bury his head under a pillow.

Ivan reported in a low murmur, "*Main floor is clear. I don't see our target. Ascending to the second. Oops.*"

Oops? Carter froze with one leg in his pants. "What oops?"

Long silence on the other end. Carter assumed Ivan was in a very tight spot and couldn't answer without giving away his position. Swearing, he jerked on the rest of his clothes, grabbed his shoes, and hoofed it downstairs.

Kyou sat in front of the monitors, and unlike every other time Carter had seen him in that position, he didn't have various windows of text and coding up. Instead, he seemed to have several camera feeds lined up on two monitors. He was lining up yet another camera feed when Carter came to a stop next to him. "Is that the mansion's security feed?"

"Ivan managed to grab the right piece of tech, for once, and plugged it into the first camera he found. I've got control of the main house, at least. Pity the vault isn't on the same system, but I guess that would be too easy. At the very least, we can watch him." Kyou didn't even look up as he spoke.

Carter eyed him thoughtfully. It was well past midnight but it was clear to him Kyou hadn't gone to bed yet. A stack of coffee mugs attested to this, as did the man's messy hair and growing panda eyes. As far as Carter could tell, Kyou hadn't moved from that chair in almost twenty-four hours. He'd adhere to the chair and grow moss soon if he didn't leave it. Kyou ran on caffeine and determination, it seemed. He might have to intervene later and make the man rest, if Kyou didn't have the good sense to do it himself.

For now, he needed the answer to a different question: "Where is he?"

"Near the stairwell." Kyou pointed to the top right corner of the feed.

Ari appeared at Carter's side and put his hand on the small of Carter's back as he leaned in, peering at the screen. "I don't see him. Is he folded up behind that table?"

"Yes." Two bulky shapes went past the cameras, guards on their rounds, and everyone fell silent until the two had passed through the room and out the other side. "Ivan, go."

Ivan rose smoothly, just a figure in black, and padded up the stairs like a wraith. Carter had to admit seeing the man in action was damn impressive.

"Ivan?" Ari asked softly. There was no need to modulate their voices, only Ivan could hear them through the bud, but they automatically did so anyway. "Do you have a vehicle nearby?"

"*Took the metro,*" Ivan admitted and he sounded entirely too pleased about that. "*But don't come get me unless this becomes zanuda.*"

Carter assumed that last word to mean 'pain in the neck' or 'shit hits the fan.' Context told a lot. "I take it you have an exit plan?"

"*Mm. And not much traffic in this area at night. It'll be too obvious if you try to lap the block and pick me up.*"

Ah. There was that.

The hallway appeared to be a long stretch, the wide expanse and décor something belonging to a museum—polished hardwood floors, carpet runners, priceless antiques on pedestals in alcoves. Other than entering rooms, there wasn't anything to really duck behind and use for cover. The hallway was, in effect, a very long kill box. A nicely decorated kill box, but a kill box nonetheless. On camera, Ivan ducked into the first room, then was back out in the hallway in five seconds. The nice thing about this was his quick and clean search. Either the right painting was in the room or not. He didn't have to tear apart drawers and search for hidden panels for smaller targets. In theory, he could clear the house under thirty minutes. Assuming he dodged every patrol.

Carter found himself holding his breath as he watched the thief dart from room to room. Ari leaned in against his side, a warm press, and whispered into his free ear, "He's alright. Breathe, caro."

"Unfortunately, we've seen him do stupider stunts than this," Kyou agreed sourly, still not taking his eyes off the cameras. "Eidolon, you've got the patrol heading back up your direction via the other staircase. Your window is closing in ten, nine, eight—"

Ivan ducked into a room and then went further. Carter could hear the soft snick of a door opening and closing again but he couldn't quite tell where the thief was. No cameras had been placed in the individual bedrooms or bathrooms. Or at least, he assumed, as every camera feed Kyou had pulled up was for a public room. It only made sense, of course. No one wanted cameras in their bedrooms or bathrooms.

The guards didn't even bother to check the bedrooms, just walked the hallway. From their body language, it was clear they were chatting about something. They passed Ivan's hidey-hole none the wiser and went back downstairs via the main staircase.

"Clear," Kyou announced.

Ivan appeared again in the hallway, then waved at the camera with a thumb's up.

Carter shook his head in disbelief. He'd heard of adrenaline junkies, but Ivan took it to a whole new level. He really was having a blast in there.

It took another twenty minutes to completely check the mansion. Carter held his breath the entire time and only partially because it got Ari to rub his back soothingly. Ivan really was scaring the crap out of him, going in like that without backup on hand, but mostly he liked having Ari pressed up close against him. Ari had initiated contact for the first time, and Carter was selfishly enjoying the moment.

"*Alright, going dark.*"

Carter blinked back into focus and shared a look with Ari. Surely that didn't mean what he thought it meant?

Groaning, Kyou sat back with a gesture of disgust towards the monitors. "And now we can't even track him by camera.

Don't bother asking where he is, Carter. He's up in the vents, or skittering along the roof, or some other route he's found to avoid all the cameras. Not that he'll tell you later."

"*Trade secret,*" Ivan sing-songed.

This surprised him. "I thought you three were a team?"

"No, not really," Ari corrected with a slight shrug. "We pull together to do jobs often, but we don't do every job together."

"We're more friends who pitch hit for each other." Kyou picked up the coffee cup at his elbow, took a sip, then grimaced. "Cold. Figures. Eidolon, you sure of your exit strategy?"

"*Sure. It's same way as I got in.*"

Which told them precisely nothing. Carter really didn't like this. It made him uneasy. Not even knowing Ivan's path out meant they couldn't help if it all went suddenly south. His fingers itched for keys. He wanted to drive over there and be on hand for the thief. If Ivan hadn't expressly told them not to do that very thing, he'd already be on his way.

Fortunately, Ivan didn't seem to have a problem with narrating his own escape. "*That's a nice face. I should come back for that face.*"

Not that the narration was in any way helpful. Carter turned again to Ari, eyebrows lifted in question. Ari just shrugged, resigned, and went to get comfortable on the couch.

"*Three blind mice, three blind mice, see how they run, see how they run—wait, how does the rest of that song go?*"

Carter really hoped Ivan wasn't singing somewhere where sound carried. Not knowing what else to do, he set his shoes down next to the door and then joined Ari on the couch. The other man made room for him and Carter snuggled into his side. He might have been yanked out of a sound sleep because of a crazy thief, but at least he got cuddles out of it. Life could be worse.

"*Aww, someone's watching Princess Bride. I love that movie.*"

Carter wished the mics were sensitive enough to pick up more environmental sounds. At least that way he'd be able to guess where Ivan currently was and if he were anywhere close to making it outside.

Several minutes passed before Ivan snickered and repeated

theatrically, "*My name is Inigo Montoya. You killed my father. Prepare to die!*"

"IVAN," Kyou snapped in pure frustration. "Don't tell me you stopped to watch the movie!"

"*Fine, I won't tell you.*"

Carter held the sneaking suspicion Ivan deliberately did things in order to get a rise out of Kyou. Part of it, he felt sure, was just the thief's own nature, but he seemed entirely too gleeful at Kyou's reactions. Ari didn't seem nearly as worried, relaxed as he was into the couch and smiling faintly at Ivan's antics. Carter sensibly decided to take his cue from Ari. Following Kyou's example would likely lead to an ulcer or a migraine. Possibly both.

"*Nose, njet,*" Ivan abruptly mourned. "*Awww, mouth, njet. Wiiiig, not you too. Chert. There goes that.*"

Carter didn't even lift his head from Ari's shoulder. "You need us after all, Eidolon?"

"*Hmm? Njet, no, I improvise. It'll be fine. I have my bedsheet.*"

Bedsheet. Right. Two could play this game. "I'm just curious, but when you say sheet, do you mean the fitted sheet or the flat one?"

Kyou turned in his chair in creaking degrees and bent an evil eye on Carter. "Are you encouraging him?"

Putting an innocent hand over his heart, Carter gave his best impression of wounded, naive protest. Ari laughed silently, his chest jerking with the motion.

"*Of course it makes difference,*" Ivan retorted, sounding every bit as innocent. "*Flat sheet easier to fold.*"

"Yeah, exactly," Carter agreed.

Kyou threw up his hands and pointedly turned away, not willing to be dragged into their pace.

Snickering, Ari put his mouth against Carter's forehead to murmur, "Don't tease him so hard. When he's this sleep deprived and stressed out, Kyou has no sense of humor."

These men knew each other so well. Why wouldn't they officially team up? What stopped them from doing so? Was it the lack of impetus to carry them to that final mark? Or were they naturally such lone wolves the idea hadn't even occurred to them?

"*Oooh, look, a threesome! Squirrels are getting more action than I am.*"

Ari asked what they all suspected: "Are you finally out of the mansion?"

"*Da. Give me a few more minutes, I'll be outside the fence. Yes, squirrels, carry on. At least someone's getting some.*"

Kyou ran a hand roughshod through his hair. "Ari, Harrison, will you stay up until he's in? I can't take anymore of this, I'm going to bed."

"Sure," Carter agreed instantly. Kyou really did look like a typhoon had run him over. "Go sleep."

Waving a hand in thanks and acknowledgement, the slender man slouched towards his room.

Silence and semi-darkness wrapped around them. Carter could tune out the nonsense Ivan occasionally spouted and he focused more on the man stretched out against him. He tilted up enough to catch Ari's mouth in a gentle kiss, more asking than demanding. Ari returned it but his body tensed up at the same time. No-go.

Carter lifted off immediately, giving him room so Ari didn't feel so pinned. Something about the way he'd shifted his weight more onto Ari's torso had flipped the wrong switch. Carter felt bad about it. He'd thought it would be okay, since Ari had invited him into his space.

"Porca troia," Ari sighed, a flush on his face and his eyes anywhere but meeting Carter's. "Sorry."

"Don't apologize," Carter whispered back. He shifted to the other side of the couch, back braced against the arm rest, one foot on the floor, leaving plenty of room open as he extended a hand toward Ari in open invitation. It didn't matter to Carter what position they were in. He just wanted to touch the man, and he wanted to build more trust between them as he could.

Ari's tongue darted out to lick his lips and he eyed Carter's open position for a long second before caving into his own desires. Uncomfortable he might have been, but not enough to kill the mood. He rolled to his knees and then settled a little gingerly between the vee of Carter's legs.

He braced a hand against the couch, the other on Carter's

ribs and leaned in. Ari caught his mouth in another kiss, picking up where they'd left off. It was languid and easy, an exchange of affection not meant to rile either of them up. Carter enjoyed the weight of the man in his arms and the sweetness of the kiss.

"*The two of you are making out on the couch, aren't you?*" Ivan groused. "*Everyone's getting some but me. Chert. You've got a bedroom, go use it.*"

Ari broke the kiss to breathe against Carter's mouth, "Not until you're safely back here."

"*You're going to—what's that American expression? Get all bothered while waiting on me and make me jealous, aren't you?*"

Carter grinned, pleased when Ari looked back at him with the same level of mischief. "Payback's a bitch, Eidolon."

"Next time, you should invite me in on the fun," Ari tacked on before resuming his steady, thorough exploration of Carter's mouth. Carter hummed approval and snugged the man in further so their groins pressed together.

Ivan just sighed.

21

ARI

Ari came into the kitchen for a cup of coffee—never mind that it was mid-afternoon, he needed the caffeine hit—but paused partway inside when he found Carter, Ivan, and Remi all sitting on the bar stools. The fingerprint kit lay open off to the side, and multiple sheets organized in three stacks sat in front of them.

It took him a second (caffeine input required), but he finally remembered. Right, they couldn't wear gloves on this job. Wearing latex or leather gloves was out. It would look too suspicious for the 'workmen' coming in to be wearing gloves, a sure sign to security something was fishy. They planned instead to paste fingerprints and palm prints onto their hands in a transparent latex to confuse anyone who investigated later.

Remi poked at one of them and read carefully, "Elvis Presley. Who's that?"

Ivan looked at him with accusing eyes. "Just what are you teaching her, that she doesn't know the famous rockstar?"

"She's only eight," Ari defended himself mildly. "I think I have time to introduce her to all the different music through the years. Carter, you picked a set of prints out yet?"

"Not yet," his mercenary answered while holding up two different sheets. "I'm having a hard time choosing. Do I want to be Lucille Ball or Rock Hudson for this job? Who do you normally choose?"

Ari poured himself a cup of coffee, dumped two sugars into it, and came back to the bar before answering, leaning his weight casually against it. "Cary Grant's usually my pick. That man was damn fine."

Carter gave him an analyst's salute. "No arguments. I think I'll go Lucy this time. I grew up—" He paused as the phone on the bar rang. Picking it up, he looked at the screen, a grimace pulling at his face. "Well, hell. It's Emura."

Kyou's chair slid so that he could look into the kitchen. "Seriously?"

"Probably doing a check-in. Do I ignore it?"

"No," Ivan commanded. "Do that, he finds someone else to take the job. We don't need another team bungling in."

Carter apparently agreed, as with a deep, heartfelt sigh, he swiped to answer and put the phone on speaker. "Hey, Emura."

"*Hello, Mr. Harrison. I'm just checking in.*"

"Yeah, well, I'm doing good so far. Got a team together, and we're mid-prep right now."

"*Excellent! Does that mean you'll have the job completed by deadline?*"

"Probably earlier than that. Have to, as they plan on switching out hardware."

"*So you're well on top of things. I'm happy to hear it. If you run into any problems, let me know, I'll do my best to assist.*"

"Thanks, Emura. I'm good for now."

"*Very well. Talk to you soon.*" The phone call ended.

"Smarmy little prick," Carter grumbled, sliding the phone back away from him on the bar. "Kyou, the site admins still haven't done their thing?"

"Apparently not. I'll follow up with them. I have found a way to discreetly contact the director of the Met—I'm waiting to hear back from him. If all goes well, we can just go to him directly."

Ari personally hoped for that outcome, because otherwise, it wouldn't be a simple pay day for them. But he absolutely wasn't going to trust Emura—or Banks, as he knew him—again. No way would he trust a double-crosser.

Turning in her chair, Remi regarded Carter seriously, lips pursed. "But what about your call sign?"

Returning her stare, Carter cocked his head a little to the side in question. "Is it really bugging you that much, sweetie?"

"'Cause everyone *else* has a call sign, even me," she said with growing impatience, "But you don't. I don't think that's fair."

"Fair, huh."

Kyou called to them from the living room, "She has a point, you know! And you don't want to give any hint you were on this job!"

"That's a fair point." Carter shrugged, smile on his face. "But I don't know what to choose. There's not much distinctive about me. How about some suggestions?"

"Killer," Ivan suggested with a wicked snicker.

Carter gave that suggestion all the attention it deserved. That was to say, none at all.

Attempting to be helpful, Ari threw in, "Snookums."

Those blue eyes rolled his direction, Carter's expression wry. "Yup. Gonna nope right out of that one."

"Dumpling," Ivan suggested, excited like a child.

Carter just sighed. "Next."

Knowing he would get the military reference, Ari couldn't resist. "Roo."

Carter nearly choked on his own spit.

Remi looked between them in confusion. "Roo?"

Okay, maybe he hadn't thought that through. Ari's open style parenting notwithstanding, did he want to explain to his daughter that Roo was short for Romeo One Oscar—'rub one out?'

Patting her on the head, Carter promised, "I'll explain that one when you're eighteen. Next!"

Kyou's next bright idea was, "Cupid."

Looking around, Carter asked the air rhetorically, "I feel it was a poor life decision to ask anything of you guys. Yeah. My bad. How about I come up with something without your input?"

"Sounds less fun," Ivan informed him, still smirking in evil amusement. "Bambi?"

Ignoring him completely, Carter slid off the barstool and asked, "Ari, how about we get some spirit gum? The one in the kit's mostly gone."

Ari would like some time to talk with him anyway so he shrugged agreement. "Sure. Bye, you three, stay out of trouble."

Ivan *tsked* him while shaking a finger in correction. "If you don't get caught, it never happened."

Keys in hand, Carter paused to look at Ivan doubtfully. "I'm...I'm not certain that is correct."

Taking hold of his shoulders, Ari urged Carter out the door. "Don't get sucked into his pace. He'll drag you down to his level and then beat you with experience."

"The Gentleman!" Kyou suggested, not able to disguise his snicker.

Ari's grip on Carter didn't falter until the door was closed behind them, cutting off the rest of the (entirely ridiculous) suggestions. Sometimes, like now, you had to take it one are-you-fucking-kidding-me at a time.

They took Carter's Jeep, as he knew DC better, and it just made sense for him to drive. Ari pulled up different stores selling theater makeup, scrolling through the options to find the closest one.

"After we deal with the painting, I'm taking you on a proper date."

Ari's head came up in surprise. That had come out of nowhere, but one look at Carter's face showed his seriousness. "Date?"

"I don't care if we're in tuxes or in jeans, but we're doing a proper date."

"Date sounds...good," Ari said slowly, picturing it. It was quite the picture with him and Carter alone and able to indulge in each other's company.

Carter paused at the stop sign and gave him a quick study, smiling at what he saw. "I thought you'd be on board with this plan. There's just too much I don't know about you. I know dating's supposed to help you learn about the other person, but I have a lot of frustrating gaps with you."

For that matter, Ari felt the same. He'd caught hints of Carter, what made this amazing man, but he had no details. Sad truth, he knew more about most of his former targets than the man sitting next to him. "We don't have to wait for an actual date to swap basics, do we?"

"Naw, I wouldn't think so. Okay—wait, which store we going to?"

Ari twisted sideways to set his phone into the cradle on the dash so Carter could just read the map himself and navigate.

He took a second to get his bearings, grunted, then turned right. "Where do you want to start? Something easy? Like, I don't even know what foods you like/dislike."

Ari felt comfortable with this topic and nodded. "Sure. Really, I like food. I'm not all that picky, I just don't like high concentrations of spice."

"What's too much for you?"

"Like, kimchi is fine. Hot salsas with habaneros, that's too much."

"Good to know. I personally love spicy food. Given a choice, though, it's Chinese."

Ari looked at him strangely. He never in a million years would have guessed that. "Really? Chinese?"

"Chinese. My default has always been Chinese. And I'm very, very repeatable with food. I can eat the same thing for three days before I get tired of it."

"Ages?" Ari asked tentatively. "Ballpark is fine, I just don't know how old you are. Despite all that grey in your hair, you look close to my age."

"Prematurely grey," Carter answered with a longsuffering sigh. "Runs in the family. I'm thirty-five."

"Ah. Not much older after all. I'm thirty."

"You mentioned you have a twin? No other family?"

Ari shook his head. "Not really. My brother's not like us—he's straight as a bleeding arrow. About a year back, we went hunting for my mother's family. She was kicked out as a teenager, came to the US to work. We only knew her last name, but my brother found her immigration records in the system. We traced it back to a small town in northern Italy. I went over to the area, stalked the family a bit to see if they'd changed any since abandoning a daughter. They hadn't. My brother didn't see anything on his end that made him really want to reach out, either. We're both pretty content to let it be. But I took on the family name, mostly to remember my mom by."

"Gotcha. I've got too much family to keep track of. I'd like for them to meet you at some point." Carter gave him a quick, understanding smile. "It's okay if that meeting's off in the distant future, though. They're overwhelming and sure to ask questions they shouldn't. It sounds like you get along with your brother?"

"It's...complicated." Ari grimaced because, God, that sounded like Facebook shit right there. "He and I were close as kids, but you know how foster works—you can't always stay with a sibling. We only got to stay with each other three times. We were okay, mostly, but it was rough. Then we hit eighteen and I went into the military, him to college—he's wicked smart, had all sorts of grants and scholarships. I got that dishonorable discharge at twenty and he did *not* react well. He's so inflexible. Rules are rules, you just abide by them. He doesn't know any shades of grey. We got into a huge fight about it and that's when the relationship broke. Not bad, I don't mean that."

"But it's strained now; you can't really talk to him," Carter said in understanding.

"That sounds like personal experience."

"Yeah, I've got a brother I can't say much to. And I say very little to my dad. It's easier talking to my sister and mother, so I get what you're saying."

"I figured you'd get it. Anyone in this business has similar problems. Things have improved since Remi, though. He's super happy I would take someone in—I honestly believe he'd thought I'd gained a black heart or something—and he adores her. Talks to her every chance he gets. Right now, we have something we agree on wholeheartedly: Remi. It makes talking to him easier."

"Have they met in person yet?"

"Not yet. He's on the other side of the country, so meeting's a bit difficult. But after this job, I've promised them both they can meet in person."

The conversation stayed in that casual meandering way, with them discussing favorite colors, places to visit, and such. Carter admitted he had a few other houses in the world, and Ari chimed in that he had a vacation house in Italy. They touched briefly on siblings, that Ari was a twin, and Carter the youngest of three siblings. Habit stilled Ari's tongue before he could say

Luca's name, but Carter didn't seem to mind. In fact, Carter appeared thrilled to learn this much about Ari without resorting to teeth pulling in the process.

Gaining a better sense of Carter made Ari want to linger just a bit longer. They made up the excuse of having an early dinner, eating together. Chinese, mostly to make Carter smile, which he did. They sat close in the booth, holding hands under the table part of the time, and speaking in low, intimate tones. It was incredibly nice. If this was any indication of what dating Carter was like? Then Ari was definitely on board. He couldn't say it was easy or comfortable, he still found it a bit nerve-wracking, but he liked it. He liked being with this man and having Carter's attention.

With great reluctance they ordered takeout for everyone else and finally left the restaurant.

They held hands on the way back to the car, as they'd had to park a block down. Ari was the one to initiate, and it put a smug tilt on Carter's mouth. Ari had only initiated touch with this man three times (yes, sue him, he was keeping count) and it pleased Carter enormously every time. Ari wanted to make this man happy, no doubt. He was a bit lost on how to go about it, to be honest, never having had a boyfriend before. But touch seemed to be Carter's love language, and he could definitely indulge them both there.

Ari walked and schemed.

No matter where they went, Ari tried to keep the same bedtime routine with Remi. He'd read in one of those parenting books that routine was important for kids, that they liked the stability of patterns. It certainly seemed to help with her. She always brushed her teeth, changed into pajamas, and then settled into bed with him sitting next to her. He'd also read that reading to your child was important, but he felt stupid reading storybooks to her. She was past that stage, right? They settled on a book more her age level—*The Ranger's Apprentice*—and he read a chapter each night. They were on book four of the series now, and Ari secretly rather liked the story.

Remi cuddled up next to him, listening intently as he read, a sweet and warm weight against his side. She was like the kitten he affectionately called her.

When the chapter finished, Ari replaced the bookmark and set the book aside. On impulse, he kissed the top of her head, and she cuddled in a little harder, smiling. "You sleepy yet, gattina?"

"Maybe."

'Maybe' meaning yes, but she wasn't ready to let go of him yet. "Can I ask you something?"

"Yeah."

"Did you push Carter into asking me out because you really like him?" Ari feared it was for a different reason entirely.

Remi didn't answer immediately, dwelling on the question for a moment. "Yes. But..." she sighed, like a jaded, world-weary woman. "It's complicated."

Ari'd rather had that feeling. "It can be complicated. Most feelings are. What I don't want you to think is that I need to be in a relationship. Gattina, some people think you can't be happy unless you're in a relationship with someone. I'm not one of those people. Whether I'm in a relationship or not, my priority's not going to shift. You're my priority."

She peeked up at him with those big brown eyes, so innocent and trusting, staring as if she could see right through him. "But you like Carter."

"I do. I really like him. But even if we break up, I won't blame you for it, because it won't have anything to do with you. My relationship with him is between me and him. Okay?"

Remi stared at him in her penetrating manner another moment, reading his sincerity. Then she relaxed. "Okay."

Ari hadn't realized until this moment Remi had always carried this worry with her, a fine line of tension that thrummed unhappily. But the moment she let go of it, he saw its absence, and what remained was a much happier little girl. He felt relieved he'd finally gotten through to her. With one last kiss on her forehead, he slid free of the bed. "Good. Go to sleep."

She obediently slid down under the covers. He glanced back as he hit the light switch, saw her eyes still open, and on instinct said, "Ti voglio bene gattina di papà."

A happy giggle sounded from the bed. "Ti voglio, Papà."

Good, now he felt she was properly settled. He closed the door and discovered Carter leaned against his own doorjamb, half-in, half-out of the hallway. The merc watched him with open hunger, and it sent an answering thrill up Ari's spine. Hot damn, but no one had ever looked at him that way, as if they were dying to get their hands on him.

"That's hella sexy, hon," Carter husked in his low tone. "Watching you be so sweet to your daughter. Makes me want to do something to you as a reward."

That fell into Ari's plans perfectly. He strode right up to Carter and seized the man by his hips, pulling him sharply into him. Ari felt Carter's surprised exhale, but he didn't fight Ari's hold, just flowed into him. Nothing about the way he kissed the man could be called sweet. It was all hunger and heat, tongues warring for dominance. Carter's hand slid up into Ari's hair, sending tingles along his skin.

They moved of one accord further into Carter's bedroom, Ari kicking the door shut behind them. He really didn't need everyone in the house listening in on this. Carter stopped partway into the room, no doubt because he had no idea where Ari went with this, or where the line was tonight. Ari wasn't ready for full on sex with the man, not yet, but he didn't see anything wrong with them getting comfortable on the bed and having a hot and heavy make out session.

He nudged them both towards the bed and Carter followed his lead, climbing up into it first, scooting more towards the middle so they weren't in danger of falling off the edge. Ari looked at him, stretched out like that, and felt the urge to lick the man like a popsicle. He settled on top of Carter and captured his mouth again, needing to kiss him like he needed air. A moan bubbled out of Carter's throat and Ari smirked for a split second. The smirk dissolved promptly when Carter did that thing with his tongue, his hand tightening in Ari's hair. Ari lost his mind. Their noises sounded loud to his ears, everything echoing in the small confines of the room, undeniably erotic.

Ari pulled back—he had to, or he risked losing control completely. This was supposed to be make-out/cuddle time, not something more serious. But something had tripped in his brain and he'd lost his control with it. A glint shone in Carter's eyes as Ari hovered over him, watching, waiting. Carter's hair was already out of sorts, the ash brown and grey strands sticking out at odd angles, and since when was that endearing as well as hot? Oh, Ari was fucked.

And not even in the good *literal* sense, despite the position he lay in.

His libido wailed in protest and despite his better judgement, Ari rocked his hips experimentally, flushing at how warm Carter was where their bodies pressed together. Carter's eyes fluttered shut on a moan, mouth dropping at the lovely friction the movement sparked. If Ari wasn't already done for, that expression right there would have done him in.

Not enough. Suddenly, it wasn't enough for him to lay here like this. He needed skin. Ari levered up onto his knees, shirking off his shirt in one hard yank. Carter needed no further encouragement and also leaned up, pulling at his own shirt. With him still half down and Ari on top of him, he didn't have the full leverage he needed, and Ari quickly latched onto the hem and helped draw it all the way off.

Hot, firm skin met his hands and he took a moment to appreciate it openly. He'd seen Carter without a shirt on a few times now, but he'd never dared to really *look*, not like this, with eyes and hands both. He was warmth and smooth muscle and scars, and Ari's hands—completely without permission—stroked everything for a moment in fascination.

Carter squirmed a bit, a flush heating his cheeks. "Hon, if you could stop petting my chubby stomach, I'd appreciate it."

Ari didn't understand the protest. No, Carter wasn't physically 'perfect,' he probably had an extra five to ten pounds on him, but the man was beautiful to him. Was he really self-conscious about the bit of padding around his middle? "I don't want some perfect version of you. I just want you."

"Yeah?" Carter's hands slid up his back, pulling him back in. "Come here and prove it."

He went willingly, like answering a siren's call. He had to keep a hand against the mattress, keep himself from crushing the man beneath, which made it a little awkward. Ari wouldn't trade it for anything—not when it meant having Carter's lips on his again, moving in a slick slide, hot and wet. Ari began to rock into him, a gentle roll of his hips he wasn't consciously aware of, not at first. A shiver of heat crept down Ari's spine to pool in his groin. And—*hot damn*, yeah, that was the hard length of Carter's cock lining up against his, hot like a brand through their jeans.

Ari could get used to this—the feel of Carter under him, the firm muscle of hips and chest, the attentive ministration of his hands. Not even to mention what Carter had in his pants—the thought of which made Ari's mouth water, especially now that he'd *felt* it.

They broke apart for a gasp of breath, and Carter pressed lines of kisses up Ari's neck with loud, wet sounds, the scrape and burn of his stubble heightening the pleasure. Ari responded helplessly, breath hitching with every kiss Carter left on his skin, fingers flexing in the fabric of the sheets. Their rocking never stopped, only became faster, harder, with them practically grinding into each other. Ari briefly considered stopping long enough to get jeans open, hands involved, but couldn't bear the thought of separating to do it. Next time, next time he'd get this man properly naked and—Carter shifted, using the leverage of his feet to press up, and it changed the angle to something *perfect*. The tension that had been building between them coiled tight in a sudden constriction and Ari shuddered.

"That's it," Carter groaned, nearly snarled in dark satisfaction. "That's it, come for me, come with me—*unngh*."

Ari's climax snapped through him, hard and fast, his vision going dark around the edges. His balance deserted him and he collapsed on Carter's chest, breathing hard, riding the rise of his endorphins with a blissed-out tranquility. His brain went off into la-la-land for several minutes as he checked out of reality.

Or at least it did until soft lips kissed his temple, Carter's hands roving over his ass.

"Why are you squeezing my ass?" Ari asked, not really bothered. He didn't even lift his head, just muttered the words against the side of Carter's neck.

"It's a nice ass."

Ari mulled this over. "That's a good reason."

"So this is what you're like after sex, huh. All blissed out and boneless."

The first thread of worry wound itself into his brain. "Am I crushing you?"

"It's a good sort of crushing. Don't move."

Well, that was alright, then. Ari stayed flopped where he was, enjoying Carter's hands wrapped around him. He'd never had an afterglow like this before. It was damn nice. Ari now understood the appeal.

He expected questions from Carter, about why Ari had suddenly made a move, or...well, any of this, really. But Carter just held him, stroking a hand idly up and down his back. Maybe he didn't want to disturb the afterglow, either. It strangely felt... connecting? Ari wasn't quite sure what else to call it. He just knew that for every moment he lay in this man's arms, he felt closer to him. That the anxiety and fear riding so hard at his heels started to slowly fade.

Ari had feared he couldn't relax enough to have sex with Carter. He'd been afraid that letting his guard down might well be impossible for months yet. Turned out, it was the fear of the thing that had stopped him more than the actual reality. Now that he'd experienced it, he only felt anticipation.

He did need a minute to recover, though. And since he had Carter alone, his curiosity took over. "Carter. Can I ask you something?"

"Sure. What?"

"You said before you were kicked out of the army for insubordination. What did you do?"

"Ahhh. Long story short, I was in Afghanistan. We were ordered to pull out of one of the villages. But there were still civilians trapped in the line of fire, and there was no way we could take them with us. Not enough room in the vehicles. So I gave the order to stay until we could get them out. Got my CO really hot under the collar that I disobeyed him, but I wasn't leaving kids behind as fodder for bullets."

Of course he'd gotten into trouble shielding people. Ari wasn't even surprised. Feeling like he'd needed to give tit for tat, he offered, "I was kicked out for insubordination too."

"Yeah?" Carter's head turned a little toward him, tone lilting up with curiosity. "I figured you were army, but what did you do?"

"I was in Iraq. We figured out where the leader for the local troublemakers was, but no one would give the order to take him out. Or do anything. We had people getting killed because of the indecisiveness. So I snuck out one night and put two rounds into his head."

Carter huffed a laugh. "Of course you did. How long were you in?"

"About a year and a half, all told. I was out of sniper school for barely two months when that bullshit went down." Ari shifted as the wet spot in his boxers became sticky and uncomfortable. Maybe they should clean up a little before resuming the pillow talk. Or at least strip.

Carter's tone was soft and gentle. "You still good, hon? You're fidgety."

Ah, so he was worried on some level. "No regrets. I want a repeat. Just feeling a little sticky. I think pants should come off."

"Oh. Well," Carter's hand squeezed one ass cheek, his voice going into a deep growl ringing of sex. "We can definitely do that."

Ari firmly set everything else aside and sank into the moment. Doing anything else with a sexy man in bed was a sacrilege and Carter definitely deserved his full attention.

22

ARI

Ari woke up to a little girl bouncing on his stomach. "Gattina, pietá!"

"You have to wake up," Remi insisted, although she thankfully stopped bouncing. "Uncle Kyou says there's a problem."

Not another one. Groaning, he rolled, taking her with him and playfully pinning her to the bed. She wriggled and squirmed and used the rolling technique he'd taught her to get out of it. "I'm up. Get Carter up."

"He's making coffee for you," she reported, pleased with her alarm clock skills.

Bless that man. Ari needed the coffee. They'd stayed up rather late last night, indulging in having a quiet space to themselves. They'd ended up giving each other hand jobs after that lovely frottage, which was a first for Ari. He'd never had sex with the same partner twice in a row before. Neither of them felt like ruining a good thing by pushing for more, so he'd retreated to his own bed at some early hour of the morning. He'd planned to sleep in a little this morning, but that plan was apparently a wash.

Remi bounced ahead of him as he zombie shuffled his way into jeans and a random t-shirt. Not exactly looking his sexy best, but Ari didn't have the luxury of a shower if Kyou said there was a problem. He made it down the stairs before a yawn caught him.

A mug of steaming coffee wafted in front of his face and he latched onto it, sipping, a smile curling up the corners of his mouth. Delightful. Morning coffee made him feel like he had his shit together. He didn't. But it felt like it. He took another sip to fully appreciate it before blinking into focus.

Carter watched him with obvious amusement, mouth kicked up on one side. "Morning?"

Closing in, Ari kissed him soft and sweet, lingering for a moment. "Morning. Thanks for the coffee."

Licking his lips, Carter murmured, "I definitely need to give you coffee more often."

"Hey, lovebirds!" Kyou called from the living room. "Focus, we've got a problem!"

Groaning, Ari went past him, his brain slowly booting online. If Kyou had woken him up at—good god it was barely six. Did the man sleep? Anyway, Kyou waking anyone up always meant a serious issue.

Entering the living room, he saw Ivan stretched out on the couch, Remi snuggled in with him. The thief did not look awake, but then, he was still on his first cup of coffee. It took more than one for him to really join the land of the living.

Ari sank into the couch, Carter joining him, close enough to brush up against each other but not snuggled in. Taking another sip of his coffee, Ari gestured for Kyou to lay it on them.

"Right, now that we're all present," Kyou's look at Ivan expressed doubt on whether he thought the thief was mentally there or not, "I've got bad news. Our timetable just changed."

Ari's posture straightened, his mind suddenly much more awake than it had been two seconds ago. "How much time do we have to work with?"

"Three days. Max. Two to be safer."

Carter groaned and slumped over the side of the couch. "Whyyy?"

"They're moving the painting." Kyou ran a hand roughshod through his hair, and it was only then that Ari realized the man was more than sleep deprived. Had he managed any sleep at all before his alerts woke him back up? "I think it's because they don't want anyone to see the painting in the vault. Their security guys are one thing, but new people coming in to change out the hardware? The more people who see that painting, the more rumor's going to spread. I don't know the reason, but that's my guess. Could be they just want it in a different location. All I know is that they scheduled an armored truck this morning to move it in three days."

Ari whimpered. Three days?! "Porca troia. I hate people."

Ivan held out a fist and Ari bumped his against the thief's knuckles.

Remi, adorable child that she was, didn't seem disheartened. "Uncle Kyou, we can still do it, right? I know you said you'd need another week to get all the cameras for the street. But if I help, we can still do it."

His first, instinctive response was no way. Yes, Kyou had been teaching Remi computer stuff since nearly the first week he'd met her. Five months of training wasn't anything to sneeze at. But this was different from idly hacking blogs and sites for practice. Kyou tested her sometimes on harder things, just to see how well she could adapt what she'd been taught on the fly. To Ari's knowledge, she didn't succeed very often, but again: eight-year-old child and only five months of training. He didn't expect her to. It was on the tip of Ari's tongue to gently set her down.

"Actually...maybe?" Kyou stared back at Remi with a thoughtful expression, head canted as he thought it through. "I'll do the actual hack. I'll teach you how to link the feeds so we can watch and loop them, create the blind spots our guys need. That'll speed up the process a lot."

Remi beamed at him, pleased to be included.

Lifting up, Carter stared at the two, his face reflecting Ari's own astonishment. "Wait, she knows enough to actually do that?"

"Well within her skillset," Kyou assured the group as a whole. "It's not complicated to begin with. The hack itself is the hardest part. We're actually in a decent position, all things considered. Thanks to Ivan's two field trips, I have access to the main parts of Knowles, at least. We've gotten a lot of the initial prep work done."

"Just no time to do any simulations or dry runs. We don't

even have the timing worked out for this." Carter looked at them all and a trace of the hard, ruthless mercenary seeped through. "Be honest. Is this doable or do I pull the plug? Tell the client to find someone else?"

Ari forced himself to really think of the logistics, of what it would take to pull this off, and not just trust his gut reaction. Even after he thought it through, his mind agreed with his gut. "I think we can do this."

"I know we can," Ivan responded. "You can't take the route I did in—only a single person could make it. And it's not possible to take anything bigger than a small pack in. Painting would be impossible. We'll need to stick with our plan. I have only two questions: Kyou, you still want these two to go in?"

"You're a little too famous, Ivan," Kyou said apologetically. "Even with my best buffers, you'd trip their internal security if I tried to put your picture into the system. Better to send them."

Ivan accepted this with a nod and not a word of protest. "You still want my drone up in the air to give you a visual on them?"

"Yes. And to be on hand for a distraction, if it comes to that. Guys, I'll be frank, I hate rushing like this. Makes me hella nervous. But if we want to do the job, we gotta move."

"A good plan violently executed now is better than a perfect plan executed next week," Ivan stated in a sage tone.

"So we're doing this?" Carter sat up straighter and looked them over. "We're crazy."

"Best kind of luck, insanity," Ivan intoned grandly. "Kyou, you said it moves in three days. We need to go in tomorrow."

"We'll need all of today to get the last-minute stuff done. And at least a mental simulation where we try to get the timing down." Kyou reached out and without apology, stole Ari's half-drunk cup of coffee. He downed it in one long pull. "God, I needed that. Alright, can I trust you guys to do the odds and ends? Rems and I have to focus on the cameras. And make sure your IDs are still solid in the system. And—"

Ari held up a hand. "We got the picture. Do your magic. Carter and I will pick up the rest of the work uniforms. I think we're only missing shoes at this point. Kyou, badges are done, right?"

"More or less. Need to print them."

"Okay. Ivan, let's hold a planning meeting when we get back, see if we can't nail down the timing."

The thief nodded amiably enough but a frown drew his brows together. "We haven't had a chance to figure out traffic patterns around that place yet."

"Don't remind me," Ari groaned. "Unfortunately, taking the metro for this is right out. They'll expect a company SUV or van. And trying to navigate the DC metro system with a portfolio is a big No Thank You in my book."

"I want a Plan B in case Plan A doesn't work, too," Carter threw in. "I don't trust any plan to survive first contact."

"None of us do." Kyou held both hands to Remi, and she promptly abandoned Ivan for him. "Come on, kiddo, time to work. I've got a separate keyboard set up for you, and our computers are networked together, so I can throw you stuff, yeah?"

Ari left them to it. He'd need a five-minute shower, just so he didn't get scrutinized in public while buying something.

It just figured that nothing about this job would go according to plan. It was Knowles, after all.

They hooked Kyou's printer up, prepping to print their employee IDs. Ivan was out testing his drones, making sure everything worked as they should, and the buzz of the machines could be faintly heard through the window. Since the rest of the house had been more or less taken over, they'd set up in the mostly empty dining room on a folding card table.

Ari really hated this truncated timeline. Not just on the professional level, either. He'd been banking on having several more weeks with Carter on this job. Ari had so little experience dating, he really didn't know what to expect. Would they just go back to their own houses after this, work the relationship long distance, and meet up when they could? Carter had mentioned different houses he owned around the world. Ari had a similar setup. Would they even be in the same hemisphere?

Now that he had this man, he didn't want to lose him because of poor planning. Or assuming things would work out. He'd finally settled in his skin with Carter. He felt like he was at the hump, that he was right on the verge of being really invested in this relationship. Losing that burgeoning connection to Carter scared him down to his marrow.

While he might not know how relationships worked in general, Ari was confident on one point. He could ask Carter anything. Carter had never once scoffed at him for not knowing something or being uncertain. He'd always patiently listened. Even if this came off as awkward, Ari had to ask. Before the uncertainty ate a hole through his stomach.

As Carter's ID printed, Ari voiced his question as carefully as he could phrase it. "So, uh, after the job is done...what then?"

Carter met his eyes levelly across the narrow table. "Well, I hoped to talk you into a mini-vacation. Maybe hit up Disneyland; Remi would like that. Or the beach. I want proper time with the two of you that doesn't involve timetables and crazy jobs. And after that, we figure out how to stay in the same area so we're not doing some crazy long-distance relationship."

Ari let out the breath he didn't realize he'd been holding. Yes. That was the answer he wanted. "Disneyland, huh. Rem's will love that. Sure, I can do Disneyland. And I've got at least one house in the same state as you, I think we can stick close."

Coming around the table, Carter slipped an arm around his waist, hugging him lightly. "I know you're a little nervous with this. I'm not used to dating, either, honestly. Last time I attempted it was a good three years ago. And I've never dated a single dad, so I might screw things up from time to time. I want to do this right, Ari. I like you. I like Remi. The more time I spend with you, the more I want to keep you both."

'Being kept' was such a strange concept, as he'd never really been kept before. His friendships and relationships with other people had been hit and miss until Remi. That had been the turning point, when he had someone constantly with him, day in, day out. Having Carter like that, on an everyday basis, sounded potentially amazing to Ari. He'd never put his faith in the future before. It wasn't until he'd taken in Remi he'd even planned very far into the future. It seemed folly to do so. *Wanting* a future was strange—a jittery feeling in the pit of his stomach. Nerves and hope battled it out and Ari wasn't sure which would win. What helped was Carter always putting his cards on the table. Ari never had to second guess his intentions. It created a path, something he could see, and surer footing of how to move forward with him. "I want more time with you. I know you'll have jobs, I will too. And we can't spend all of our time together—"

Carter shook his head. "If you take a job, I want to watch your back. It scares me you don't have backup with every job. Let's work together, sweetheart. Don't give bad luck a chance to get its foot in the door."

Oh. Yes. That was what was missing. Ari had never once had a dedicated partner for work. Kyou and Ivan were the closest he'd come. Remi had asked if he'd work with Kyou and Ivan from now on, but he'd not had the chance to really talk to them about it. And he did feel like he'd have to talk them into it. Carter saying this to him felt wildly different. The idea of always having support opened a door in his mind Ari hadn't realized had been nailed shut before this. It felt like Carter had just taken chains and ripped them off, freeing Ari to move. The longing of his inner child to have a dedicated protector practically beamed with satisfaction. Carter had fulfilled that wish perfectly. His voice came out husky as he answered. "I like that idea. You sure?"

"Really sure. I realize we're barely into dating but I'm not risking you. I won't risk you. Let me shield you, Ari. No one should go it alone."

Yes. All of that, yes. Ari hugged him tight, breathing the clean scent of the man in. Carter held him just as tightly, dropping a kiss against the side of his head. Ari's guard dropped completely for a moment and he relaxed utterly into Carter's arms. A feeling he knew, but normally associated with Remi, bubbled inside of him. The words left his mouth in a rush. "I want you safe and with me, Carter. I don't know exactly how to manage that. I've never tried before with anyone."

"We'll figure it out together, step by step. We don't have to have an answer right now," Carter breathed against his hair. His palm rubbed a soothing circle against the small of Ari's back. "I just needed to know if we're on the same page."

"We are. We stay together. We work together. We'll figure it out as we go." The words felt strange in his mouth but *right*, in a way very few things in his life had. The last time he'd been so sure, he'd adopted Remi. That alone said a lot. Maybe he should stop listening to his fears so much. His gut made better decisions.

"Daddy, do you—uh. Oops."

Ari pulled back enough to look towards the open doorway. Remi had stopped at the threshold, watching them with a sort of smug delight. It had done something to his daughter as well, seeing him with Carter. She seemed to settle more. "Hey, kiddo. Whatcha need?"

"Uncle Ivan was going to order in Thai," she reported, still grinning at them. "You want anything?"

"Yeah. We'll put in an order."

Carter released him enough to face Remi properly. "Remi, after the job is done, what do you say we go to Disneyland?"

Delight consumed her, Remi shining like a second sun rising. "REALLY?!"

"Yeah. I think we all deserve a vacation, don't you?" Carter grinned down at her. "I take it you're on board with this plan?"

"You bet!" She launched herself at him and hugged him tight around the waist.

Carter cradled the back of her head, his expression soft and affectionate. "And your dad and I, we decided to take jobs together from now on. You okay with that too?"

She propped her chin on his hip and looked up at him with that expression that reminded Ari too much of an adult. It was an odd look on a child's face, and hearkened back to the time when she'd had only herself to rely on. "I think that's good. You can watch out for each other. What about Uncle Kyou and Uncle Ivan, though?"

"Yeah, we'll talk to them properly about it, as well," Carter surprised him by saying. "I honestly don't know why the three of them aren't already an official team. I think they should be."

"Me too. See, Daddy, told you."

Ari spluttered, eyes bouncing between the two of them. Now wait a second, when had this become a done thing? Kyou didn't always take jobs that needed outside help. Neither did he or

Ivan. There wasn't a good reason to...well...his train of thought abruptly derailed as he remembered his relief and happiness of only a moment ago. If it felt like this to have Carter, a dedicated partner at his side, wouldn't it be even better to have two of his closest friends with him too?

Huh. Why hadn't he realized that earlier?

Carter watched him from the corner of his eye, his expression sardonic. "Just realized it, didn't you?"

"Shut it," Ari growled, already resigned to being teased about this for a while. "Assassins are lone wolves, alright?"

"You three are all lone wolves, but you best get over it. I want a team. And I like you."

"Is this something like being adopted by a cat?" Ari couldn't help but ask.

Carter grinned and shrugged, no denial on his lips. "Let's go put in our lunch order. I'll wrangle all three of you into agreeing to my master plan later."

Somehow, Ari didn't doubt that he'd get his way.

23

CARTER

Tomorrow was the day. They'd spent the whole day prepping, and it was late into the night now. Whatever hadn't been done would be either taken care of early in the morning or left undone. They were flat out of time.

Everyone had unanimously agreed to turn in and get some good sleep. They'd need it. Carter had seen too many jobs go bust because the team hadn't been rested. Sleep-deprived people weren't as quick to react and they made stupid decisions. He was glad to see these three had better sense than that. Kyou actually took Nyquil to make sure he slept soundly.

Carter still felt a little too tense from all that had happened today and chose to take a shower, see if that helped relax him any. It wasn't just the job tomorrow, of acting well ahead of schedule, that had him wound up in knots. It was also the emotional impact of baring what he wanted to Ari. He'd been walking something of an emotional tightrope ever since he'd met the man, and while it was worth every second of effort, it had taken something of a toll on him. Like yesterday. Carter felt like he'd been pushing his luck, laying everything out now. But he'd also been afraid of losing his connection to Ari once the job ended.

It seemed, though, what held Ari back from him was uncertainty. He'd needed to know exactly where he stood with Carter. He'd been much more relaxed with Carter after their mutual decision to stay together. Hell, if he'd known that was all the man needed, Carter would have said something well before now.

Ari had been adrift most of his life. Some of what he'd told Carter gave him that impression, at least. If he was to make any headway, have any prayer of keeping him, Carter had to make sure Ari knew he'd catch him. He was the safety net. He'd not let Ari fall.

This was something he'd need to think about more carefully, but not tonight. He didn't have the brainpower, honestly, not after a full day of planning. And the shower was meant for him to relax, start powering his brain off so he could sleep. If the shower didn't work, he'd borrow a page from Kyou's book and down some Nyquil.

With a bone deep groan of pleasure, Carter stepped under the spray. The heat and force of the water acted like a mini massage and he turned his head this way and that, letting it beat against the back of his neck for a minute. Ah, better. Reaching for the body wash, he soaped himself copiously and then leaned his shoulder against the cool tile as the water sluiced him clean. His eyes drifted shut as he relaxed fully. A slight displacement of air stirred through the moist heat and his head came up partially. Air conditioning or something else?

Something soft and fabric hit the tile floor and Carter's dulled senses kicked back into life. Turning, he regarded the shower curtain and the figure that he could see through it. Oh. Oh, really? He'd never in a million years expected Ari to ambush him in the shower.

The shower curtain drew back with a hiss and cooler air flooded the shower. Ari stood there uncertainly, not a stitch of clothing on him. What a truly, lovely sight. So that golden, sun-kissed skin was completely natural, huh? Carter's libido perked up and took notice. Nudity clearly didn't phase the man, as Ari wasn't exhibiting any signs of shying away from Carter's eyes as he was swept from head to toe. But something about his body language suggested vulnerability. He hung back, one arm wrapped around his waist, like Ari wasn't clear if he was welcome or not.

Silly man. Carter smiled and held out a hand. "Join me?"

Those wide shoulders relaxed as Ari stepped in, pulling the curtain back in place behind him. He wasn't shy about getting his own eyeful of Carter either as he came in closer, lips parted, dark brown eyes going black with hunger.

"I wanted some time with you," Ari confessed lowly, hands coming up to cage Carter's hips. "Hard to arrange with a curious eight-year-old in the house."

"You can join me in the shower anytime, hon," Carter assured him huskily. He let himself be maneuvered backwards, Ari crowding him in against the tile. Carter groaned low in his throat and pressed into that warm body, Ari rapidly becoming slick from the spray of water.

Ari lifted up a little on his toes, tilting his head to close the two inches of height between them, and his hot tongue teased over Carter's lips, demanding entrance. Carter gave it with another groan, enjoying the kiss immensely. It was heady to be skin to skin like this with him, for once nothing barring the way, and Carter let his hands roam free. Ari's cock stiffened against his own, and he smirked a little. He wasn't the only one enjoying this. Carter slid his hands down to the small of Ari's back, encouraging the man to rub up against him, and Ari did in small circles. Damn, that was good.

Pulling away, Ari's mouth trailed down towards his neck, nosing the short hairs at the nape of Carter's neck. He took the muscle between his teeth. Carter whined low in his throat and pushed into the contact, unable to repress a shiver. Oh yeah. He was more than ready to rumble now.

Ari groaned his name and licked where he'd bitten. Pain and pleasure signals sang along Carter's nerves and he shuddered again. He did like it a bit rough, to be honest. Ari rumbled and pulled back, sinking down onto his knees. Carter stared down at him, a little surprised. He hadn't expected Ari to take the more vulnerable position, not this soon. Sure, he'd relaxed his guard considerably after sex the other night, but he'd not thought it was *this* much. He'd really hit the right button in the man, hadn't he?

Ari looked up at him under his lashes and Carter damn near came from that expression alone. It spoke of all hunger.

Tracing a thumb over Ari's bottom lip, Carter husked,

"That's damn sexy, that look on your face."

Ari's pink tongue flicked out at Carter's thumb, teasingly. Then he leaned in, using that mobile tongue to catch Carter's cock and draw it into his mouth.

Oh god. His knees might not hold him.

Ari's hair was like a slick, black oil spill against his head. It gleamed in the light the way only deep ink black hair could. He looked sleek and sharper, somehow, and Carter's thumbs traced along his cheekbones in a loving sweep, hands trailing down to palm the sides of Ari's neck. He kept the touch carefully light, a caress. Not a threat. Ari hummed at him and took his cock deeper, tongue laving along the underside in a hot rasp.

Carter's eyes nearly rolled into the back of his head as he fought the urge to thrust. His breath became sharper, shorter, as a spiral of pleasure tightened his gut. He absolutely wouldn't last long. The combination of sight and sensation was undoing him, and he couldn't even regret it.

Even as the thought crossed his mind, he had only a moment to squeeze Ari's neck once in warning before orgasm ripped through him. His head nearly slammed into the tile as his vision whited out as pleasure took over.

Holy shit.

Carter's legs felt shaky. He honestly didn't know if Ari had swallowed or not, that was how out of it he was for a second. Ari pressed a kiss against the inside of his thigh before slowly standing. There was a smugness to him now, feline somehow. Carter had to taste that smirk. There was a trace of bitterness, which answered the question—he had swallowed. Well, hell. Carter hadn't expected that either.

"You going to let me return the favor?" Carter murmured against his mouth.

"Please," Ari breathed in return.

The man was as hard as a rock against him. Carter hadn't expected a different answer. Still, polite to ask. The question was the mechanics, because putting Ari's back against a wall was just—no. Bad idea. Ari was currently relaxed, but they weren't over that instinctive reaction yet. He knelt where he was instead so that Ari could lean over him and brace his hands against the wall. Trailing kisses along Ari's abdomen, he found a few thin scars but he ignored them for now. Following the happy trail down, he stumbled across at least one ticklish spot that had the man squirming and laughing, which pleased Carter. Sex should be fun, dammit. Not stressful. If he could have Ari laughing, that was for the best.

The tub wasn't quite wide enough for him to do this comfortably, his knees pressed against the walls, but he ignored that for now. Ari had done the same, after all; only fair. Ari's palms slapped the wet tile and Carter wished he could bottle and drink the noises pouring out of Ari's mouth.

Carter focused on mapping Ari's cock with his tongue. It was an unhurried exploration—firm, slow suction and wet licks. Ari didn't try to rush him, although he whined a few times, clearly fighting the urge to pump and speed things along. Carter tightened his grip on both hips. He had an idea in mind, and it wouldn't work if Ari rushed him. Carter relaxed his throat and concentrated on physical sensation of the stretch and burn. Gradually, he was able to take more of Ari inside; not a full-on deepthroat, but damn close.

Ari shuddered from head to toe, making the most pained and breathy noises above him. Carter gave him a smack on the ass in encouragement to have at it. Ari didn't need to be told twice. He fucked Carter's face with enthusiasm, one hand dropping down to cradle the back of his head as he grunted in pleasure. Carter fought to keep his gag reflex dormant and let his mouth be used. Bit of a challenge—he hadn't done this in a while—but worth it for Ari's obvious pleasure.

"Ca-Carter," Ari gasped in warning, his name strangled and barely discernable.

Carter knew already. He could feel it in the way Ari's balls had tightened and drawn up. Ari pulsed down his throat and Carter swallowed, or did his best to, coughing when the volume exceeded his ability. Ari slumped against the wall as he came down, panting for breath.

Carter needed a moment himself. He shifted to give his knees a break but otherwise let his head rest against Ari's thigh, re-learning how to breathe. His throat felt like he'd swallowed a sword. Maybe an ostrich egg. He didn't care. It was a distinct pleasure bringing Ari over the edge like that, and he'd do it again in a heartbeat.

Questing fingers came down and stroked through his hair. Carter turned his head enough to kiss them before turning his face up and sharing a smile with Ari as if passing along a naughty secret.

"Tonight," Ari started, only to falter and stare at him another moment, as if he wasn't sure of something.

"Tonight?" Carter prompted encouragingly.

Ari swallowed visibly before he tried again. "Tonight, I want to try sleeping next to you."

Carter tried to tamp down an insane urge to crow, but there was no disguising his smile. "You can. And if you're not able to sleep, it's fine if you retreat to your own bed."

Those agile fingers kept stroking through his hair. "It took me months of being around Ivan and Kyou before I could relax with them in my personal space. Remi was never a problem. But she's a kid, so that just makes sense. It's weird with you. My instincts are all mixed up. But most of the time, I feel as safe with you as I would with Remi."

The openness of that confession was hard won—Carter could see that clearly. He tried to respond in kind, to reward his lover who was trying so hard to reach him. "I want you to feel safe with me. I know it's rare in this line of work—I've never had partners like yours. I've had some jobs where I only slept in cat naps because I couldn't trust the men I was with long enough to really hit a REM cycle. I get it, Ari, I do. You don't need to push yourself to the straining point. I can wait for you."

Ari shook his head, jaw set in a line of determination. "I don't want to wait. I'm still jittery sometimes, I can't help that, but I don't want to wait. I want to know what it's like to sleep next to you."

God, this man was going to just ruin him. Absolutely ruin him. Carter felt like he would either crack and say something he shouldn't or latch onto him like a koala bear for the rest of the night. In desperation, he fell to teasing instead. "Well, to start with, I snore—"

He got a solid flick of the fingers against his forehead for that.

Chuckling, Carter pressed a kiss against the warm skin

under his cheek. "Come on. Water heater's about had it. We're lukewarm right now. Let's get dry and in clothes. We do need to catch some shuteye."

"Okay." Ari helped him up to his feet and then leaned in to kiss him, affectionate and gentle. "Quanto sei bello amore mio."

"That," Carter murmured against his mouth, "did not encourage me to go to sleep."

Ari laughed softly, a gentle puff of air, and pulled him out of the shower. "More sex later, caro. We've got a painting to steal."

"Steal back," Carter corrected, accepting the towel Ari handed him. "Important distinction. It's not stealing if you're stealing it back."

24

ARI

Ari might have been a touch nervous as he put on the security uniform. Nerves were actually good. Confidence could kill a person faster than anything else on jobs like this. But a touch of nerves kept a person alert. He didn't try to give himself a pep talk out of them.

Last night had been an interesting mix of success and failure. Oral sex was a rousing success, but after about an hour of lying next to Carter, he'd reluctantly reached the conclusion he wouldn't be able to sleep. And he needed the sleep. Ari hadn't shared a bed with anyone in...well...since Remi first came to stay with him. Months. And even then, he'd not gotten used to it. Before her, the only other person to share a bed with him was Luca. And they'd been kids. For once, his overactive survival instincts weren't the ones throwing up alarms and causing trouble. He just needed time to adjust to having someone in the bed with him. Ari was actually pleased by this. It showed progress on his part. Once they were through the job, he'd have time to slowly get used to having Carter under the covers with him.

Speaking of his brother, he'd promised to text Luca a head's up when they were going in. Just so he'd be on the lookout for Remi and not caught off-guard, if she had to go to him. He snagged his phone from the nightstand and typed a quick text, then tossed it back onto the bed. Let's see, ID on the lanyard, black shoes, no tie with this outfit, thank god—

The phone rang. He stared down at the screen with a sense of inevitability. Yeah, that figured. Picking it up, he answered with a resigned sigh, "Yeah, Luca."

"What the hell do you mean, going in? I thought this was days away."

"Timeline got moved up on us."

"Shit. So, in other words, you're rushed going into this. Are you going to be okay? Wouldn't it be better to just pull the plug?"

"We will if it starts looking bad. I think we can do it, though."

"You're seriously bad for my ulcer, you know that?"

"You don't have an ulcer."

"I do now and it has your name on it. Okay, so...is this an all day thing?"

"Only if things go very, very wrong. More like a morning thing. I'll call you again when we're out."

"Yeah, okay. I'll just be sitting here, chewing what's left of my nails."

His brother really was a worrywart. It's why Ari didn't tell him a lot. If Luca had any idea of everything he got into, he'd have keeled over from cardiac arrest by now. "Luca. Look, this doesn't go past you, okay?"

Sounding suspicious, his brother agreed slowly, "*Okay...*"

"I told you before that I'm not doing this alone, right? But this time we've got a new guy, a mercenary."

"Wait, you've got Remi with you. You trust this guy around your daughter?"

"He's one hundred percent trustworthy. No issue there." It was too good of a segue to pass up while he had his brother on the phone. "And, um...."

"Oh god, what else?"

"No, this is a good thing," Ari hastily reassured him. "He's my boyfriend."

Dead silence.

"Luca? You still with me?"

"Boyfriend. Seriously? You're not pulling my leg, are you?"

"Carter is his name." Ari felt a little shy telling his brother about all this, and he almost ruffled the back of his head before thinking better of the gesture. He'd have to fix his hair again before going back down. "We're planning to take Remi to Disneyland after this, and he's got a house too in Cali, so...after this, want to meet up? He's the nicest guy ever, Luca. I think you'd really like him."

"Wait. Just back up a sec. You're telling me you not only trust this man enough to date him—which is huge for you—but you trust him with both me AND Remi?"

"Yeah."

Luca made strangled duck squawking noises for a second.

"Want to meet him?" Ari reiterated, amused now.

"Hell yes, I want to meet him."

"Then plan on it. I gotta go, I'm running out of time. But I'll call you later, okay?"

"You bet your ass you will. And Ari—good luck."

"Thanks, bro." Ari hung up and released a huge breath. Wow, that conversation had gone better than he'd feared. And it felt good to be able to tell his brother happy news for once. So often their conversations were just tension and worry.

Ari slipped the phone into his pocket and finished getting ready. After a final check on his person, he deemed himself good and left the room. He made his way downstairs to find Remi already up. She was in her Batman pajamas still, hair a messy halo around her head, and a perfect match for Kyou who was in the same state. (Sans the Batman pajamas.) They were both ensconced in their respective computer chairs, hands on keyboards and mice, talking in computer gibberish. Already at work?

Coming over, he put a kiss on the top of Remi's head. "Hey, gattina. You're up early."

"Uncle Kyou woke me up an hour ago," she answered, flashing him a quick smile before she went back to focusing on the screens. "There was too much to do by himself."

That didn't sound promising. "Kyou? Did you sleep at all?"

"About five hours. It's all good, we're almost there. By the time you three get into position, we'll be able to cover you. One thing—" Kyou paused and craned his neck to look behind him. "Ah, good, there you two are. Ivan, Carter, I found something good this morning. The original blueprints to the vault."

All three men leaned over Kyou's shoulders as he pulled up the blueprints on the middle monitor so that they could see it. "It looks like we actually have three levels to contend with—you've got the top story, the one we can see, then two basement levels. The elevator inside is plenty wide for any cargo, but the stairs are not."

"Elevator," Ivan repeated in disgust.

"Kill box, more like it." Carter sounded just as disgusted. "You really think stairs are a no-go?"

"You'll have to carry the painting upright, not horizontal to use the stairs." Kyou shrugged, indicating that was their call to make. "It'll be awkward and slow you down."

Carter caught Ari's eye, silently asking which way he preferred to go. Ari's gut said stairs, but it might be better to make that call when they were on site and got a better idea of what they were dealing with.

"I've also pulled up traffic patterns over the past two weeks. Looks like we have two windows where the traffic tapers off enough that its feasible to get in and out quickly. From 9:30 to about 11:00, then again from 2:00-3:00. Which window do you guys want to hit?"

"Morning," Ivan stated without a second of hesitation. "If we need to do a false start, we can pull back and try again this afternoon."

Ari nodded in agreement. "If you're ready? You don't need a few more hours?"

Kyou groaned, rubbing fingers against both temples. "I need a few more days. But I think Rems and I have the basics down. You three just need to be your sterling professional selves and do the rest."

It was a bit tight and Ari could admit to himself, privately, that he didn't like jumping into this without more prep. But on the other hand, he hated having to follow an armored truck to an unknown destination, where he'd have to start from scratch all over again to break into yet another secure storage facility. They just didn't have that kind of time, to chase something across the country. Assuming it stayed in country. He caught Ivan's eye, then Carter's, silently confirming with them. Both men nodded back. Yes, still a go.

"We're crazy," Carter sighed, but an excited grin spread across his face. "Let's do it. We don't have a lot of time. Skip breakfast?"

"I demand coffee," Ari declared as he moved towards the kitchen. "But otherwise, fine. We don't have time to cook or go grab something."

"I don't like stealing on an empty stomach," Ivan complained, but he readily followed Ari into the kitchen.

"You can have my Lucky Charms!" Remi called to both of them.

There were worse things to eat than sugar and coffee. Ari shrugged and hunted up the box. As he poured cereal into bowls, Carter came in close, mouth brushing near his ear.

"Was it too much last night?"

Ari shook his head minutely and shot the man a reassuring smile. "Actually, it was fine. I just couldn't settle enough to sleep."

Relief stole over Carter's face. "Okay. Try again tonight?"

"Yeah. I just need to get used to it."

Ivan stole up on his other side and whispered, "Get used to what?"

Planting a hand on his face, Ari shoved him off. Ivan sniggered like the irreverent child he actually was. "Aww, come on, share with the class."

Ari shot him the bird before pushing a bowl into his chest. "Eat your breakfast and stop being a pain in the ass."

Of course, Ivan smirked even as he did as told, and Ari had no doubt he'd bring it up again later. Just wait until Carter unleashed his plan to make them an official team—THAT would wipe that smirk off his face. Ivan was by nature even more lone wolf than Ari was.

Well. Maybe not. He'd certainly paused his life quickly enough when Ari needed help with Remi. Maybe he was a lone wolf by chance more than design. That was food for thought. Thoughts for later, as he really had no time for it now.

Remi turned her head and called over her shoulder, "But we still need a code name for Carter!"

Ari had been thinking about this for a few days now, and he had the perfect suggestion. "Smiley."

That salt and peppered head came up as Carter gave him a 'why the hell that?' sort of look.

"Because he's always smiling," Ari added, grinning at his boyfriend.

Ivan held up a hand. "Seconded."

"Thirded!" Kyou said in agreement.

"Motion carried!" the eight-year-old declared.

Carter just sighed. "I thought I got rid of mandatory call signs when I left the military."

"Nope. No such luck." Ari kissed him to soften the blow although he could tell that Carter was actually pleased.

Ari checked and double checked that they had the print of the painting to switch out, the employee IDs, the fake work cases full of their own equipment. They helped each other paste on the replica fingerprints, making sure they all stuck on firmly. The prints would have to hold up to a lot of tote and carry. This wasn't going to be an easy case of striding in, switching out paintings, and striding back out. For one thing, no security guard worth their salt would just let them take a portfolio case into the vault. They'd have no good reason to have it. It would look odd from any perspective. They had to somehow find the right timing to slip the portfolio in while distracting the guards at the vault. While also finding the right time to connect Kyou to the vault's cameras so he could loop it and cover the switch.

He'd swear, but he couldn't think of any words strong enough.

Kyou flicked a finger at him, beckoning him over, and Ari once again leaned over the back of their chairs. Kyou handed him a small USB drive, barely bigger than his thumbnail. "Wireless bridge. Plug it into the back of the camera and give me five minutes. We'll be set."

"You want me to bullshit my way through measuring for hardware for five minutes?"

Kyou patted him on the arm. "You're charming. You'll be fine."

Ari debated strangling him. Naw, he'd glue the keys together later on his keyboard. That always got Kyou in a tizzy. Pocketing the gadget, he went back to doing the last-minute things. It was already 8:30. Best to get rolling soon.

Because Ivan needed to be in a different position, across the street and on top of a taller building, he left ahead of them. It left Kyou and Remi with the choice of three cars, but in their case, it was better to hoof it for the metro system anyway. They could get lost in the subway far easier than trying to cut through traffic. Carter ended up driving the security van, Ari in the SUV, and of course they all had their ear buds in.

They slipped through traffic, and while it wasn't light, it was definitely better than sanity-destroying, bumper to bumper nonsense. They briefly went out of their way to a back alley Kyou had control over, parking the SUV as their getaway vehicle. Ari switched to the van and Carter turned them around, retracing their route a little. The familiar zing of adrenaline coursed through Ari's veins as they got closer to their destination. Some people thought him crazy, but he liked the challenge jobs like this brought him. They were more complicated than getting line of sight on a target and pulling a trigger, sure, but that was half the fun.

This job had been far more fun than any other, and he knew why. Despite all of the rushes, the setbacks, the insanity of the deadline, Ari hadn't felt nearly as stressed as he should have. Having such amazing support on his side made all the difference. Maybe Carter had a point about the whole team thing. He could get on board with this plan.

Carter stopped at a red light, and Ari couldn't resist the impulse to lean over and kiss him lightly. Blinking, Carter gave him a warm smile in return and that smile did funny things in Ari's chest. Carter was handsome enough when he stood there breathing, but smiling? Ari had no defenses for that smile.

"Was that a kiss for luck?" Carter teased him.

"If we're going to do that, I think it should be a proper kiss."

"*I think we need a new rule,*" Kyou interrupted, tone beyond exasperated. "*No kissing on the job. Especially not when you're on comms. You've got innocent ears listening in, remember?*"

"*But I like it when they kiss,*" Remi objected.

Carter sniggered and Ari outright howled laughing. "You're overruled, K!"

The hacker grumbled out a curse not precisely something he should say in front of a child.

"*Just drive,*" Kyou groused.

Ivan chuckled into the comms but didn't say anything.

At the next turn, Knowles came into sight. Ari forced his head into the game and took in a deep breath, held it, then released in a steady stream. Alright, show time. This job meant more than the two million and change he'd collect. It meant a possible future with the sexy man at his side. And Remi. And Ari would do just about anything for that.

"Showtime," Carter murmured. "Eidolon, how are you?"

"*In position, drone is flying overhead. I've got you in sight.*"

"Copy that."

Carter turned onto the short drive in front of the tall metal gates and stopped, rolling his window down and aiming a friendly smile at the guard already strolling up to the van. "Hey. We're Wilson and Miller from Assured Security. We're here to do measuring in some place called the Vault?"

The guard gave him a nod and used the walky-talky strapped to his shoulder. "Assured Security to do measuring in the vault?"

A scratchy voice responded, "*Yeah, they're on schedule, let them in.*"

Bless you, Kyou. Having them on the list was always so much easier than charming his way through. Carter gave the guard another smile and rolled up the window as the big gates slid to either side. They rolled on through, following the pavement around the house, past the parking lot in the back, and to the vault itself.

It really didn't look like much. It had all the grace and elegance of a cardboard box, actually. Flat roof, straight sides, and unadorned cement walls. Ari had seen bunkers with more imagination than this. The cameras on all corners left no blind spots on the outside, and the two guards standing outside the main door struck him as the humorless sort. Ari shared a glance with Carter, the man almost eerily calm.

"Going in," Carter murmured just under his breath. He parked directly in front of the door, as there was no other place to stop. They snagged the toolboxes and small step ladder through the side door, leaving the portfolio tucked out of sight for now. The guards were watching them too closely to sneak that in just yet.

Slamming the door closed, Ari got his pleasant face on, the one no one really looked twice at. As they strolled toward the door, Carter waved to the guards in greeting. "Hey, guys. Need to do some measuring inside."

"ID," one of the guards responded, sounding bored to tears.

They raised the badges clipped to their breast pockets. The guards barely gave them more than a glance, just checking that photo matched face before moving on. One of them swiped the door open with a keycard and they slipped through with ease.

"Two guards outside, confirmed," Ari murmured as they entered the air-conditioned building. "And damn, it's freezing in here. What do they have the aircon set at, arctic?"

"It's all of the books and parchment that they have inside," Ivan answered. *"Have to keep that climate controlled."*

"I think they're trying to preserve stuff by freezing it solid."

"You've got another guard making the rounds inside the vault right now. I think he's there to watch you two," Kyou pitched in. *"Get me access to a camera."*

"Yeah, yeah." Ari looked around the room, getting his bearings of the top floor. Art hung in a uniform line along the walls, all of it priceless beyond measure. Eight different glass cases protected different statues and one open book. It looked like an art gallery, only with more security. And cement walls. If not for the art, it would look like a prison in here.

As they entered, the elevator dinged and a new guard stepped through. This one looked a little older than the guys outside, with more of a beer gut and a relaxed air, as if he'd seen it all at least once. "Hey, you guys from Assured?"

"That's us," Carter lied glibly. "Did they tell you why we're here?"

"Measuring for the new hardware, they said. Although I thought someone already did that a few weeks ago."

"Yeah, they did," Carter agreed with an easy shrug. No skin off his nose, that was what his body language relayed. "And then they came out with the latest and greatest cameras that can do even more fancy shit. You know how it goes."

"Anything running is obsolete in the tech world," the guard agreed with an answering grunt. "So you're measuring for the newest stuff, gotcha. Alright, well, I have to follow you around."

"No problem, man. We'll need you to tell us where the breaker is and all that anyway. Let's see..." Carter made a show of looking around. "There's our first camera. Miller, you want to measure that one?"

"Sure." Ari undid the small, folding step stool he had with him and set it under the camera. He popped up with a measuring tape and made a show of measuring from the ceiling to the mount, then from the wall to the base of the camera already there. As he did so, he plugged in the pocketed USB port. "Four inches down, six inches flush."

"Huh. I think that's going to be a tight fit." Carter scratched at his chin, frowning up at the camera as if he really were thinking about camera adjustments. "You got a three prong or two prong outlet up there?"

"Three." Ari mentally applauded his bullshit ability. He'd not be able to think of ways to keep this going, not like Carter was doing. Did he even know how to install security cameras? "I don't know, man, I think we might need to change where the cameras are mounted."

"Yeah, looks that way." To the hovering guard, Carter explained, "New ones aren't as bulky as the old ones, but they're motion-sensor rigged. They'll follow whatever's moving, so we have to give them room to turn, otherwise they'll smack up against the wall. Or tear something by rubbing against it."

"Motion sensor cameras, huh. I've heard of motion sensors, but I didn't realize you could have cameras that actually tracked movement."

Carter nodded. "They've been in the works for a while. But it's only recently they've worked out all the kinks. Do you know if all the cameras are mounted the same way?"

"I think they are."

"Hmm, we better measure them all and double check."

Ari approved of this plan. That was a great way to buy them some time. Not to mention, it would be the perfect excuse to get them into the lower levels. Their painting wasn't on this one, so it had to be on the second or third level.

As they went to the next camera, ostensibly measuring it, the guard asked, "So what makes this one more spiffy, aside from the motion sensor tracking?"

Kyou supplied the answer smoothly: *"Tell him it's got an advanced 1080 sensor with 100 degree viewing angles and a low-lux sensor."*

Carter repeated the information calmly and added, "That and it's in a vandal-proof bracket. This model's good for indoor and outdoor, too. No need for two different types of camera."

"Yeah, perfect," Kyou approved.

"Okay, we're good on this level. Let's go down to the second level."

The guard, of course, wouldn't just go along with this. "But they're all set the same way for each level. You don't need to measure them all."

"Vandal dome," Kyou suggested, the words accompanied by a rapid-fire clack of keys.

"We want to measure to see if there's a possibility of installing a vandal dome," Ari offered, folding the stepstool. "Cut down on the number of cameras the security guards have to keep track of. It's not possible on this floor, you've got too many blind spots. What's on the other two levels? More statues and glass cases like these?"

The guard led them toward the elevator. "Well, some, not as much on the second floor. There's a flatter case on the third level. You think a vandal dome could cover the whole distance?"

"I mean, maybe? Our latest is also a 1080p and it's got a really crisp image."

The elevator was definitely meant for cargo. It had the width for it. They went down to the next floor and Ari tried not to crawl out of his skin. Elevators and he were not friends. He'd been stuck in an elevator too many times with bad outcomes to like taking one.

With a ding, the doors opened and he thankfully stepped out of it, looking around. Of course the painting wasn't on this level either. But it still answered the question of where it was— it must be on the third level. As long as he knew which level it was at, they could move.

Catching Carter's eye, they exchanged subtle nods.

Time to go.

"Eidolon," Ari murmured under his breath. "Go."

25

CARTER

Carter made a show of looking the ceiling over. "Miller, you got your wall scanner on you?"

"Shit, I think it's in the other tool box," Ari responded, going with their pre-planned signal. "I'll run up and get it."

He hated taking the elevator back up, but had to in order to look normal to the guard. As soon as the doors closed, he asked, "We good out there?"

"*Guards are not happy about the drone but not moving yet,*" Ivan reported, sounding irritated. "*I'll draw them out in a second, but you might need to make a show of checking for that scanner.*"

"Copy that. K, Widow?"

Kyou snarled out, "*We might have a situation. Some tech came in to do an inspection of the computer. He's decided to install an update and reboot the system.*"

That sounded potentially bad. "Uh, and what happens when he does that?"

"*The system checks all hardware for anomalies, and the bridges you and Eidolon put on the cameras get detected. I'm trying to hack his BIOS and give him a false reboot but I'm fighting against time. Be prepared to come out hot.*"

Well, shit. "I can unplug the boggle on the top floor camera real fast?"

There was a ruminative pause. "*That...might help. That*

way the main house is flagged and you guys look fine. But that means I'll have to start from scratch on the cameras in the vault. You'll be exposed for five minutes.

Not ideal, then. Dammit.

"Uncle K, I can get the cameras back. I watched how you did it."

Another digestive silence. The elevator doors chimed as they opened and Ari stepped through, although he wasn't sure now what to do. Go fetch the portfolio and switch out the paintings? Wait and see if he had to mess with the camera? Did Remi really have the skills to do this, or did she just think she did?

"You sure, Widow?"

"Do not doubt my solnishko," Ivan scolded.

Kyou sighed gustily. *"No harm in trying. Alright, Malvagio, pull that thing and pocket it for a minute. Widow, you'll need to be quick. When I say go, you'll have to react immediately."*

It wasn't dignified, but Ari hopped up lightly and snagged the boggle from the back of the camera, much like a child hopping up to reach something on a higher shelf. It took him two tries to fully get it out—which left the question of what he'd do to get it back in—but he had it. Pocketing it, he opened the door and gave the guards a laconic wave. "Forgot something."

They grunted and let him pass without challenge.

As Ari put his head into the van, pretending to search for the right tool, he listened to Kyou and Remi discuss what to do next. It was mostly Kyou teaching Remi what to do, double-checking she had it down, which...she did. Ari knew his daughter was smart. After six months with her, that had been obvious. But she only needed the one time of watching Kyou do something in order to have it down?

His chest puffed with pride. His little tech genius. He'd give her the biggest hug when they were done.

The buzz of a drone overhead came in closer, louder, and he ducked out to see the drone come in so close it nearly clipped the roof of the building. The two guards shouted and waved at it, then one of them got the bright idea to pull a gun and try shooting at it. Ivan was quick to jerk it upwards, throwing off the guard's aim. He could hear the Russian thief cackling as he zig-zagged the drone away and the guards chased after it.

Ari wasted no time in snagging both the portfolio and the tool and darting back into the building. He sprinted down the stairs, taking two at a time, and slapped his hand against the door, throwing it open as he reached the bottom level. His breath came a little sharp and quick as he worked, part adrenaline, part exertion.

Where was it? His eyes frantically bounced from wall to wall until he found the painting he wanted, hanging innocuously next to the elevator doors. He went for it, pulling it as quickly as he dared off the wall, spinning it around so that he could pull the painting from the frame. It was critical they left the frame as it was, to not make the observer question whether the painting was legit or not.

"*Shit, shit, shit. Of course he has more than one fucking update to install. Malvagio, ETA?*"

"I've got the painting free of the frame. One more minute."

"*You've got thirty seconds. I've stalled the reboot but—damn him, he just overrode the reboot. What the hell is this idiot doing, he risks corrupting his .exe file if he does that. Where did he get his certification, a cereal box?*"

Ari didn't let Kyou's chatter distract him, or the casual chitchat Carter engaged in with the guard upstairs, or anything else. He moved with smooth efficiency as he put the fake painting in, re-hung the frame, and made sure it was level. Then he slipped the real painting into the portfolio and rushed back into the stairwell.

"*System rebooted,*" Kyou reported in aggravation. "*Because he's a fucking moron and he did a hard reboot. System is now scanning. Eidolon?*"

"*I'm ok—chert. Zasranets just shot my drone.*"

Ari paused with his hand on the door. He was at the top of the stairs but wasn't sure if he could exit. There was no camera in the stairwell, but that was the only part of the building not covered. "Can I go out or not?"

"*Not,*" Remi answered firmly. "*I don't have the cameras back yet. You're exposed, Malvagio.*"

"Okay, I can't leave Smiley alone much longer. I'll leave the portfolio in the stairwell, try to get the boggle back in and rejoin him. Eidolon, are the guards back at the door?"

"*Da. But it's okay, I will save other drone for when you need back out.*"

"Okay, copy that." Ari felt the tension ratchet up several notches. It wasn't good, none of this was going to plan. The only thing going for them at the moment was that their cover wasn't blown, and he'd gotten the painting switched out. They were on the last leg, but could they make it?

He exited out of the stairwell and went back to the elevator, because he had to come back the way he'd left. Pushing the down button, he tried to think of a good way to get the painting from stairwell to vehicle. Nothing immediately leapt to mind. Maybe they could split again under some pretext? Have Carter finish the transfer?

Ari had maybe another thirty seconds of privacy to speak freely. He rode the elevator down and tried not to fidget. "K, status?"

"*I'm still trying to wrestle control of the system back. That update reset the—*" Kyou broke off in a long string of swear words. "*Of all the stupid things to do. He just unplugged the computer! Can I kill him? I want to kill him.*"

"*Why did he do that?*" Remi asked, equally puzzled and aghast.

"*I couldn't hear what he was saying over the cameras, no audio. But he seemed to realize we'd hacked the cameras and got all excited about it. Of course he fucking just shuts everything down and unplugs it instead of TRACING A LIVE SIGNAL LIKE A NORMAL PERSON.*"

The rant would have been funny if Ari's nerves weren't singing with tension. He'd likely get a good laugh about this later. Assuming they survived until later. "So can Widow get the cameras back or not?"

"*Not until he turns the computers back on. And we're of course blind, I can't see a damn thing now. He probably won't turn anything back on until he's found that compromised camera.*"

Ari'd had a feeling that was the answer.

The elevator doors opened and cut off any possibility of him replying. He went through, waggling the device in his hand as he did so. "Found it. But there's something crazy going on up there. A drone is flying around and almost ramming into the buildings."

"Yeah, we've heard about it," the guard said while tapping his walky-talky. "Looks like someone managed to shoot it down, though."

"Oh, they got it? Cool. I wonder who thought it was a good idea to fly a drone over here, though."

"Likely some kid," Carter responded, playing along. "Okay, let's hop up and do that measurement."

Ari played along, running the device along the ceiling, supposedly looking for an electric wire they could tap into and create a plug for the camera. Carter started talking about how they would need to run a new line, as it didn't look like anything was in the right area, chattering like he actually knew something about wiring and electricity. Maybe he did. There were a lot of things Ari didn't know about the man yet.

While drawing the device along the ceiling, Ari was able to get close to one of the cameras and slip the boggle back in, at least. If that idiot at the main house ever turned the computers back on, at least Remi and Kyou would have a chance to get the cameras back.

"Computers are back on, thank fuck. Widow?"

"On it," she said confidently. *"Uncle K, I need—"*

"Way ahead of you, Widow. In three, two, one, go. Eidolon, in about thirty seconds, we need you to make with the distraction."

Ivan didn't respond. Just cackled like the demented soul he was.

Trying to keep this going, Ari dropped back down on his heels and went to 'confer' with Carter. "I don't know, what do you think? These are concrete ceilings, that's not going to be fun to drill through in order to run a new line. I know they wanted to consolidate cameras if they could, but..."

"Yeah, not really cost effective. And it's going to stir up a lot of dust, which—" Carter broke off and looked around in an exaggerated way. "Considering how pricey all of this art is? I don't recommend. What do you think, Bob?"

"I'm with you on this one. No matter how carefully you

wrap stuff, dust gets places it's not supposed to. But you'll stir up dust by doing the new mounts too, won't you?"

"Yeah, it's a problem."

"*Guards are chasing my drone again,*" Ivan reported happily. "*Whoa, almost got me there. Come on, come on, durak. Make my day.*"

The walky-talky went live again, the voice a snarl of frustration. "*That idiot with the drone is back with another one.*"

Bob the Guard groaned, his head flopping forward. "This has been such a day, let me tell you. Guys, I don't know if you can finish. I might need to get out there and help. Can you come back later?"

"Sure," Carter said equably. "We'll just grab our gear. Call us when the drone invasion is over."

"We'll do that."

"*Widow needs another two minutes with the cameras. She's got all of the main level of the vault, for the interior. Working on the exterior. Whistle if you need more than the main level.*"

Ari didn't think they would. He'd already gotten the painting up to the top level, after all. Their job was done in that sense.

Hefting the tool box and step ladder, Carter said pointedly, "Okay, we're good. Let's load up. Sorry you're having such trouble today, Bob. It normally like this?"

"Naw, it's normally pretty quiet," Bob answered as he pushed the button for the elevator. "Unless they've got some grand party going on."

They stepped into the elevator as if nothing was really wrong. Ari felt an itching in the base of his spine. It was always hard keeping calm when he could see the home stretch. But he wasn't going to blow this by being antsy. How they would get the portfolio out under Bob's watchful eye, that was the question. Even if Remi got the cameras under her thumb, that door was no joke. It had a ton of pressure on it when it locked. Ari didn't have the keycard or gadget necessary to open it, and it wasn't a biometric scan—Ivan's trick of licking it wouldn't work here.

An elbow jostled his and Carter winked at him subtly.

Oh? Did his sexy boyfriend have a plan? Ari hadn't been led

astray by him yet. He decided to trust him and see what trick Carter had up his sleeve.

Bob hustled toward the front door, impatient to get outside and help hunt down the drone. He looked a little too excited about it, actually. It must be hard to have mind numbing workdays, day in, day out. The chance to shoot at something might be too much for him.

As they passed through the door, Ari saw Carter smoothly jam something into the lock, although he barely got a glance at it as he walked out. Was that paper? Something about that stirred at the back of his mind but he couldn't quite put a finger on it. It wasn't something he'd done, but something he'd heard about. Something...Ivan'd told him, maybe?

He had no chance to really chase the elusive thought down as they put gear into the van and ostensibly got ready to leave. Bob, satisfied they were out, was already jogging towards the front of the mansion to help hunt down the drone.

Ari hovered near his open door and demanded of Carter, "Was that paper?"

The grin on Carter's face was downright wicked. "A newspaper folded eight times can support a ton of weight."

It clicked in his head and Ari snorted a laugh. "You got that from Eidolon, didn't you?"

"*Of course,*" Ivan preened. "*All the best ideas come from me.*" He let out a panicked yelp and then something pinged metal. "*They're getting close. I don't know how much longer I can keep their attention.*"

"Widow, cameras?"

"*Got outside,*" she reported, smug as a cat with cream. "*You're a go.*"

She was even picking up the lingo. Ari grinned as he darted back inside, through the door and into the stairwell. It took him mere seconds to retrieve the portfolio and he spun on his heels, sprinting for the door again. He snagged the newspaper as he went through the door, erasing as much of his tracks as he could. The boggle on the camera would be a dead giveaway someone had bypassed security, but there was no helping that.

Carter had the side door open for him, and Ari carefully slid the portfolio inside before slamming the door shut and hopping into the passenger seat. He barely had his own door closed before Carter backed the vehicle out.

"Target acquired," Carter reported, still professional and calm. "On our way out."

"*Uh-oh.*" Kyou groaned.

Ivan echoed it. "*Uh-oh.*"

Pinching the bridge of his nose, Ari demanded in a sort of morose resignation, "Now what?"

"*Car accident right in front of the gate. I think someone got distracted watching the show and rear-ended the car in front of them. You can't get out.*"

Because of course that would happen just as they were about to leave.

Kyou pitched in, "*We've got a cop car and an ambulance converging on the accident. Stay cool, guys. They're not here for you.*" That would have been vastly reassuring if Kyou hadn't added, "*I think. Pretty sure.*"

Ari groaned again. With friends like him, who needed enemies?

Pulling to a stop in front of the closed gate, Carter shot him a smile that didn't completely disguise his nerves. "All we have to do is sit tight."

Considering they had a multi-million-dollar painting sitting right behind them? That was a pretty tall fucking order. Ari had done tougher, more nerve-wracking things in his lifetime than sitting in a car with stolen art while gun-happy guards ran around them.

Give him a second, he might even think of an example.

26

CARTER

Carter tried to sit still, acting as if he had all the time in the world. The one fidget he allowed was the rap of his fingers against the steering wheel, a gentle rhythmic tap. His eyes roved over the situation and tried to estimate how much time it would take to get them past this obstacle.

The accident had happened directly in front of the gate, because of course it would. It didn't look bad, all things considered. The back end of the black sedan was crushed upwards, the trunk crumpled like a sardine can. The truck that had done the damage had its front fender hanging off on one end, but otherwise looked undamaged. The truck, at least, looked like it could drive off without an issue. The car? Depended if that back axle had taken damage or if the frame was bent. If they had to wait on a tow truck to haul it off, they'd be here a lot longer.

Needless to say, he was rather eager to exit.

He felt jittery, uneasy about sitting, but Carter firmly squashed the impulse to do something stupid. Impatience killed people faster than anything else, except perhaps overconfidence. Ari, he was pleased to note, was also firmly sitting still. Of course, an assassin of his caliber would know better than to let nerves get the better of him.

The tension in the van was lethal, thick enough to slice and serve on bread. Neither of them looked at each other. No one said anything over comms, either, as if they were all mutually holding their breath.

One of the gate guards said something to his companion before opening the gate and stepping through. He went to Carter's side, and Carter lowered the window, pasting a welcoming look on his face. "Hey."

"Hey," the guard returned, exasperation heavy in his tone and expression. "Can you believe this? First that crazy drone, then an accident because the driver was too busy looking at us to pay attention."

Carter's tone was sour. "And we're stuck here waiting because of it."

"Look, I know Bob rushed you out. I can walk you back and you can finish up, if you want."

Mentally cursing him for the offer, Carter opened his mouth to refuse when Ari beat him to it.

"We were done, actually, but I think I left a tool behind. It's on the second floor. You mind if I go fetch it real quick?"

What the hell was he playing at? Second floor, they didn't leave anything—in a flash, it hit. The boggle on the back of the camera. Of course. Ari hadn't been able to grab it, not in the time they'd had. It had been too tight for comfort getting the painting out without anyone noticing. True, if they could get that boggle back, they'd erase all signs they were ever there. Kyou fully planned to purge their pictures and 'employee' records from the system as soon as they were clear of the grounds.

"Sure, man, that's fine."

Ari thumped him on the shoulder, catching his eye firmly. "I'll be back in a sec."

"Okay," Carter agreed around a dry mouth. He really didn't like them separating but it would look odd for them both to go back to fetch a tool. That wasn't a two-man job.

The guard and Ari went off, both of them bemoaning loudly the idiot with the drone. It was still buzzing away, although at the back of the grounds now. Carter rolled the window back up and watched them like a hawk in the rearview mirror. "K, you got eyes on him?"

"Not really. He's not in range of the vault outside cameras yet. Breathe, Smiley, he'll be fine. It was quick thinking on his

part to go back in for the boggle."

He knew that. Intellectually. But his heart beat in his chest like a scared rabbit looking for a break. The added tension of not being able to make a clean getaway was likely why he was more nervous than usual. Carter couldn't say he liked this situation all that much.

"*Got him,*" Remi announced, and she sounded relieved. "*He's still talking with the guard.*"

A gunshot rang out and Carter tracked it instinctively, twisting in his seat as he tried to see through the van's tinted windows.

"*Drone, njet,*" Ivan mourned. "*My poor babies.*"

Second drone down, eh. Carter couldn't say he was surprised.

The thief bounced back in the next second. "*On my way back. Smiley, Malvagio, you want me to stick close just in case?*"

"*No, you can't. They're looking for the drone operator. You're too close, they'll spot you in a few minutes. Get out. Smiley, I've got word through dispatch that they've got a tow truck almost there. Just sit tight another ten minutes.*"

Ten minutes sounded like ten years just then. Carter swallowed hard. "Yeah, okay."

"*Malvagio's back out,*" Remi updated him. "*Guard still talking to him.*"

Carter's eyes flew back to the rearview mirror and it was true, Ari was back out and walking toward him. He said something to the guard, waved, and the man peeled off to go toward the back of the lot. Ari walked along toward him, casually, as if he had all the time in the world.

"*Got the boggle,*" Ari informed them all smugly. "*He didn't even follow me in, it was easy. Breathe, caro.*"

"I'm breathing." Carter was also promising himself he'd make better backup plans than this. Granted, they'd been beyond rushed with this job, with no real time to plan every detail out. But still. This flying by the seat of their pants was not fun.

Ari slid into the passenger seat and closed the door with a soft whump. He practically radiated satisfaction although his eyes still stared hard at the two mangled cars, the police car, the ambulance, and the spectators. "Come on, tow truck, come on."

A policeman came up to speak with the guards, then returned to the truck's driver. The man looked like a gardener or landscaper, and the truck had the logo of some company on the driver's side door. The driver nodded, gestured a few times, then shrugged. Between cop and driver, they wrestled the bumper completely off with some hard tugs, then threw it into the back bed.

Carter straightened up slowly. Was the policeman trying to clear enough space they could at least get out? Or was he trying to buy some room for the tow truck? Both, perhaps?

They sat tensely and watched it play out. The truck slowly drove off, merging with traffic, and the cop waved them forward.

"*Yes*," Carter and Ari hissed at once in triumph.

"*What, what?*" Kyou demanded.

"They're letting us out," Ari reported even as the big black gates swung inwards.

Carter gave it a respectable distance before driving slowly through. He waved at the cop in thanks, smile unfeigned. The cop nodded back, already turning away to deal with the traffic and the sedan still sitting there. He carefully merged with traffic as well, using all the right signals and speed to not draw anyone's attention.

Three blocks away, Ari punched a fist into the air. "YES! God, I can't believe we did it."

"*I know we had a lot of issues, but good work guys! Seriously, I can't believe we tackled that place with such little planning and pulled it off.*"

"*It's because we're that good,*" Ivan interjected smugly. There was a bit of background noise accompanying his voice, no doubt because he was driving back to the townhouse.

Carter knew the next part of the plan was losing the van and uniforms, and quickly. They couldn't be caught with any of this, as they were no longer employees. They'd leave the van behind to be boosted. K had already arranged for someone to pick the vehicle up, wipe it clean, and re-sell it.

Ari was already unbuttoning his shirt and getting ready to lose it. "What's our ETA on getting out of the townhouse? We still aiming for two o'clock?"

"*I think that's still doable. Widow's already shut down all non-essential processes and she's packing stuff up for me. Don't worry about the furniture, it was all rented, and I've got the company scheduled to come and pick it up tomorrow.*"

It was actually impressive how quickly Kyou had set this up and could take it down again. It made Carter wonder how many times he'd done so. Carter wasn't actually accustomed to long-term heists. His sort of jobs usually involved quick turn arounds and bullets. He had to admit, even though parts of it were nerve-wracking in the extreme, he'd rather enjoyed this better. Or was that because of the team of men he was working with?

"*Daddy, I'm packed. Should I pack you?*"

"That would be awesome, gattina. Did you sweep the bathroom too?"

Remi let out an aggravated gasp. "*No, I forgot.*"

"Do that for me and you, okay? But it's okay if you forget something, I'll do a sweep as soon as I'm in."

"*Okay.*"

Kyou gave a grunt of satisfaction. "*Your employee records with Assurance are scrubbed. You officially don't exist. How close are you to parking?*"

"Parking now." Carter pulled into the narrow alley and wasted no time exiting the van.

"*I'm five minutes out from the house,*" Ivan reported.

Ari hauled the portfolio out and they left the vehicle unlocked, keys inside. Their boosters would be here to collect it in the next fifteen minutes. They shifted the portfolio and tools over to the SUV and shucked the employee shirts, which they tossed into the back of the van. Ari slid into the driver's seat and pulled steadily out of the alleyway, joining the crazy DC traffic. He caught Ari's eye as they waited for the red light, and they broke out into irrepressible smiles. They weren't home free yet, but it was so close they could taste it.

"K," Ari requested, still grinning at Carter, "Tell me something good."

"*They have no idea that the swap's been made. We're good. I still want out of town in the next two hours to make sure that we don't invite bad luck on our heads. Smiley."*

"Yeah?"

"Finally got a reply from our client. He's okay with us taking the painting directly to him, and he's anticipating us tonight. Said he'll wait for us, as he's pretty anxious to get his hands on the Monet. Actually...I know we talked about you going to turn in the painting alone to the client, but I'm not really good with that option anymore."

Carter sensed that this had nothing to do with him. "Why?"

"Because the director's anxious. This guy isn't a hardened criminal, I could practically hear him sweating. Just in case he does something stupid, I think you shouldn't go in alone."

Frowning, Carter considered this. "Okay, that's a good point."

Ari's smile morphed into a thoughtful frown. "In that case, he's definitely not going alone. I'll follow him in. Eidolon, K, you two play backup."

"I'm good with that," Carter agreed.

"Good. I'll start breaking down."

It meant that Kyou wouldn't have eyes on them the rest of the way, but that was fine. He hardly needed to. They still had their earbuds in, they could tell each other if something went wrong.

He and Ari slid through traffic, which fortunately wasn't crowded at this time of the day. They remained alert to their surroundings the whole trip, not wanting to let their guards down at the last second. Carter frankly wouldn't really relax until he had the painting delivered and money in his account. Still, his free hand slid into Ari's, and they held hands the entire trip.

When they entered the front door, they were met with a round of applause. Carter laughed and kicked the door shut. "Anyone want a good look at it before we take off? Probably your only chance outside of a museum."

"Later," Kyou admonished.

"Da," Ivan instantly agreed, already heading for the portfolio.

Kyou threw his hands up and went back to packing his computer carefully into the various crates and boxes.

Carter handed it off to the thief as he didn't really have time to admire it. He needed to pack the rest of his personal belongings and throw them into his car. As he moved, he asked Kyou, "So do I tell Emura the job is finished or not?"

"I think we should skip him altogether. We can still pay him the fee, just so he can't scream about being cheated later. We don't need that kind of tarnish on our records. But the site will boot him soon and really make sure he can't do business again. It was embarrassing enough he snuck back in once—they'll double down on security measures to prevent another black eye."

Sometimes reputation was the only saving grace in this business. Carter agreed with that. "I'm fine with all of that, but are we seriously going to just walk through the Met's front doors with a stolen painting?"

"Why?" Ivan queried. "It's supposed to be in the museum, isn't it? Let's just put it back."

Put it back...? As in... "Wait, you want to break into the Met yourself and switch them out? Seriously?"

Ivan cackled.

He was joking. Wasn't he?

Ivan did not win the argument about switching the painting out, fortunately. Ari didn't even have to break in and mediate the argument, which made Carter think Ivan had been yanking Kyou's chain all along. They drove the four and a half hours to New York caravan style with no issues. While Carter and Ari headed into the Met, the other three waited across the street at a coffee shop, on hand just in case things went south. The director of the Met greeted them at the door and escorted them in. Security never even got a chance to look at the painting nestled in the portfolio.

The director of the Metropolitan Museum of Art didn't look very distinguished, despite the suit he wore. Thinning brown hair on top, average build, a sort of everyman look to him. What did stand out were his nerves, as he kept glancing behind him, tracking that they were still with him, and wiping sweat from his forehead.

It was an impressive building, to be sure. The Metropolitan Museum of Art was built of light grey stone, looking as impressive as any Grecian structure with its tall columns near the doors and the high, domed ceilings overhead. The tiled floor echoed every footstep from the visitors, and the art wasn't cluttered together. It was all spaced out by several feet to give people the ability to really look at it individually and appreciate each sculpture, each painting, on its own. Each area also had its own designation for countries, the architecture reflecting the country of origin. Carter had spent a few hours here once, just enjoying the art and culture.

They passed by the information desk, going up the stairs and to the third story, then on towards the back of the building where the staff offices were. Carter had the painting in hand, his gate loose and easy. Ari strode like a shadow at his side, taking in absolutely everything. Nothing looked out of place to him, but he hadn't lived this long without looking for a double-cross. He was sure whatever he missed, Ari would spot.

The director opened his office door and stepped through. A woman waited inside with an open authenticating kit on his desk. Ari closed the door behind them and then leaned casually against it. No one was coming in or out without moving him first.

Director Lofland gave him a leery glance before clearing his throat, smoothing down his brilliantly red tie as he did so. "Gentlemen. You'll understand if I want to check the painting first."

"Of course," Carter assured him. "Here, please take it. We can wait until you're satisfied."

"Yes, thank you." Lofland deflated a little when he didn't get an argument and quickly unzipped the portfolio so his colleague could get to work. The woman pulled free the tools she needed and bent immediately over the painting.

As the director hovered, Carter came to stand at Ari's side and watched for a minute.

"Nothing looks suspicious from out here," Kyou threw in. *"I've tapped into the director's and the museum's phones, and he hasn't alerted anyone. Bank account is ready for him to*

transfer the money to."

"*All clear out here as well,*" Ivan reported, sounding bored.

The authenticator knew her business. She ran three tests and then sat back with a relieved smile and nodded to Lofland. "It's genuine."

Lofland's unease died an immediate death and he beamed at Carter. "Mr. Harrison. Thank you so much. When you took the job, you didn't think it would be possible, but you pulled through beautifully."

"I fortunately found the right team for the job," Carter replied modestly. "If you could, transfer the payment to this account."

Lofland took the card with the printed account and routing number but frowned uneasily at it. "What about Mr. Emura?"

"You can send his share directly to him."

"He stipulated I was to pay through him, and he would divide the funds..." Lofland paused, dark eyes narrowed suspiciously. "Your colleague explained to me that Emura was not trustworthy, but you've experienced this for yourself, Mr. Harrison?"

"He's apparently done this trick before. Don't use him in the future, Director. I'll leave you my contact info. You can just directly hire me."

"Ah. I'll gladly take it, but I'm sure you'll understand if I say I hope I never have to hire you again."

Carter returned that smile with a soft chuckle. "Understandable."

"Here, let me transfer the payment." Lofland pulled out his phone and tapped for a while into it, his bottom lip caught between his teeth as he concentrated.

"*Aaaand it's transferred. We're good. I'm divvying it out to everyone else's account now.*"

"Thank you, Director." Carter shook hands with the man and then they were free. As he walked out of the museum, he took the first full breath for what felt like eons. It was definitely months. He caught Ari's eye and couldn't help but think that if not for this wild, crazy job that he'd taken on, he'd never have met the man. Or Remi. Or Ivan. Or Kyou. He'd considered himself insane for taking it on, but...maybe his insanity had worked out for the better.

Remi's hopeful voice piped up in his ear. "*Disneyland?*"

"Yeah, gattina," Ari responded, and the expression he had on his face was utter contentment. "Next stop is Disneyland."

EPILOGUE

ARI

Ari had his hands full as he juggled his bag, Remi's, and tried to open Ivan's door at the same time. They'd had fun at Disneyland for a full week. They'd even squeezed in having dinner with Luca twice, which had gone rather well. Carter had been his usual charming self. Luca had been very obviously delighted to see Remi face to face and curious about his brother's new boyfriend.

In between amusement rides, Ari and Carter had discussed how to move forward. It wasn't easy, in their line of work, to have any sense of permanency. But they wanted to stay together and really give this relationship thing a try. Carter was adamant that he didn't want he and Ari to take jobs alone anymore, too.

To that end, Carter had set up this meeting. Ivan had a house in California, so they went there to crash for the night. Well, in theory. Carter had every intention of pressing his agenda.

The door opened under Ari's hand, and Ivan stepped back to let them through. "There you are. Carter got here a half hour ago."

"Yeah, well, he was on the road faster than we were." His boyfriend(?) had left early to swing by and pick up a few things from one of his safehouses nearby. Carter, it seemed, had just as many places to crash as Kyou. Or Ivan.

"Solnishko," Ivan crooned, holding out his hands for a hug. "How was Disneyland?"

"Dreamy," she sighed happily, closing in around his legs and hugging him tightly. "I want to do it again."

"Next birthday," Ari promised her, swinging the bags to a stop, tucked out of the way from the main path. He'd not actually been in Ivan's house before. It had a very modern, Santa Fe look going for it, what with the stucco and red tiles and the open concept floorplan. Even the floors were a polished cement. Ivan went for white walls and bold furniture colors, the sofa and chairs red or black. It didn't actually look like something the man had decorated himself. Ivan's taste was a little different than this. It made Ari think the man had bought it and then hired an interior decorator to finish the house off.

Remi excitedly started telling Ivan every detail and Ari left her to it, hunting for his sexy man who was supposedly in here somewhere. He found him in a back bedroom, where he was offloading a truly interesting collection of guns, knives, and was that a new drone? The box didn't even look opened.

"There you are," Carter greeted, straightening. He skirted around the bed and greeted Ari with a kiss that was meant to be quick but Ari drew him back in, lingering. They'd not had a proper kiss this morning what with an eight-year-old pleading to stay a day longer, and the general chaos of trying to get packed up and out the door. Carter hummed approval even as he kissed back, hand gliding up to catch the back of Ari's head.

"Why hello," Carter purred at him, eyes twinkling. "Is that a promise for later?"

"Yes," Ari promised in a growl. "Ivan can distract her."

"Sounds like a plan to me."

"You two stop kissy-kissy!" Ivan called from the main room. "Kyou's ready to talk!"

Ari wasn't actually sure on this point: Was Ivan the bigger cockblock or Remi? Some days, it really was a flip of the coin either direction. Sighing, he pulled back. "We're coming!"

Apparently able to read the look on his face, Carter gave him a reassuring nod. "It's fine. I think they'll agree."

"I'm not sure if this will work out the way you think it will," Ari warned him. Again. He'd said this at least three times already. "We're all pretty independent."

"I think you've been independent because you didn't really

think you had another option. Let's at least put it out there for them to consider, yeah?"

Ari still harbored his doubts, but he followed Carter into the living room. The big screen had Kyou's figure on it, the hacker swathed in a worn-in sweatshirt, a cup of some steaming liquid in both hands. He looked more than a little worked over, as if he'd been on a work binge ever since the last job completed. Which, knowing Kyou, wasn't outside the realm of possibility. Remi and Ivan were stretched out on the couch as if anticipating movie time. All they were missing was the popcorn.

"*Alright, we're all here,*" Kyou stated, his voice scratchy. It could have been exhaustion or disuse. When he got into a hacking binge, he didn't go outside or speak to people for sometimes weeks at a time. "*What's this about, Carter?*"

Carter came to stand so he could face all four of them, his arms crossed over his chest and a stubborn tilt to his jaw. "I want a team. I want *you* to be my team."

Letting out a low whistle, Ivan stared at him and, for once, the charming thief wasn't anywhere present. He was closed off entirely, hiding his true thoughts. Kyou didn't look all that surprised, more a mix of pensive resignation.

"*Carter, I think I said this before,*" Kyou said slowly, carefully non-confrontational. "*But our jobs don't always overlap with the others' skillset.*"

"They do often enough, though. Ari's told me how many jobs the three of you have tackled together in the last five years. More than half of them, you did together. The other half, it was a mix of either working with just one of you as a partner, or going solo. Even solo, you sometimes pulled the others in halfway through the job. Look, I know the three of you think you need to be independent, I get that. I'm not suggesting we're hobbled together at the ankles. It's just, wouldn't you like for this to be official? To not need to question if the other two will have your back, but to *know* they will?"

Kyou fell silent, sipping at his cup in an obvious bid for a moment to think. Ivan was staring silently down at Remi, and Ari could just see the calculations flash through his friend's head.

Sensing his win, Carter pressed his point. "You say that not every job you take needs all the specialties. Okay, that's fair. I'm not demanding we do every single job together. But on the ones where you don't need everyone's help, just read them in. That way, if something goes wrong, you have automatic backup. You don't have to explain the situation or find a way to reach us first. We already know."

Ivan's head came up, and he stared at Carter for a full five seconds before a slow grin broke out. "You make a good argument. Alright. I'm in. Ari?"

"You think he hasn't already talked me into this?" Ari retorted with considerable asperity. "Besides, Remi's over the moon for this idea."

Remi pointed her puppy eyes at the screen with perfect timing. (Suspiciously perfect timing. Ari suspected she'd been coached, and he knew exactly by who.) "Uncle Kyou, you don't want to play with us?"

Whatever defense Kyou had got utterly derailed. *It's not that, it's just...oh hell. I really can't think of a good reason not to, it's just you realize we'll have to figure out how to split every payment for a job—*"

"Do it like we did the last one," Carter countered, the epitome of reason. "Four ways. Or two ways, if only one other person helps you."

"*—and what about who takes lead? I mean, just trusting four guys to go at it never works out well; you always need a team leader.*"

"So, the person who specializes in the right field for the job takes lead. Only makes sense, right? He'll know best what to do."

"*And what about location?*" Kyou really was grasping at straws. He didn't look argumentative so much as curious to see if Carter had an answer to this, too. "*Remi needs to go to school at least part of the school year. We're constantly in and out of jobs; none of us really have a fixed location.*"

"So we put our heads together and figure out where we'll be based from. We'll pool together our safehouses so we all know where they are and use them depending on where the jobs take us." Carter splayed his hands to either side, body language saying, *See, easy.* "This isn't rocket science, Kyou. And isn't it more fun to work jobs together anyway?"

"*You're a people person*," Kyou accused as if he were actually an axe murderer.

Carter grinned and shrugged, no defense on his lips.

"Come on, K." Ari knew his friend would fight this the hardest. Ivan was always the easiest sell of the two. "It's not like we bite. And we can help you keep an eye on that guy you're stalking."

"Protecting," Kyou corrected instantly, then made a face. "*I don't really have much choice on this, do I? Remi's already pouting at me.*"

"I'll pay you in vodka," Ivan offered.

"*The vodka is tempting....*" Kyou trailed off. Was that a hint of a smirk?

"Don't make me kidnap you," Ari threatened. "You need a life outside of that guy and your computers."

Kyou sighed, as if put upon, and he couldn't understand why they were being so mean. "*Fine. Fine, dammit, you win.*"

Remi let out a loud whoop and bounced in place. Carter looked ready to join her. Ivan, of course, actually did while Ari and Kyou looked on in amusement. Considering how easy it was for Carter to talk these two into it, it made Ari think he'd been right all along. They'd already been a team. They just hadn't officially called themselves that or recognized it for what it was. With it now out there, and agreed upon, Ari felt like another door of possibilities had just opened out in front of them.

Really, the future promised to be so much more fun with them working together.

Curious why Remi chose Ari? Turn the page to find out!

AFTERSTORY

REMI

She watched the scene play out behind the abandoned convenience store with solemn eyes. The handsome man—the one in the leather jacket—she didn't know him. He'd not been around here before. But the other one—the man he'd taken down so ruthlessly—she knew him. Everyone in the neighborhood knew him. He sold bad drugs and hurt people. Sometimes shot them.

Mrs. Havera, the lady who lived across the street, she'd warned Remi about men like him. The ones who carried guns, who didn't look or dress like the people in the neighborhood. Those were the ones to watch out for. The ones who came to kill someone. She said when you saw someone like that, go home, stop playing, to take cover until the fight was all over.

Normally, she'd have listened. But she'd snuck out of the house because her stepfather had gone from drunk to bad-drunk, so it wasn't safe to be there right now. And something about the handsome man drew her attention. She found herself watching instead. She hugged the side of the building, staying small and still. Years of living with her abusive stepfather had taught her how to be very, very still. Stillness meant his eyes would pass right over her without seeing. She kept her breathing soft and steady so nothing about her drew the man's eye.

It was brutal, the beatdown. The drug dealer was crying and begging for mercy, then with a swift boot to the head, even that stilled. The girl he'd been dragging away, the one who had screamed for help, she was huddled nearby, shaking and staring with wide eyes. Really stupid decision. Sarah could have told her she should have run for it while no one was paying her any attention.

The handsome man, the one who killed for money (according to Mrs. Havera), he bent down and rifled through the man's pockets. He brought out several rolls of cash, enough to fill both hands. Then he carefully approached the girl still shaking on the ground.

"Hey." He crouched down, slowly, extending both hands the blonde girl. "You take this, okay? You take this and you run for it, find a new city to live in. Cut ties with that toxic father of yours."

The blonde teenager stopped shaking, but she didn't move. After a long moment, she croaked, "Why are you giving me this?"

"I don't prey on kids," the man said patiently. "I was here for another job entirely. I dealt with him 'cause he pissed me off. So you take this, okay? You get on a bus, or a plane, or whatever. You get out of here so that bastard father can't sell you again."

She nodded and finally took the money, hugging the rolls against her chest. Sounds choked, she whispered, "Thank you."

This man didn't like abusive fathers. He didn't like it when people hurt children. Mrs. Havera said people like him hurt people for money. All of these facts whirled through Sarah's mind and a plan started to form. Could she hire him? Would he stop her stepfather from hurting her?

Sarah didn't really remember a time when she was safe. Her mother used to slap her when she was frustrated, or when Sarah asked for food. Her stepfather now hit her just because he was drunk and angry. This idea that someone was against hurting a child was odd to her. There were adults like that?

But there must be, because this man had said he didn't hurt kids. He helped a girl and was gentle with her. This man was kind.

Sarah eased back and watched as he left the cracked parking lot, heading down the street. She had her secret stash of change on her, the one she'd collected over the past several months.

She wanted to save more, but it was hard around her stepfather. He spent every dime he made. On beer, mostly. It wasn't much, what she had, but maybe the handsome man would help her anyway.

On silent feet, she padded after him, trying to work out what to say. The girl hadn't said anything to him to get rescued, so that didn't help Sarah any. She chewed on her bottom lip for a moment before the split pulled painfully.

The more she followed him down the dirty, trashy street, the higher her tension rose. Surely he'd parked nearby. If she didn't call out to him soon, she'd lose the chance entirely. But she didn't know what to say. Doubts started to creep in, too. What if he didn't want to help her too? He'd already helped someone else tonight. What if he was tired, or just wanted to go home, and chose to ignore her?

He abruptly stopped under a street light, not turning, just still. Sarah stopped too, as she didn't understand what he was doing. She lingered behind a trashcan, hiding, as hiding came naturally to her when she didn't understand what adults were doing. Hiding was always the safest option.

"Hey," he said calmly. "This whole cat and mouse thing ain't cool, okay? How about you come over here, in the light, and you tell me what you need. I might be able to help you out."

He was offering to help? Sarah peeked out at him, hope rising hard and fast in her chest. She still didn't quite know what to say, how to ask, but he was listening. It still unnerved her, approaching this strange man. He'd been gentle with the girl, but Sarah had seen him beat a man bloody. She was under no illusions. This man was capable of bloody violence, too. A lifetime of being someone's punching bag made her cautious. But the patient way he waited for her encouraged her to try.

And really, if she didn't get someone to stop her stepfather soon, she'd probably not live much longer. Sarah was grimly certain of that. No one else would stop him from hurting her, and every day, he got angrier. More violent.

The thought propelled her forward more than anything else. She had to get help. She simply had to. So even though her hands shook, and not from the cold, she approached him.

The assassin turned slowly, keeping his hands to the side,

a faint smile on his face. He really was handsome, like the men in those action movies. His smile dropped when he saw her and Sarah almost bolted. Why had he stopped smiling at her?

Sarah quickly spoke, because she didn't want him to change his mind and leave after all. Looking up at him, she swallowed hard before speaking, words raspy. "I'm Sarah. I saw you beat up Hardy back there."

Slowly, he sank to one knee. Sarah breathed out shakily when he put them on eye level. He'd done this for the other girl, too. He'd come in and knelt and spoke gently. Oh good, he wasn't going to leave. He'd at least hear her out.

"Yeah, honey, I did. He was a bad man. His face needed rearranging."

Sarah nodded, as she agreed with that. But it didn't answer her main question. "Do you beat up bad men as your job? Mrs. Havera, she said that you kill people for money."

"Yeah, honey, I do. Why?"

From the pocket of her sagging pants, she drew out all of her money, and held out both hands to him. It was a jumbled collection of change, perhaps two dollars altogether. She looked up at him, pleading. "Can I hire you? Will you stop him?"

The look on the man's face was murderous rage. Sarah almost flinched from it, but instinctively she understood it wasn't meant for her. This man was angry on her behalf. That was a strange feeling. She'd never had someone angry *for* her sake before.

His voice was soft, the anger a live hum in his words. "Who's hurting you, honey?"

"My stepfather. Momma left last year, and when she did, he got mad. He..." she trailed off, eyes falling to the pavement. This was hard to say. She didn't want to talk about it. But he needed to know, otherwise he couldn't help her. Her chin firmed and she squared her shoulders, meeting his eyes once more. "I need you to stop him."

He held out both hands, taking the change from her. "You just hired yourself an assassin, sweetheart."

Relief ran through her and she dumped the change in his hands. Her instincts had been right, after all. This man was kind and would help her. "He lives at 314A Osborne Way."

"Tell you what, kiddo. You come with me, stand just outside the house, okay?" He pocketed the change, standing.

Sarah nodded, fell into step with him, taking two steps for his one. He noticed, and slowed down so she wasn't jogging to keep up with him. She liked that, too, that he was thoughtful of her.

"Honey, you got any relatives? Grandma, grandpa, uncles, anything like that?"

Shaking her head no, she kept walking. This worried him, Sarah could tell from his expression. It was odd that he was so worried when people who'd known her longer than five minutes didn't care she was being hit all the time. But she liked that he did care. She knew he wasn't a prince—assassins couldn't be princes, could they?—but he looked like Prince Charming from *Cinderella*. She liked him. Or maybe he was more like Flynn Rider from *Tangled*. He did bad things, but for good reasons. Like now. That idea made her happy.

The happiness was short lived. They reached the house. Sarah honestly hated the house. She never went there unless she had no other option. The house meant pain and fear. It meant being absolutely still for hours at a time, not even breathing loudly for fear of discovery. Sarah would do anything to make sure she didn't have to go into it again.

She didn't know what would happen to her after her stepfather was dealt with. Maybe she'd go to a cop. They were supposed to help kids. Either way, right now, she felt nothing for the man sitting inside. A vicious sort of satisfaction filled her chest. Finally, finally, he'd know what it was like to be the weaker one. Finally, there was someone to stop him.

The only sign of life came from the flickering light in the window, clearly from a TV. Kneeling, the assassin put a light hand on Sarah's back, drawing her eyes up to him. Concern showed in his eyes and he asked her in a low voice, "You change your mind, sweetie?"

Shaking her head, she pointed to the door. "It's not locked."

"You stay on the porch, okay? If someone comes to get you, you scream for me. I'm going to take you to a safe place after this."

"You are?" Why? He hadn't done that with the other girl.

He'd just given her money and told her to run away. Was it because Sarah was younger?

"Yeah, honey. Can't leave a kid on the streets. That's non va bene, you get me?" With a pat on her head, he moved toward the house, stride becoming quiet as he moved.

Sarah was surprised he could move that silently. She'd learned how by pretending she was Black Widow. It made her happy she could move quietly like him. Like a real assassin. She'd thought about being an assassin when she grew up. Bad men didn't hurt Black Widow, after all. She beat people like that up. Maybe if Sarah became an assassin, people wouldn't hurt her, either. She wanted to be an assassin like the one helping her now—the type to help people just because they could.

Rather than a prince, she'd take an assassin coming to her rescue any day.

The door stuck a little and the assassin shouldered it aside before entering. Sarah could clearly hear every word as her stepfather slurred out, "Who the fuck're you?"

"I'm here because of Sarah."

"That runt? You into kids?"

Sarah went cold at those words. She'd heard them before. She knew what they meant. The kid sold off had never come back.

"Five hundred dollars, you can have'er."

Two gunshots rang out in quick succession. Sarah jumped, not expecting them. After that, dead silence. She didn't need to look to know. Her stepfather was dead. She stared at the open doorway, the door warped by time and too many kicks. No part of her felt sad for the man who'd been her stepfather. Rather, overwhelming relief swept through her from head to toe. For the first time ever, she felt like she could breathe.

The assassin came back out and stared down at her with an odd look on his face.

She smiled up at him. "Thank you."

He seemed to come to a sudden decision and said seriously, "Tell you what, kiddo. How about I adopt you? I can't trust you to the foster system. I gotta tell you, I'm probably not good dad material, but you'll be safe with me. And no douchebag will get his hands on you again, I can promise you that."

She cocked her head up at him, hope gradually rising. Keep her? He wanted to keep her? That sounded so much better than going to the cops and hoping things turned out alright. This man she could trust. And he'd be able to help her become an assassin, right? Because he was one, he'd be able to teach her. "You're an assassin, right? Can you teach me to be like Black Widow?"

He grinned at her. "Yeah, kid, I can teach you the moves."

Her smile hurt because of her split lip and bruises, but she couldn't stop. This was really, really so much better than being rescued by a prince like in the movies. "Then please adopt me."

"Sure thing." He reached out with both hands, picking her up, settling her into his arms. "Anything you want from inside?"

It felt strange, to be picked up again. After a moment, she decided she might like it. It felt far safer here than anywhere else she'd ever been. Shaking her head no, she latched onto his collar with both hands, fingers tangled in the fabric. "You really, really want to keep me?"

"Kid, I like your guts. Not many adults have your kind of savvy, to walk up and make a deal with me. But let's discuss details after we get out of here, okay?"

"Okay."

Really. So, so much better than being rescued by a prince.

DICTIONARY

Russian Dictionary:
Solnishko – Sunshine
Milij – Dear/precious
Horosho – good
Njet – no
Da – yes
Chert – damn
Zasranets – asshole
Durak – fool
Svoloch – bastard
Zanuda – very boring person, pain in the neck

Italian Dictionary:
Quello non va bene/ non va bene – That's not right
Capiche/capisci/capisco – got it/understand
Vaffanculo – fuck off
Stronzo – asshole
Figlio di puttana – son of a bitch
Porca troia/porca putanna – Shit! Son of a bitch!
Cazzo – dick (used like Shit!)
Quanto sei bello amore mio – You're so beautiful, my love
Ti voglio bene gattina di papà – Papa loves you, kitten.
Ti voglio, Papà – Love you, Papa.
Caro – dear
Basta ti prego – stop, please!

Books by AJ Sherwood

<u>Legends of Lobe Den Herren</u>

The Warden and the General
Fourth Point of Contact

<u>Jon's Mysteries</u>

Jon's Downright Ridiculous Shooting Case
Jon's Crazy Head-Boppin' Mystery
Jon's Spooky Corpse Conundrum
Brandon's Very Merry Haunted Christmas*

<u>Unholy Trifecta</u>

How to Shield an Assassin
How to Steal a Thief*
How to Hack a Hacker*

<u>Short Stories</u>
Marriage Contract*

*Coming soon

AUTHOR

Dear Reader,

Your reviews are more important than words can express. Reviews directly impact sales and book visibility, which means the more reviews I have, the more sales I see. The more books I sell, the more I can write and focus on producing books you love to read. You see how that math works out? The best possible support you can provide is to give an honest review, even if it's just clicking those stars to rate a book! (I won't even complain it if 4 stars, honest.)

Thank you for all of your support. See you in the next book!

AJ's mind is the sort that refuses to let her write one project at a time. Or even just one book a year. She normally writes fantasy under a different pen name, but her aforementioned mind couldn't help but want to write for the LGBTQ+ genre. Fortunately, her editor is completely on board with this plan.

In her spare time, AJ loves to devour books, eat way too much chocolate, and take regular trips. She's only been outside of the United States once, to Japan, and loved the experience so much that she firmly intends to see more of the world as soon as possible. Until then, she'll just research via Google Earth and write about the worlds in her own head.

If you'd like to join her newsletter to be notified when books are released, and get behind the scenes about upcoming

books, you can join her NEWSLETTER or email her directly at
sherwoodwrites@gmail.com and you'll be added to the mailing
list. You'll also receive a free copy of her book *Fourth Point of
Contact*! If you'd like to interact with AJ more directly, you can
socialize with her on various sites and join her Facebook group
: AJ's Gentlemen.

Made in the USA
Coppell, TX
10 November 2022